BECOMING BETTY

Books by Eleanor Wood

My Secret Rockstar Boyfriend
Becoming Betty

BECOMING BETTY

ELEANOR WOOD

MACMILLAN

To Alexis Maryon – who was there while I wrote this entire book: in a borrowed tower block, at favourite tables in Tout Va Bien and Café des Tribunaux, and on a few cross-channel ferries – with love and gratitude always

First published 2017 by Macmillan Children's Books
an imprint of Pan Macmillan
20 New Wharf Road, London N1 9RR
Associated companies throughout the world
www.panmacmillan.com

ISBN 978-1-4472-7838-2

Pan Macmillan does not have any control over, or any responsibility
for, any author or third-party websites referred to in or on this book.

1 3 5 7 9 8 6 4 2

A CIP catalogue record for this book is available from
the British Library.

Printed and bound by CPI Group (UK) Ltd, Croydon CR0 4YY

To Do

1. Become cool.
2. Make new friends.
3. Decide WTF I'm going to do with my life.
4. Possibly stop making lists?

Lizzie:

Soooo, it's almost time for my Big New Start . . . I'm going out today to buy a whole new wardrobe before I go forth and be awesome – are you two with me in my epic quest??! xxx

Daisy:

Lizzie, you are your own perfect geeky self just the way you are. You don't need new clothes. YOU ARE AWESOME.

Jake:

Come on. Let's be real. You're nice and everything, Lizbot . . . But a few new outfits wouldn't go amiss. It can't hurt.

Lizzie:

See? I can't just go there with a stupid plan like 'be myself'. That would defeat the whole object.

Daisy:

Nonsense, my love. What you should NEVER do is listen to Jake. You're like Mary Poppins: Practically Perfect in Every Way.

Jake:

Except your hair. Your hair isn't perfect. It's kind of meh. Please note that I am telling you this because I love you. Constructive criticism. Real friends are honest, Daze.

Lizzie:

Um, thanks?

Jake:

WELL, YOU ASKED.

Daisy:

Don't listen to him, Lizzie. Are you really going to take hair advice from someone who has a Pinterest board entitled 'Hair Goals' that ACTUALLY INCLUDES A PICTURE OF JUSTIN BIEBER?!

Jake:

Girls. Hilarious as this is . . . Where are we meeting for this exciting shopping expedition?

Daisy:

Churchill Square, Urban Outfitters side. No lateness excuses will be tolerated from either of you. Lizzie, no obsessing over what to wear. Jake, no staring in the mirror and losing track of time. K?

Today is the first day of the rest of my life. That is official.

I mean, I might say that fairly often. Which I suppose makes today something like the two-hundredth first day of the rest of my life. And today looks quite a lot like all the other first days of the rest of my life did.

But this time it's different. This time I'm actually making it happen. So I am outside Urban Outfitters, waiting for my friends and trying to look nonchalant, with a feeling of genuine excitement. The sun is shining on the busy Brighton street, but the chill of autumn is in the air – along with the promise of the new term and new beginnings. My headphones are playing some appropriately inspirational vintage Bruce Springsteen. I made a playlist especially for today, heavy on the motivational power pop. I need it to get me through the necessary evil of shopping for new clothes – I know it's for the greater good, but I'd rather spend my money on records than clothes. Record shops don't have changing rooms, mirrors and unflattering lighting.

Luckily my soundtrack is working, which is the beauty of music and the perfect playlist. All things considered, I'm feeling basically . . . OK.

Even more so when I see Daisy get off the bus and wave like a hyperactive windmill as soon as she spots me. Daisy is like an excitable puppy, and she has the same way of making you feel better about yourself with a big enthusiastic welcome. Not to mention that she's always excited about coming into Brighton for any reason other than school – her parents live out in a 'picturesque' country village in the South Downs, and Daisy can never wait to escape from there any chance she gets. This is why she spends most of her time round at mine or Jake's.

'Lizzie!' she exclaims breathlessly, as if it's an amazing coincidence that she should see me here, rather than something we've been planning for ages.

She envelops me in a huge hug that smells very strongly of strawberries. Well, kind of like synthetic strawberry sauce with sweets on the top. She read in some Buzzfeed 'Top 10 Ways to Make Boys Fall Madly in Lust with You!' or similar that strawberries are an aphrodisiac, and she's been dousing herself in sickly scented pink products from the Body Shop ever since. She won't listen to polite reason from me, or much more direct insults from Jake, and she wasn't even deterred by the wasps that kept attacking her at the beach all summer.

'You look gorgeous!' I say to her, focusing on the positives and ignoring the smell as best I can.

She makes a disbelieving face in response. Daisy is one of those classic girls who doesn't realize that she's pretty, even though I'm always telling her. I would kill for her naturally blonde hair and perfect skin, but she's always telling me to shut up and saying she's too short and too fat. She says I'm as bad as she is at running myself down, so I can't criticize, but then again I'm not as gorgeous as she is.

'Hey, look – there's Jake,' Daisy says, grabbing my hand. 'He's obsessing over the mannequins in the Topman window. We'd better go and save him from himself.'

She's right – Jake is staring pensively at a mannequin wearing a bright yellow suit jacket and the tiniest shorts I've ever seen. I mean, if the mannequin actually had balls I'm pretty sure you would be able to see them. Experience tells us that if we don't talk some sense into Jake, he will soon convince himself that this should be his latest new look. Then he will ask us why we didn't warn him, when all he ends up with is an empty bank account and non-stop mockery from all sides.

Jake loves the idea of looking like a high-fashion model, but unfortunately for him he's more like a ruddy-faced farmer. He's built like a rugby player, and could probably be one if he didn't hate physical activity and the outdoors so much. He keeps hoping that he might catch cheekbones from all the fashion magazines he reads, but it's a lost cause.

'Do you think I could pull off those shorts?' Jake asks right on cue, without bothering with such niceties as saying hello.

Daisy rolls her eyes behind his back.

'No,' I tell Jake. 'Sorry, but . . . just no. And if you dared to try, I can guarantee that nobody else would want to pull them off either!'

'That's so rude, Lizzie. Rude. I've been one-hundred-per-cent supportive about this little gothic orphan Annie eyeliner thing you're doing these days. I haven't said a single bitchy word.'

I automatically raise a hand up to my face, suddenly

self-conscious. I suppose it must be obvious I've been trying out a new look, but I was sort of hoping nobody would notice, while at the same time finding me inexplicably more attractive. I've been trying to change my image gradually, over the course of the summer holidays, via stealth. Like if anybody knew I was trying to look different, they might be like 'Who do you think you are?' As if I should just stick to being boring old Lizzie Brown, like I've always been.

Only two months ago, before I became known for being a complete freak, I was officially the most boring girl in the world's most boring school. *B* for effort, *B* for achievement. Ten *B*s at GCSE. Not one of the high-achieving geeks of the class – and let's not forget that this is the age of the geek, where nerd-status is cool – but not one of the seriously cool girls either. Always somewhere in the middle.

But not any more. All that's about to change. That's why today is the first day of the rest of my life. Or whatever. While Daisy and Jake are staying on at West Grove to do A levels, tomorrow I am starting at sixth-form college. It's my chance for a brand-new start, where nobody knows me and I can be whoever I want. It's scary, but I am so, so excited.

'Come on,' Daisy says, as if reading my mind. 'Today is supposed to be about Lizzie. We need to find an outfit that will knock them all dead on her first day at her new college.'

'While we're still stuck in the world's most hideous –

and most *burgundy* – school uniform,' Jake grumbles. 'It's so unfair.'

The original plan was that we would all embark upon the adventure of sixth-form college and new horizons together. Daisy, Jake and I had this scheme to reinvent ourselves and become cool. Finally. This seemed like a brilliant plan for about two seconds, but Daisy and Jake, who both have much stricter parents than mine, weren't allowed to leave West Grove Secondary for sixth form, as the school is renowned for its results and university applications and all that stuff.

My parents, cringe-makingly, are kind of the 'cool' parents of our group. Well, my dad is, and he usually manages to talk my mum around. Daisy has too-good-to-be-true, super-religious parents, who are like something out of the 1950s, and Jake lives with his 'very involved' hippie therapist dad. Sometimes I envy them, in a weird way. Still, my parents said it was up to me where I went. In the spirit of optimism and reinvention, I decided to be brave for once and go it alone.

So this is my chance. And I'm doing it for all of us. I have to get it right.

'Let's shop!' Daisy commands. 'Just think: what would RuPaul do?'

Just as Jake spends his life inhaling fashion blogs and hoping his life will start to resemble the images within the pages, Daisy is inspired through the medium of reality TV. The motivating words of RuPaul are her current favourite. She is also a fan of waddling around like a duck sticking out her bottom, after watching the Kardashians, and putting on an affected accent and flipping her hair around a lot in the manner of a Chelsea girl.

'Well,' I interject, 'it's more like what would RuPaul do if he had a total of fifty quid left from his summer-job savings . . .'

'So basically we're looking at either one nice thing from Urban Outfitters or a whole bag of Primani swag . . .' Jake muses.

'And I definitely want money left for chips after,' I remind him. 'And a milkshake.'

'Priorities, priorities . . .' Jake tuts. 'We're talking about your all-important brand-new image here!'

'He's right, Lizzie,' says Daisy.

'Don't worry,' I tell them. 'I've already thought it through. We can go to Beyond Retro.'

If I'm making a whole new start, I want to be different. And there are loads of racks of weird, cheap old clothes there. I can buy myself a whole new vintage image and still have enough money left for chips.

An hour later I'm happily eating my chips in the American diner on the seafront. At my feet I have a shiny yellow carrier bag containing a vintage dress with a bright 1960s pattern. It's made of flammable man-made fibres and feels a bit like a dishcloth. I love it more than I have ever loved any item of clothing in my whole life.

'Not being funny, Lizzie, but it looks like my nan's curtains,' Jake proclaimed when I came out of the changing room in it. 'My eyes actually hurt.'

'He's right, you know,' Daisy agreed. 'It's like something out of the drama costume cupboard at school.'

I ignored them and bought it anyway. They might laugh, but this is the different kind of look I have always dreamed of and never had the guts to pull off.

I love the new brave me.

'You know,' Daisy says, slurping her milkshake and changing the subject, 'I really think this is the year I'm going to get a boyfriend.'

'Yeah, and this is the year I'm going to win *X-Factor*,' says Jake with a roll of his eyes.

Have I mentioned I also love my two best friends?

'Well, it *might* be,' I say, jumping to Daisy's defence. 'If I can go off to college all by myself, there's no reason why all our dreams can't come true. Finally. It's about time, right?'

'Yeah, yeah – all right. Dial it down a notch, Pollyanna Sunshine.' Jake throws a chip at me.

'I'll eat that if you're not having it,' Daisy says quickly, snatching it up off the table and slathering it in mayonnaise. 'But seriously, this is going to be our year. I can sense it.'

We are all the same. This is why the three of us are friends. An unkind person, like most of our classmates back at West Grove, might say that the three of us are mostly friends because nobody else wanted to be friends with us – to be honest, we were sort of thrown together. But the three of us are actually all the same: our friendship is based on the fact that we are all incurable daydreamers. In fact, against the odds, we are pretty much a perfect little gang.

For years now we have been sitting around and talking about what we're going to become, one day in an unspecified near future, and how awesome it's going to be – eventually. Our time together mainly consists of fantasizing and making up stories, and each of us humouring the others about the actual sad state of reality. Our big ideas have always been so far removed from real life, it's like some sort of depressingly aspirational sci-fi novel: *Do Losers Dream of Electric Sheep?* or *The Wannabes' Guide to the Galaxy*.

Jake wants to be famous, only he's not sure how, so his planned means of doing so vary. Popular options include: boyfriend of footballer, or one of those weird people who has loads of plastic surgery and ends up looking like a cat, just because, as he says, 'It would be a lol.'

Daisy's sole ambition is to get a boyfriend. She flips between sometimes not caring who it is, as long as it's someone – *anyone* – and sometimes insisting he has to be the world's most perfect male specimen. At one time she was convinced it was going to be Harry Styles, but she claims to have grown out of that. She has eyes out on stalks whenever we walk down the street, looking out for the special person who will turn out to be her one true love.

Jake and I keep telling her she shouldn't worry so much – she's just the sort of person who is likely to

11

blossom later in life – but boys at school don't tend to look twice at her because she's so wholesome and young-looking. They have no idea that she's secretly boy-crazy.

We might all be bordering on delusional, but at least Jake and Daisy both have some idea of what it is they want out of life. I don't really have a clue. I just know that I want *something*. Something different, something more. It's just that I have literally no idea what that might be. I've always been so envious of people who are really good at a particular subject, or a sport, or a musical instrument.

When I was a kid I was forever searching for my favourite new hobby – so much so that it became a running joke in my family, until my parents realized that it was genuinely upsetting me and contributing to my 'generalized anxiety', which was yet to be diagnosed but evident in full force even when I was a small, nervous child.

There was the time I was desperate to be great at gymnastics – but really I just wanted the leotard and was too scared even to attempt a cartwheel in case I hurt myself. The violin lessons I begged my parents for and then dreaded so much I used to hide in the school loos every week and cry. That time when I was fourteen and decided to 'go emo' and everyone just laughed at me.

Going to college is finally my chance to change all of that. I'm ready – I have never felt so ready for anything in my life.

'A toast, guys,' I say, raising my chocolate milkshake

and grinning around the table with my mouth full. 'To new beginnings.'

'To new beginnings,' the other two dutifully chorus.

'And to me having sex,' Daisy adds.

'And me becoming a reality TV star,' Jake adds after her. 'And to Lizzie finally becoming cool – but not so cool she gets new, better friends and forgets all about us.'

'As if!' I laugh. 'But I *am* going to be really cool.'

'In your hideous polyester nightmare dress.'

Lizzie:

Guys, I just wanted to let you know that The New Lizzie isn't AT ALL nervous about starting college tomorrow. I'm totally cool, just chillaxing, eating three platefuls of my dad's macaroni cheese for dinner . . .

Jake:

Dude, I've experienced your dad's macaroni cheese. I think the world would have to end before I was too nervous to eat three platefuls of that stuff.

Daisy:

PLEASE don't even talk to me about it. I can't take it. My mum's put me on a diet again. I had chicken salad (no skin, no dressing, NO FUN) for dinner.

Jake:

At least you're allowed 'food with a face' in your house. I don't even like chickens and their stupid beady eyes, but my dad has this lame 'respect for all living creatures' thing going on. Lizbot, please tell me your dad did the mac and cheese with the bits of bacon on the top. DROOL.

Lizzie:

Affirmative. Also peas on the side, which doesn't sound all that exciting but is in fact AMAZING. Give peas a chance, guys!

Jake:

SO WITTY.

Lizzie:

Oh, and Daze, I feel your pain.
Salad for dinner – that's way harsh.

Daisy:

It's fine, I've found a pack of choc buttons at the back
of my desk drawer and I will enjoy them all the more
knowing that my mother would disapprove.

Jake:

THAT'S THE SPIRIT.

15

'You're not feeling too nervous about tomorrow – are you, Lizzles?' my dad asks.

'Of course not!' I say brightly, shovelling another massive forkful of pasta and molten cheese into my mouth. 'I'm really looking forward to it.'

'Lizzie, I thought you said you went out for food with your friends earlier,' my mum interjects.

'I only had chips,' I mumble with my mouth full. 'And that was hours ago.'

'I just wondered; you don't have to sound so defensive,' she replies. 'God bless your appetite – that's all.'

I don't think my mum means to sound so disapproving half the time. I try really hard not to take it personally, and to get all stroppy and teenage as a result – I don't want to be a cliché. It's just hard not to take it that way sometimes, when she's so perfect.

When my mum was my age she was an actual part-time model. Not even joking. In a box in the loft there are pictures of her in magazines from the 1990s, wearing weirdly fitting jeans, headbands and floaty spaghetti-strap dresses. Even though it seems to have been an era of brown lipliner and greasy hair, she was ridiculously gorgeous. To be fair, she's still ridiculously gorgeous now – she looks like a mum, with her smart haircut and work outfits, but a really tall and pretty one with great cheekbones I can only dream of.

Unfortunately for me I look just like my dad, who is much more ordinary-looking, nay, geeky. And can also put away the macaroni cheese like it's going out of style.

My parents met because my dad worked at one of the magazines where she went for a casting. He worked in the advertising department and looked then, by all accounts, exactly as he does now – glasses, cardigan, weird man-bag. He is still fond of telling the story of how she walked into the room and he fell madly in love within literally thirty seconds.

'It was like the first time I ever heard an ABBA song,' he likes to say. 'You know, ABBA are a really underrated band. Those are perfect, life-changing pop songs. Just like Annabel's perfect face when I saw it that day and my life changed forever. It wasn't just love at first sight – it was an epiphany.'

My dad's a bit weird. Plus, if he wasn't my dad and always banging on about my mum's beautiful face and – grossly – snogging her in the kitchen (and the hallway, sitting room, dining room, etc.), I'd probably think he was gay. When they first meet him, everyone assumes my dad is gay.

Anyway, he followed her out of the magazine office and down the street and – unsurprisingly – she thought he was a total creepy weirdo. He pestered her for months before she agreed to go out with him. It's one of those stories that would be really cute if it happened in a film starring, say, Emma Stone and Ryan Gosling. But when it's your parents, it makes you feel a bit sick.

My mum wanted to be an actress and only gave up on the idea when she got pregnant with me. She and my dad then started up an 'online marketing and social-media agency' back when that was a new thing. Now they have an office near the seafront in Brighton and loads of people working for them. It's one of those 'lifestyle' offices, where there's table football and 'pizza Fridays' and stuff – it's actually really fun; I'm allowed to work there in the summer holidays, stuffing envelopes and answering phones and other tasks that I can just about be trusted not to mess up. That's how I was earning money all summer – which was supposed to be saved up for my complete new wardrobe and change of image, but ended up going on chips and milkshakes and bus fares until there was only enough left to buy one new vintage dress.

Anyway, now it's my sister Grace who wants to be an actress. After years of being the star of youth theatre, she went out and got herself an agent – without even telling my parents she'd done it until she needed them to go with her and sign the contract. Since then she's been in two adverts and – in a coup that made her the class celebrity and got her a week off school – an episode of *Hollyoaks*. She's only fourteen, but she seems so much more advanced than me. That's the problem with little sisters when you're as stunted as I am – they make you feel terrible about yourself. Plus, Grace isn't exactly sympathetic about it.

'Well, as long as you're not feeling nervous about your first day at college tomorrow,' my dad goes on. 'If you're worried about it, I hope you'd tell us.'

'Honestly, I'm really looking forward to it,' I say.

It's almost insulting how concerned he is. Luckily

nobody is actually that interested, so Grace takes the opportunity to start talking about herself.

'So, today me and Chelsea and Tina went to the beach, and this guy started talking to us, and he thought I was that girl out of that TV programme about models – you know, the pretty one, not the annoying one. It was so funny, but then Chelsea got really annoyed that he didn't think she was anyone. He kept asking if he could take photos of me. Then he wouldn't leave us alone, so we made him buy us ice creams and then we ran away. It was hilarious.'

'Um, how old was this person?' my dad asks, brow furrowed, doing his awkward twitchy thing. 'Was he the same sort of age as you?'

Grace shrugs elegantly. 'I dunno. Why?'

'Because he sounds like a paedophile, Grace,' I explain helpfully. 'He was grooming you. You shouldn't really let old pervs buy you ice creams.'

'Well, he was pretty old, I suppose.' She cocks her head to one side as she thinks about it. 'At least nineteen. I told him I was eighteen. But don't worry, we weren't interested. We just really wanted ice cream. By the way, Dad, can you lend me twenty pounds?'

He looks at her for a moment like he's going to tell her off, then bursts out laughing. He slaps his forehead in mock horror, but he can't stop. She just stares at him with a scathing expression on her face, while he laughs and laughs. That's the thing about my dad; he's ridiculously good-natured.

'What's so funny?' Grace asks. 'I saw this bag in Topshop that I really need, and me and my friends are going shopping on Saturday.'

'I *think* what your father's trying to say,' my mum interrupts, 'is that you shouldn't be talking to strange men on the seafront, and you already have a perfectly good school bag. So, the answer is a big, all-round no. Oh, and you're grounded. That's what your father meant. That's what you meant – wasn't it, darling?'

'Well, that does seem a bit steep,' my dad blusters, his eyes darting between my mum and my sister, vaguely panicked, not sure which of them he's the most terrified of – a dilemma I totally understand. 'It wasn't really her fault that—'

'*Nicholas*,' my mum says in a warning tone, 'that *was* what you meant – wasn't it, *darling*?'

'Yes! Of course, that was exactly what I meant,' my dad says, clearly trying not to burst out laughing again.

'This is so unfair,' Grace rages. 'I made a ton of money from that Clearasil advert, and you kept it all for yourselves. I only want twenty quid for a bag in Topshop – it's not bloody Chanel! You two are so *crap*.'

My mum rolls her eyes. 'Grace, that money has gone into an account that you can access when you are twenty-one. I hate to say this, but you will thank me for this when you're older.'

'I'm going up to my room. You can leave my pudding outside the door.'

My parents exchange a glance as Grace flounces from

the table and then thinks better of it, coming back to refill her plate with macaroni cheese before storming off again.

'Honestly, I think we're going to have to start getting tougher with that girl.' My mum sighs. 'Pass the wine, Nick.'

'At your service, m'lady.'

My dad can be guaranteed to diffuse the tension and cheer my mum up. Which is almost a shame, because this is a subject where for once I agree with her, and I would like to hear the full conversation. Grace can be a total nightmare and she seems to be getting worse – I swear she gets meaner by the day. Dad pours Mum a glass of wine and extravagantly kisses her over the table. I involuntarily make a disapproving face.

'Sorry, Mary Whitehouse,' my dad says. 'Listen, are you sure you're OK about tomorrow? All set?'

'Dad, it's lovely that you care so much, but you honestly don't need to worry about me.'

If know he's trying to help, and my dad gets very emotional about things, but if he keeps going on about it, it will only make me *more* nervous. Besides, for once he doesn't need to worry – everything's going to be fine. In fact, it's going to be great – I know it.

Lizzie:

Guys, are we really sure about the new vintage dress???

Jake:

TBH I was never sure about the new vintage dress.

Daisy:

Not helpful J. Lizzie, you LOVE the dress! It's so YOU!

Lizzie:

OK, cool. I was just feeling weirdly nervous. Stupid, right? Maybe I should just wear jeans and my Sonic Youth T-shirt. Not look like I'm trying too hard.

Jake:

Srsly, if you wear those depressing old jeans I will never speak to you again. And don't even get me started on your saggy old 'ironic' jumpers – if you wear any sort of KNITWEAR, I will actually kill you. OK thanks bye.

Lizzie:

OK, you're right. I *do* love the dress. It's all going to be GREAT! YAY!

Daisy:

Yup. GREAT. YAY! Hadn't you better go if you're not even dressed yet? You'll be late for your big day!

Jake:

Spare a thought for us. Back on the chain gang in our nasty school uniforms, all the same old faces, no excitement . . . SOB.

Daisy:

You're the trailblazer, Lizzie! You'll be AWESOME! Knock 'em dead.

Jake:

Not literally! (Oh, and break a leg . . . again, not literally.)

Lizzie:

Thanks, guys! OK. The dress is going ON! Wish me luck . . .

I do love my new dress. But everything seems a bit scarier without my friends around to back me up. We've been pretty much inseparable since Year Seven and this is really the first time I've faced the world on my own. I'm excited, but I'm not going to lie – it's a little bit terrifying as well. I suppose a few last-minute nerves are inevitable. Right?

And it's an important decision. This outfit might define the rest of my life. Well, the next two years, which is a really long time. When I think about it like that, no wonder I've spent the last twenty minutes messaging my friends for their advice, standing in front of my open wardrobe wearing a turquoise leopard-print Primark onesie and a stupid expression.

'Lizzie?' My mum's voice bellows up the stairs, reminding me that I really do need to get a move on.

I force myself to take a deep breath. I will be brave. I remind myself that today is the first day of the rest of my life. Or the second day of the rest of my life. Whatever. I'm going to go out there and make a big success of it. It's going to be great.

'Elizabeth Brown!' My mum's voice is getting louder and louder. 'I know this is a big day for you, but I've got to get to work. Five minutes, or I'm leaving without you!'

I know from experience that this is actually true, so at least it forces me into action. I can't hang around in my bedroom obsessing over my wardrobe forever. I've got to get out there.

So – sod it. Fortune favours the brave. I grab the lurid

polyester vintage dress and awkwardly scramble into it – not giving myself the chance to chicken out. Then I chuck on tights, leather jacket and trainers, hoping this will tone it down rather than make me look like a charity shop has thrown up on me.

I grab my bag and run out the door. I only allow myself a quick glance in the mirror on my way out – the new vintage dress makes me smile involuntarily, which must be a good sign. I really do love it – I'm glad I decided to be brave; it's the way forward today. All things considered, I think I look just right. Time to stop obsessing and go for it.

'You look . . . different,' my mum says, her head cocked to one side and her voice vaguely suspicious.

'Thanks!' I reply cheerfully, sticking with my Positive Mental Attitude.

I'm not sure if she quite means it as a compliment, but I'm choosing to take it as one.

'Not too nervous, are you?' she asks briskly.

She's not big on feelings – which is sometimes good, as my dad is *very* into feelings. I love my dad, but if he was here he would definitely hug me a lot and possibly even cry – this morning for once my mum is the preferable parent.

'I'm fine, thanks!' I reply.

'Good girl. Now, I'm working late this evening, so I won't be able to pick you up. I've got a call with New York later on – but your dad's working at home, so he can come and get you if you need him to.'

'Thanks, Mum. It's OK though – I'll probably just walk.'

'Well, do me a favour and text him to let him know how you get on, OK? You know he'll only worry otherwise. Right, I've got to dash – so I'll drop you here. Have a great first day!'

I actually surprise myself with how confident I feel as I watch Mum drive away. Maybe a bit of her confidence has rubbed off on me. I smile and wave as she disappears around the corner at speed.

I force myself to take a deep breath and hold my head up as I cross the road and walk towards the college gates, stopping only to rummage in my bag for a minute until I find my headphones. I scroll through my music options and settle on some 80s Madonna to keep me feeling brave and badass. Again I marvel at the effect that music can have on my mood. That's why I like making playlists for every possible occasion, to pull out when I need them. The right soundtrack can make all the difference.

My dad got me into music at a young age – my parents always say I must have been the only three-year-old to know all the words to everything from David Bowie to De La Soul via Nirvana. It's always stuck with me – and right now it does the trick. I secretly pretend I'm in a music video and even manage a little swagger in my step as I walk through the gates and into my future.

Lizzie:

Guys! It's going GREAT so far.

Daisy:

THIS IS SO EXCITING! WHAT'S HAPPENED??!

Lizzie:

Well, nothing has actually *happened* . . . I haven't gone inside yet. Right now I'm just walking up to the main entrance. But I have a really good feeling about this.

Daisy:

Have you seen any cool people yet?

Have you talked to anyone? Any fit guys???

Lizzie:

Not yet – but I bet I will! I mean, the thing to remember is that nobody knows anyone yet. We're all new, not just me. So everyone will want to make new friends. RIGHT???!!!!

Daisy:

Exactly!

Jake:

This is very touching and all . . . but maybe get off your phone and actually talk to these people. Next time you text us HAVE SOMETHING TO ACTUALLY TELL US. OK?

27

The nearer I get to the building, the less confident I feel. I am actually deflating. The place is so *big* and I have no idea where I am going. I slow down with every step until I'm standing motionless, like an idiot in everyone's way in the entrance. I can feel any trace of optimism slowly start to drain out of me, like blow-dried party hair on a rainy night.

I force myself to put one foot in front of the other down the endless corridor and follow the scrappy printed signs that seem to be taped to every available wall, saying 'New Student Induction'. Even then I'm not going quickly enough and a few people shove past me without stopping or saying a word.

I dawdle so much that the main hall is pretty much full by the time I arrive. It's totally overwhelming, and I feel worryingly panicky as I just stand there in the doorway. These people must all be the same age as me. Statistically some of them must also not know anybody. It's impossible that I'm the only person here who knows nobody, but that's exactly what it feels like. Why do they all seem so much older, so much more confident, so much *more*?

I try my very best to hold my head up and regain a little bit of the optimism I felt only a few minutes ago, but I have no idea what to do or where I'm supposed to sit. I can't bring myself to actually instigate a conversation with anyone, but I try to smile hopefully as I walk into the room and hope somebody might approach me. This doesn't happen, so I select a chair right at the back, by itself and separated from anyone else by a few spaces so as to avoid any potentially humiliating human interaction, as a man who looks even less cool than any of my teachers back at school did walks on to the stage. I make a vague attempt at eye contact with a girl down the row from me, so that perhaps we can bond over this observation, but it doesn't really work, as she starts talking to the boy next to her and I pretend I was looking at the clock behind her head. Smooth, Lizzie – well done.

'Ah, welcome, everyone.' The teacher spends ten minutes clearing the frog out of his throat before he introduces himself as Mr Stark. 'But if you find yourself in my history class, you might end up calling me David. You see, that's the thing – A levels, or whatever course you are doing, are much more challenging than GCSEs. You will find college to be a very different environment to school. But if you are prepared to act like adults, we will treat you like adults.'

Despite my state of mounting anxiety, his voice is so monotonous it could put anyone to sleep. I'm tuning out already, and everyone else in the room seems to be as well – at least that's one thing we all have in common; I'm not a total anomaly.

And then she walks in.

I swear mine is not the only head to turn. Even though she enters at the back of the room – with a bang of the heavy door and a resulting shrug – there is some kind of energy about her that makes everybody turn around and look.

When I see her, just for a second I imagine what it must be like to *be* her. To look like that, to wear those clothes, to have that face and cool hair and air of not caring what anyone thinks. Because if you look like that, then why would you worry about *anything*?

If I thought I was being cool and different with my vintage dress and my cheap fake leather jacket, it very quickly becomes apparent that . . . I'm not. Her outfit makes mine look like something a mad auntie might wear, or maybe a costume from some twee 'retro' school play. Her dress is a bit like mine but a million times sexier, and set off with dyed platinum-blonde hair and perfect eyeliner. She sits down right at the back, on the opposite side of the room to me.

I have to force myself to look away so she doesn't think I am some kind of psycho. I try to concentrate on: a) the world's most boring speech (official); and b) not hating myself and my own mediocrity/cowardliness/mentalism too much. Both of these tasks are almost impossible.

Lizzie:

OK, so you said not to text until something ACTUALLY HAPPENED . . . Well, what do you want to know first???!

Daisy:

I want to know about the MEN, obv. Any fitties? Have you talked to any?

Lizzie:

OMG. Daze, you would be in HEAVEN. The boys here are so much hotter than the ones back at school.

Jake:

Yeah, thx a lot. I AM a male, you know. I think you two forget that sometimes. It's insulting. So have you actually talked to any of these amazing superior beings yet?

Lizzie:

Of course! We had this induction thing in the morning and we all had to introduce ourselves and chat and stuff. Bit cringe but quite good for meeting people in my classes. Everyone seems really friendly. I met a really cool girl as well.

Daisy:

Hope you aren't going to meet any new cool girls who you like more than me?! What's this girl called? I hate her already!

Lizzie:

Listen, I've got to go! There's loads going on here, it's bonkers. More later . . .

Until *right now* I didn't know how lucky I used to be. Why didn't I appreciate my brilliant sad little life before? Before it was too late.

I was such a baby. I complained all the time about how bored I was, how rubbish everything was; me and my friends talked non-stop every single day about how we couldn't wait to get out. We were *so* sick of being stuck there in the world's most boring school.

Daisy and Jake don't know how lucky they are, and I really don't want to disappoint them by telling them the truth. But really I'd give anything to swap places. If only 'dull' and 'boring' were all I had to contend with now. Instead of low-level panic and a sense of my own general rubbishness.

It is now officially 1.57 p.m. and nobody has spoken to me since my mum dropped me off this morning. That means I have not spoken all day to another human being who I am not related to. Including teachers, who have so far delivered pre-prepared speeches to the wall somewhere above the top of my head, rather than ever addressing me personally – speaking directly only to those brave enough to stick up their hand and ask a question, which certainly does not include me.

My fellow students have, if anything, been even less communicative. It can't be possible that they all know each other and have already formed terrifying, impenetrable gangs – so why does it feel that way? Even the people who look mousier and less cool than me seem to know something I don't. Maybe they all scuttle off together to the library or the computer room or something. Because whenever I try to spot someone to approach, to try being friends with – just to make eye contact and smile at in the hopes of starting a conversation – there's literally nobody. I've given up already.

So far today I have invented several strategies for trying to look busy, so I'm not just standing around on my own like a total loser as everyone else goes about excluding me from their social lives:

1. Texting. More specifically, texting Daisy and Jake pointless (totally made-up) drivel, just for something to do. I feel weird and a bit terrible about this, but I can't let them know the truth – then they'd probably be just as depressed as I am. There's no point taking them down with me.

2. Staring at my phone and pretending to text. For when I've run out of pointless (totally made-up) drivel to send Daisy and Jake.

3. Putting my headphones on, hoping this makes me look occupied and that the music might distract me – unfortunately I am now on approximately the tenth repeat of my motivational first-day playlist and the desired effect seems to have worn off. There are only so many times you can listen to 'Don't Stop Believing' in one day and still be moved by it.

4. Gazing into the middle distance while looking casual and glancing occasionally at my watch, as if

waiting for someone. This one works quite well for those interminable 'in-between' times.

5. Buying a hummus-and-salad sandwich in the canteen at lunchtime, then, unable to spot any empty tables and not having the balls to sit down in close proximity to strangers, finally deciding to bring the sandwich to eat in the loo. In possibly the most depressing and least hygienic culinary experience of all time. Admittedly, the sandwich is quite delicious.

Oh, actually, I told a lie. Precisely one person has spoken to me today. The lady who sold me the sandwich in the canteen said:

'One pound ninety . . . Ten pence change . . . You're welcome. Next.'

So I have had nine words directed at me today. Actually, I suppose the 'next' must have been intended for the person in the queue behind me. So technically eight words.

This calculation makes everything seem very real all of a sudden. The thought is so depressing I can hardly stand it. I know there are wars and starving people in the world, and I can't shake the feeling that I'm just being silly and spoiled . . . but I feel miserable.

Just this morning I was so confident. So hopeful. So stupid. And now look at me. I am locked in a toilet, trying not to cry and dreading going back outside.

I don't think I can take two years of feeling like this. I

really didn't see it coming, but now I can't believe I ever thought I could do this. What an idiot.

I'm going to go home tonight and tell my parents I want to go back to West Grove for sixth form after all. If nothing else, it's got to be better than this. I don't care how embarrassing it is; everyone will soon forget all about the whole thing, right? It will be like I was never away . . . right?

Suddenly it occurs to me that they might not even *let* me come back. I've technically left, and I know there's a waiting list for the sixth form there, as their A-level results are generally excellent. In fact, it's the sort of school where my very average GCSE results were considered a bit of a disappointment – loads of people did really, properly well. The best I ever got on my school reports was 'Lizzie's such a trier'. It was like even the teachers felt a bit sorry for me.

Oh god, they're not going to let me back and I will be stuck here forever. Maybe I'll have to play the loony card. Maybe I can make everyone feel bad for me and then they'll have to . . . No, stop it, Lizzie. Even if I could, after everything that happened it wouldn't be worth worrying my mum and dad all over again.

I am not a sad person. I may have my stupid anxiety issues, but I'm actually very good at being a cheerful, just-getting-on-with-it sort of a person. I have had to be.

I am certainly not a crier. Daisy is the crier. Daisy cries at everything – movies, adverts, puppies, when she's hungry . . . The list goes on. I hardly ever cry.

So it happens without me even noticing it. For a second I wonder what that weird high-pitched whining noise is. Then I realize that my face is wet and it is me. There is actual snot dripping down my chin before I have fully understood what is even going on. And once I start I can't seem to stop.

In fact, my entire crying fit probably only lasts for about thirty seconds. It starts to become quite an enjoyable sensation. I should cry more often, I think. Unfortunately, this thought distracts me from the crying, and I find I've stopped before I've even really got started.

Then I hear another noise, and I am so intrigued that I forget to cry altogether. The door to the toilets bangs open, literally making me jump, but the expected echo of it is drowned out by the sound of singing. Proper, real-life singing. Loud.

'*One way or another . . .*'

I hold my breath, my ears out on elastic, on high alert to try to figure out exactly what is going on. For a second I wonder if it's a radio. But, no, it really is a girl's voice. Not any girl I have ever heard singing in real life before though. This voice is belting out a tune without the slightest trace of volume control or self-consciousness. It's a great voice, but not in some school-choir or *X-Factor* kind of way. This is proper belting, rock 'n' roll style.

'. . . *I'm gonna getcha . . .*'

I can't resist. I stop cowering in the toilet stall like the world's biggest loser. Quickly I unspool a massive wodge of loo roll and hurriedly wipe my face.

I hear the hand dryer start whirring, and I'm so worried I might miss this one random window, I burst out of the toilet cubicle like there's a fire in there. Still the singing doesn't stop. In the mirror I catch sight of The Girl with the Voice and I am pretty much dumbstruck. This has got to be the weirdest lunch hour ever. Including the year when I was having 'behavioural problems' and had to eat my lunch in the science lab while Mrs Fowler the biology teacher did things like dissect mice and build models of reproductive organs around me and my Marmite sandwiches.

Anyway, It's *her*. The girl I saw earlier. All bleached blonde hair and eyeliner. Not to mention that she is tall and voluptuous and looks like some kind of pin-up model. The coolest girl I've ever seen – and properly, legitimately beautiful, even close up.

'That's Blondie!' I practically shout the words out; I've been so desperate to say them. 'The song, I mean. Blondie. Debbie Harry. "One Way or Another".'

She stops singing and starts laughing. 'Wow. I can't believe you know that,' she says. 'I'm sure most people around here probably think the 1D version is the original. I love Debbie Harry. She's amazing.'

She rummages inside her giant suitcase of a handbag. Eventually she fishes out a fat eyeliner and starts topping up her make-up. Then she fluffs up her already perfect hair with her fingers. I just watch. She doesn't seem uncomfortable at all. After my big opening with the Debbie Harry reference, I am completely lost for words.

Should I:

a) Say something else – anything. Oh god, what can I say? Inane questions, the weather, Syria – like I said, *anything*?!

b) At least smile, rather than staring at her with a frozen expression like an antisocial weirdo or possible stalker?

c) Just stand here like an absolute moron and wish I could be someone else, who has even an ounce of charm and brilliance?

Oh, OK. *C* it is. Luckily, while she does her make-up, she catches my eye and grins at me in the mirror. Then she starts doing enough talking for both of us. I can't believe it – she's actually really friendly and nice, and bothering to talk to *me*.

'My name's Viv. Well, Viviane really, but nobody calls me that. My mum's a moron. No wonder I don't speak to her any more. So, Viviane Zoe Weldon. For some reason she wanted to give me the stupidest initials of all time. What's your name? Love your outfit.'

So of course I could:

a) Attempt to come up with an amusing anecdote around my name like she did and make myself sound interesting.

b) At least say thanks for the compliment on my dress, which I'm suddenly glad again that I wore, after a whole morning of feeling like I was standing out for all the wrong reasons and wishing I had just tried to blend in.

c) Not manage either of these very basic and obvious things.

Although these options run through my head at lightning speed, presenting themselves in multiple-choice succession, no prizes for guessing which one wins in real life.

'Um, Lizzie.'

'Like, short for Elizabeth, or something else?'

'Yeah, Elizabeth.'

It dawns on me that I actually have the most boring name in the world, to go with my boring personality. I'd never really thought about it. I should have come up with a more interesting abbreviation before now: Beth, Eliza, Elly . . . *Anything*. Not just boring old Lizzie Brown. Everything about me seems boring compared to this girl.

'So, Lizzie – are you new? How are you finding it?'

'Um . . .' I have no idea what to say – now that I'm having an Actual Conversation with a Cool Person for the first time since I got here, I don't want to blow it by admitting that I am the most pathetic person she could possibly have met and she would be better off making friends with anyone else. 'I don't really know anyone here . . .'

'Oh, thank god! Neither do I. Do you want to skive off

this afternoon and go for coffee? I don't really feel like hanging around.'

Of course I know what the sensible answer to this question would be – I am well aware that this is a really, really bad idea, and all the trouble I could get into, and how given my track record that could be a complete and total disaster. I'm the girl who's scared of everything, particularly getting into trouble. I've never broken the rules in my life.

And look where that's got me. Crying by myself in a toilet cubicle. I have the sudden feeling that this girl could be a 'bad influence' on me, but I find for the first time ever that I literally do not care.

'OK,' I say.

'Cool. Let's go. By the way, I kind of love what you've done with your make-up. Very post-goth.'

I've been so busy staring at her, I hadn't even noticed. It seems so unbelievable that five minutes ago I was crying my eyes out in a toilet cubicle. As a result, my eyeliner has set in artful streaks all the way down my face. I smile at my own reflection and then turn to follow Viv wherever she is going.

Lizzie:

So, just heading into town with my cool new friend Viv – NBD.

Daisy:

Whaaaaaaaaaaaaaaaaaaaat?

Jake:

Shouldn't you be like *learning* or whatever? Are you skiving?! Surely not. This is very unlike you and your uncool fear of authority.

Lizzie:

Yeah, just going into town for a coffee. Skiving isn't really a big deal here, it's different at college. So it's going to be FINE.

Jake:

YOU HATE COFFEE!!!

Daisy:

Where are you going?
What's happening????!

Lizzie:

Sorry, better go. Bye!!!

'Hey, Lauren. How are you doing?' Viv stands up and actually *hugs* the waitress as she comes over to our table in the coolest cafe in the Lanes – Cafe Vinyl, famous for its great coffee and its perfect soundtrack. Being a total vinyl geek, I've always wanted to come in here, but have been too intimidated by the hipster clientele. Daisy and Jake prefer the tacky 50s diner on the seafront, and I could hardly come into a place like this on my own.

Viv seems to know everyone here and feel completely at home. She is so relaxed I feel practically Amish by comparison.

'A black coffee, please,' she says.

'Like you need any more caffeine,' the waitress – bobbed hair, great eyeliner – laughs. 'You're always hyper enough as it is, Miss Viviane.'

'Oh, by the way, this is my new friend Lizzie,' Viv says, beaming at me and literally making my day. 'This is Lauren. The hottest waitress in town, obviously.'

'I'm not *just* a waitress though – I'm Brighton's most promising up-and-coming photographer,' Lauren adds, nudging Viv.

'Oh, of course, and that. When I'm a famous rock star, you're going to be my official photographer, right? It's happening, babe.' Viv says it like it's already settled – coming from her, this actually sounds plausible.

'Yeah, right.' Lauren rolls her eyes. 'In the meantime, in this brief window before we become rich and famous – what can I get you to drink, Lizzie?'

I pause just a fraction too long as the inevitable list forms in my brain.

a) Copy Viv and ask for a coffee, even though I hate the stuff. And might be sick over myself. Which might negate coolness of coffee order.
b) Cup of tea. Safe. Classic versus boring?
c) Hot chocolate. A lovely, delicious hot chocolate. I would love a hot chocolate so, so much.

I wish I actually had time to text these options to Daisy and Jake, to gauge the group's opinion as usual. Left to my own devices, I'm more clueless than ever. Now things are finally looking up, I don't want to blow it.

'Yeah, I'll have a black coffee as well, please,' I hear myself saying.

'Cool. I'll bring them over in a minute. Nice to meet you, Lizzie.'

I feel weirdly disappointed in myself as Lauren walks away. They always say it's important to be yourself, and I can't even be myself when I'm ordering a hot drink – but I'm not taking any chances. My natural self really isn't that great. It hasn't done much for me so far anyway.

'So, that's Lauren,' Viv says. 'Like she said, she's an amazing photographer. She took some photos of me that I'm planning to use as publicity shots one day.'

'Wow . . . So,' I venture, 'what was that you were saying about being a famous rock star. . . ? Your singing sounded great. Do you have a band or something?'

'Well, that's the plan. For now I'm Brighton's most famous unknown. But I've got big ambitions. I've been singing forever – you know, not your usual *X Factor* crap, real music. That's what I'm going for anyway.'

'Cool!' I exclaim.

'So, a while ago I thought that if I'm actually going to make it out of my bedroom, I need to be able to do more than just sing. I've been learning guitar and writing some songs, trying to get a band together. It's early days but I'm going to get there. Watch this space. You never know, maybe one day you'll be able to say you knew me when.'

'If anyone can do it, I bet you can.' As soon as the words leave my mouth it occurs to me that this is a weird thing to say, considering that I don't even know her – it just slipped out before I could stop it. This is why I usually have to be so guarded – otherwise I find myself accidentally saying stupid things like this.

'Thanks, babe,' is all Viv says, sounding actually pleased, and I feel myself relaxing a tiny bit. 'Well, in the meantime, even if I'm not a rock star yet, at least I can try and look like a rock star. Maybe we can go shopping in the Lanes after this. I love shopping. Of course.'

'Great – me too!' I find myself saying.

This is not true in any way, shape or form. Everyone who knows me would burst out laughing if they heard me say I love shopping. Shopping, and clothes, and communal changing rooms, and doing battle with sizing and feeling like people are looking at me and worrying about my bikini line or if I look too fat or too short or too flat-chested . . . well, just the thought is enough to make me break out in a cold sweat. I guess if the brave new me wants to wear cool vintage dresses, I'm going to have to get over it – after all, I can't wear this one outfit every day for evermore. Still, there's a big bit of me that would rather just wear my comfy old jeans and spend my money on records. But that's the same bit of me that just wants to stay indoors and preferably never talk to another human being again, so she's not actually very helpful.

'Hang on just a sec,' Viv says. 'I must go for a wee; I'm bursting. Then we'll finish our coffee and blow this pop stand.'

I can't take my eyes off her as she deftly picks her way through the crowded cafe, waving at a couple of people on her way. I'm so deep in thought that I actually jump slightly when I hear a voice right next to me. Going off into my own world when I'm in a public place is one of my worst habits – it was always one of the running jokes about me at West Grove.

'Hey.'

In the seat that Viv has recently vacated, a boy has appeared. Not just any boy. A ridiculously hot boy. Seriously, I am *so* glad I met Viv and skived off college with her. Who knew such great things could come from breaking the rules?

The first thing I notice is the most perfect hair I have ever seen. I have to stop myself from reaching out and touching it. It's just the right balance between long and short, artfully dishevelled but not trying too hard. Of course the hair tops off a retro-cool outfit that includes the obligatory skinny leather jacket, drainpipe jeans, battered Converse and band T-shirt. This guy is so good-looking he looks like a young Elvis playing a modern day hipster. Let's face it – he looks like all my dreams come true.

He smiles at me and I find myself smiling back, feeling as though I have been bathed in sunshine. Then I tell myself to get a grip. Dude, seriously. The inevitable lists spool through my head like an out-of-control matrix, but none of the possible multiple-choice options are any help.

'Um, hi,' I say.

He puts a vintage-patterned plate in front of me. It seems like a very strange thing to do. Is this some sort of code I ought to know about?

Still, I forget about everything else when I get a burnt-sugar whiff of gooey warm flapjack and my stomach gives a gigantic rumble in response. I shift awkwardly in my seat, crossing my arms as hard as possible over my lap.

The boy laughs. 'Flapjack? Sounds like you need one.'

'Oh . . . Um, I didn't order this. Sorry.'

'It's on the house. And it's the best flapjack in Brighton – and I should know. Made with my own fair hands. The secret is a mixture of golden syrup and black treacle. Obviously I can't tell you the ratios or I'd have to kill you. Seriously. Try a bit.'

I take a small bite of flapjack, trying to forget the fact that this boy is staring intently at me while I eat. A clump of oats sticks to my lip and I wipe it away with the back of my hand, barely noticing that I have taken off half my lipstick with it, all the better to match my destroyed eyeliner – as it is, in fact, truly the best flapjack I have ever tasted.

'That *is* the best flapjack I have ever tasted,' I tell him.

'You've got to love a flapjack.' He grins. 'I'm a bit obsessed with them. I'm thinking of starting a blog about flapjacks. With all my secret recipes, and flapjack puns. You can't beat a good flapjack pun. My theme tune is "Don't Stop 'Til You Get Enough" by the Flapjackson Five.'

'So you're basically a flapjack artist . . . Flapjackson Pollock.' The words came out of my mouth unexpectedly, and I am gratified to see that his face breaks into a wide smile. That sunshine feeling washes over me again and I find that for once I want to keep talking, to make him laugh and look at me with those wide smiley eyes.

Our eyes meet – mine dull and brown, with their messy, cried-off eyeliner; his the most beautiful shade of green and with unexpectedly long eyelashes. They are so thick and black I wonder for a second if he is wearing mascara, and so I forget to look away when I'm supposed to. I just keep staring at him.

Suddenly he's the one who looks the other way – right over my shoulder – and I look back down at the flapjack, examining it intently.

'Here she comes,' he says. 'Flapjackie O herself.'

I follow his gaze and see Viv sashaying – yes, literally

sashaying – back from the loo.

'Oh, good, I see you two have met,' she says. 'You're not boring poor Lizzie with tales of flapjacks and fairy cakes and the perfect cup of tea, are you?' she says, shoving Indie Elvis out of her seat and sitting down.

I can't believe she actually knows him. Maybe he will think I'm cool by association. Maybe my luck is about to change.

'Actually, we haven't officially met yet,' he says, raising his eyebrows at me in a question mark.

'Well, then allow me to do the honours,' says Viv. 'Lizzie, this is the infamous Rex Matthews. He works here, as you may have worked out. Rex, this is my new friend Lizzie. Lizzie, this is terrible, we've been new best friends for over an hour and I don't even know your last name. Hit me.'

I feel so ordinary it's embarrassing. I wish I could actually make something up.

'Brown,' I mumble apologetically. 'Lizzie Brown. The most boring name in the history of the world. I don't even have a middle name.'

'I like it,' Rex says.

I smile back goofily at him before I can stop myself. As well as being so ridiculously handsome, I notice that he also has a kind face, underneath all that hair.

'Hey, at least it's less of a mouthful than Viviane Zoe Weldon.' He shrugs most appealingly. 'And a hell of a lot easier to spell. So count your blessings.'

'Wow, you even remembered my middle name!' Viv

exclaims. 'Rex, that's so . . . romantic.'

As she says this she puts her arm around him. For a second I think it must be some kind of ironic joke – her tone is so sarcastic that maybe they are just friends. I don't know why I'm holding my breath, hoping desperately that this is the case, when I only laid eyes on this guy five minutes ago and I barely know either of them. I may as well be watching this on TV; that's how involved I am in the situation here.

Then they smoosh their faces close together as if they are posing for the world's coolest-looking, best-combined-hair selfie, and he kisses the side of her face – on her cheek, but just catching the side of her mouth.

Embarrassing confession alert: I have never actually been kissed in any way before – except once, by Jake, who is obviously gay, when he was drunk on a bottle of sherry he won on the tombola at the school Christmas bazaar – so I would not venture to call myself an expert.

However, even in my limited knowledge, and from watching an awful lot of rom-coms with Reese Witherspoon or Sandra Bullock in them (with my dad; they're his favourites), I'm fairly certain that was not a kiss between platonic friends. It could be something to do with the way that he closed his eyes for a moment as his lips touched her flawless skin.

Unreasonably, my heart sinks. Then I instantly hate myself for it. What did I *think* was going to happen? They're both so perfect – *of course* they are a couple. You're an idiot, Lizzie. Maybe one day I'll learn not to get my hopes up like this. It never ends well.

'Don't ruin my lipstick, Rex! So I just got a text from Jess – she's going to be the bass player in my band. I have to go round to her house,' Viv says, simultaneously texting as she talks. 'Sorry, Lizzie – I know we were going to go around town together after this, but I'd better go. See you soon, yeah? Tomorrow at college.'

'Yeah, nice to meet you,' I say lamely, feeling sad that it's all suddenly over.

'Look me up on Facebook – there's not many people with my name so you'll know it's me.'

She's already putting her coat on and I'm too embarrassed to start the whole long and boring story about why I don't do Facebook. Or Instagram or any other social media. I look at my watch just for something to do, and then realize that I actually need to go as well – by the time I get home, it will be around the time I should legitimately be back if I hadn't skived off all afternoon. Dad's working at home, and even if he didn't notice, Grace can be such a little grass when she wants to be.

'Bye, then,' Viv says, standing up and – of course – kissing Rex on the lips this time, 'I'll see you at home, OK?'

Home?

'See you guys.' Viv waves over her shoulder as she strolls off.

'Well, I should be getting on,' Rex says. 'Stuff to do, people to see, flapjacks to make . . . I'd better do some work; I can't just sit around and chat. I guess I'll be seeing you around as you're Viv's new mate, yeah?'

'See you . . .'

He's turned away and started talking to somebody else before I've even finished the two syllables. Now that Viv's gone, of course there's no reason why he would want to hang around and talk to me.

With nothing else to do, I set aside my untouched cold coffee, pick up my bag and struggle into my leather jacket – which, incidentally, now looks cheap and plasticky and really unauthentic compared to Rex's.

I notice out of the corner of my eye that he shrugs out of his, standing behind the counter in his Clash T-shirt, simultaneously pouring a coffee and putting an old Iggy Pop record on the cool old-fashioned turntable.

I walk out of Cafe Vinyl slowly, practically walking backwards, feeling like I ought to make the most of this day while I can. Why can't I shake the feeling that this was all some sort of weird dream and I am never going to see any of these people again?

Lizzie:

Just on my way home from Cafe Vinyl, NBD . . . How was your day?

Jake:

Dire. While you were skiving off college like some kind of badass, I got detention for NO GOOD REASON. School is the worst. You're so lucky.

Lizzie:

What happened?

Daisy:

Well, I am on your side, J . . . But it wasn't *exactly* no good reason.

Lizzie:

What happened????!!!

Jake:

NOTHING. You can read all about it one day in my memoirs.

Lizzie:

He got detention for wearing make-up. Then having an argument about it with Mr Parker.

Jake:

See? I did nothing wrong. I was discriminated against for not being binary in my gender. That school is so bigoted.

Lizzie:

OMFG. This sounds awful. Are you OK? Your dad must be furious with the school. How dare they?!

Daisy:

Well, Mr Parker was actually being pretty nice about it (and pointed out that nobody – male or female or otherwise – is allowed to wear make-up at school). It only kicked off when J called him an ugly old man and told him he should try using a BB cream.

Jake:

See? That's not so bad.

Daisy:

I think it was when you attacked him with your Batiste that things took a turn for the worse. Lizzie, he literally sprayed him in the face.

Lizzie:

Sorry, guys – really want to chat but I've got to go.

Jake:

SHE'S FORGETTING ALL ABOUT US ALREADY, DAZE.

Daisy:

Shut up. But don't forget you're both coming round to mine on Saturday night, OK. My parents are out!

'So, how was your day?' my dad asks.

For once I can hardly wait to start talking. I'm basically like our cat Maurice when he has caught a mouse and is just desperate to dump it in my bed.

'It was *great.*' I choose not to notice the surprised looks my parents are casting both at me and each other – apparently me being socially functional and having a good day is so hard to believe. 'Fantastic,' I add for good measure.

'Oh. Gosh. Wow.' My dad blinks from behind his glasses. 'How so, exactly?'

'I met this girl. She's called Viv. She's really cool. I think we're going to be really good friends. We went out for coffee . . . I mean, after college was finished, so it was fine. She likes really good music and she's a singer. We went to that cool place in the Lanes, Cafe Vinyl, and I met some of her friends, like this girl who's a photographer. It was brilliant.'

Saying it out loud feels like a magic spell. If I say it, it is real. It will happen. This will be my new life.

'So, what, are you a lesbian now?'

Grace sounds totally matter of fact – like, even if I am, this isn't exciting news to her.

'No, Grace, I'm not a lesbian. Although I'm sure you'd be cool with it if I was. Because that would be fine. There is nothing wrong with being a lesbian. But I am not one.'

'Oh, I just wondered,' she says. 'Because of your clothes and everything.'

I sigh. 'Well, actually, we wear pretty much the same

sort of clothes. It's just that I look different in them.'

More like a lesbian, apparently – whatever that means. Grace looks me up and down with the cold appraisal of a department-store makeover person.

'That's so funny,' she says. 'You're actually right. Who knew?'

Have I mentioned that Grace is ridiculously gorgeous? Not even in an easily mocked, generic sort of way. She's actually beautiful, and a bit weird-looking in a way that makes everyone else appear like a boring lesser species. People literally stare at her in the street. She has the face of a pretty space alien, with wide-apart eyes and gappy teeth – a face so improbably perfect that it actually suits her severe short haircut. She drifts around like some sort of sexy teenage Bambi, all limbs and eyes. She's basically like this long, leggy creature made of eyes.

I'm resigned to it now, but I always used to hope she might go through some sort of awkward phase. I mean, she's fourteen, for goodness sake. When I was fourteen, I was spotty and a bit overweight and liked to wear a onesie outside the house, just to 'make a statement'. I think the statement was probably something about watching TV and eating biscuits, as that was pretty much all I did back then, but I can't really remember. Anyway, Grace only shows signs of getting more striking every day. No wonder she lacks any of the self-esteem or confidence issues that basically every other teenager has. She's the coolest girl in her year; she has hordes of boys after her and she is already taller than her average-to-short big sister. As you may have gathered, she's also mean, which gives her an armour I really envy. I try my best not to be jealous, and to remind myself that I have other qualities that I bring to the table – like being a nice person and not being a sociopath – but it's really hard sometimes.

'Yeah, it's not really your clothes.' She is still staring at me. For some reason she won't let this drop. 'Mentally I always sort of picture you in, like, a tracksuit or something. But that outfit is actually not that bad. It's a shame we're not the same size or I might even borrow it.'

'Gosh, thanks, Grace. What a compliment. Shame I'm three sizes bigger than you.'

'Grace, can we leave Lizzie alone, please?' My dad's voice is diplomatic, his face worried – in a way I find that more insulting than Grace's naturally insensitive manner.

'What? I was just *saying*. God, I wasn't *insulting* her or something. You're being homophobic. Like, you assume I mean "lesbian" as an insult.'

'OK. Thanks for that, Miss LGBT Poster Girl. I'll try not to be so hateful next time. But let's change the subject. Lizzie, I'm so glad you had such a brilliant day. That's fantastic.'

'What about your classes?' my mum cuts in. 'Do you think you've chosen the right A-level options?'

'Yeah, fine. It was all fine. I had quite a nice sandwich for lunch as well,' I say as vaguely as possible, feeling suddenly guilty. 'From the canteen. And the best flapjack ever . . . I mean seriously, it was the best flapjack I've ever tasted.'

'Right. You seem strangely enthused about flapjacks, but what subjects did you have today?'

'Um, sociology and geography this morning. Then, um, media after lunch.'

I have no idea what I'm going to do with any of these subjects. The fact that I didn't go to half of these lessons will probably make no difference to my future life. Unlike most people I know, who seem to have some sort of a plan about what they want to do next, I just picked the subjects I did OK at for GCSE. I'm hoping inspiration might strike at some point, but it seems doubtful.

'Speaking of media . . .' Fortunately my dad interrupts. He is no good at concentrating on one subject for longer than five seconds. This is bound to be a tenuous connection. 'What are you girls up to on Friday night? Mum and I thought we might go and see that new French film. You know the one about the nuns in the war, with a title I can't even begin to pronounce. Looks a riot. Are you in?'

'Oh, and I read an excellent review of that new Vietnamese restaurant near the cinema; maybe we could go there for dinner afterwards,' my mum chips in.

Bless my ageing hipster parents. When they're not being annoying, I do have to remember that they can be pretty cool.

'No, I'm fine, thanks.' Grace's tone is arch as ever. 'I'm probably, like, busy. Thanks anyway. Is it OK if I go up to my room now?'

My dad just nods. I think he might be a little bit scared of Grace.

'No Netflix until you've done your homework though,' my mum warns as Grace shoots out of the dining room. 'Otherwise I'm switching the Internet off. And no one wants that.'

'But I'm already so far ahead it's not even funny,' she sighs as she goes out of earshot.

And she's right. That's the mildly annoying part. As well as being beautiful, Grace is also a genius with a photographic memory. Life can be so unfair sometimes.

'So, how about you, Lizzie?' my dad asks. 'What are your plans?'

'I'm not sure yet. But I think I might keep it free for now. If you don't mind. You know, just in case . . .'

Neither of them asks me in case of what, thankfully. We all know. I'm actually hoping I might have something exciting to do this weekend, for once in my life. I used to love weekends, but they're always the same – going out with my parents, hanging out with Daisy and Jake.

I think of Viv – and Lauren and Rex and all the cool people in Cafe Vinyl – and what they might be doing now. What they do on a Saturday night. I have this feeling that life might be about to change. I'm keeping all my fingers crossed.

How I can be more like Viv

- Wear better clothes – maybe overcome morbid fear of shopping.
- Be more confident – maybe try self-help books, picturing people naked (that's supposed to work, not just make me a perv, right??), etc.
- YouTube eyeliner tutorials?
- Dye my hair blonde? Oh god, but what about my monobrow? This is never going to work.

Daisy:

No offence, but I'm kind of bored of talking about Viv already.

Lizzie:

Oh. Sorry, Daze. Sorry for being SO BORING.
I just thought you were interested. Never mind.

Daisy:

I was JOKING, Lizzie!!! Don't panic. You are coming to my house on Saturday, right?

Lizzie:

Of course, wouldn't miss it.

'Hey, there you are!'

I pull my headphones off and blink behind my cheap rip-off Ray-Bans. I was dreading going into college by myself, but I can't believe it – it looks as if Viv has been waiting for me outside.

'I was hoping I'd find you,' she says. 'I couldn't face going into college alone. I didn't have your phone number, and it turns out there are about a million Lizzie Browns on Facebook. I think there are over a thousand just in Brighton. Hey, nice T-shirt.'

Thank goodness the distraction means I don't have to explain the whole Facebook thing. I'm so happy she's noticed my Sonic Youth T-shirt. Which, let's be honest, I kind of wore specially. It used to be my dad's, which I guess is a bit weird, but it is my all-time favourite item of clothing.

'Oh, thanks,' I say. 'It's original, from their 1991 UK tour. Vintage.'

'Cool.'

'Yeah, Sonic Youth are great,' I enthuse, pleased to get on to a subject I know about for once – it hardly ever happens in normal conversation. 'I was actually just listening to them – their album *Goo*? I love it. They're one of my dad's favourite bands so I kind of grew up on their music.'

'Wow, your parents must be cool . . .' I can't believe it – Viv actually sounds interested in what I'm saying. Maybe even a little bit impressed.

I shrug. 'Well, they're parents, but I suppose they are.

In some ways anyway. They're really into music and films and it kind of rubbed off on me.'

'That's how you know all about Blondie and Sonic Youth and all the rest of it. I wish my parents were like that. But I don't want to talk about my terrible family and my tragic life . . .'

I'm not sure what to say to this. 'Well, if it's any consolation, my dad wears a lot of cardigans and has a really weird love of Abba.'

'Hey, that's weird.' Viv perks up instantly. 'Rex likes Abba as well! He's a total music snob, but always says he'd kill to write songs as good as Abba. They're "underestimated modern classics", he says.'

That truly is weird. Those words could be my dad talking. If my dad was the hottest boy I have ever seen in my life . . . Urgh. The idea of hot Rex being like *my dad* is disgusting.

'Rex writes songs?' My voice comes out sounding wrong and I mentally kick myself.

'Yeah, of course. He wouldn't be much good to me if he didn't! I'm just kidding – but he's basically a musical genius. He can play any instrument. He's teaching me guitar.'

'Wow. It sounds like it's all happening—'

'Urgh. Don't even ask.' Viv turns suddenly gloomy and makes a face.

'OK,' I say. I take this literally; I won't if she doesn't want me to.

Then she looks at me like she's expecting something,

and I'm not sure if she really does want me to ask her about whatever it is or not. I keep quiet just to stay on the safe side.

'I am *so* pissed off this morning,' she goes on, regardless. 'That's why I'm so glad I bumped into you. Listen, I genuinely don't think I can face college today. Not this early anyway. Will you come with me into town to get a coffee? Please?'

I really want to, but I automatically falter. Just out of an entrenched fear of authority. I never once skived off school at West Grove, and now it looks as though I might be doing it for the second time in as many days.

Viv seems to read my mind. 'Oh, come on, Lizzie. Please? This isn't the same as school, you know. You're allowed to do what you like. Honestly, nobody cares. I should know – I've been to so many of these kinds of places.'

'Really? How come?'

But Viv just starts walking in the direction of town and I follow, no further discussion. I'm too intrigued. Even though she has chunky high heels on, she is walking so purposefully away from college that I find myself trotting in my Converse to keep up. Damn my Shetland-pony legs.

'Well, I've been to loads of different schools,' she explains. 'I like to blame my parents and their unsettled ways, but I expect it was a combination of that and my own shocking behaviour. My mum lives abroad and my dad's hardly ever around. I used to go to St Catherine's –

you know, that posh girls' school? It was awful, full of weirdos and *so* snobby. I hated it. When I started there I was put back a year because everyone there is basically some sort of freak genius. Luckily I did so badly in my GCSEs they wouldn't let me go back for sixth form. They didn't want me there messing up their league tables, when everyone else there gets straight *A*s and has no life. So, here I am, starting again.'

'How old are you?' I ask.

'Eighteen. You?'

'Nearly seventeen.' My birthday's not until February, but this sounds preferable, given the discrepancy. It's not that big a gap, but no wonder she seems so much more advanced than me. Embarrassingly so, when I think of all the things that she can do and I can't. She might as well be light years ahead.

This brings me to my next question, which I've been dying to ask. 'Do you and Rex live together?'

'Yeah. Can you believe it? I've only known him for a couple of months. He's in his first year at uni and he was living in halls . . . My dad's all wrapped up in this new girlfriend he's got, and I was in disgrace after failing my AS levels, so he didn't want me hanging around. It was all my idea that I could get a flat and Rex could move in – I talked my dad into paying the rent; the only condition was that I come back to college to do my A levels. Which is all right really. Pretty grown-up to have my own flat, right?'

'It's *insanely* grown-up. I can't even imagine,' I say

honestly, without even thinking about it, 'what it must be like to have a boyfriend who you *live* with. I've never even really had a proper boyfriend.'

This might be the understatement of the century. There's no point over-sharing my tragic spinsterhood too much at this stage. The most meaningful relationship I've ever had is with a cardboard cut-out of *Dirty Dancing*-era Patrick Swayze, which I bought off eBay. I know he's old enough to be my dad, not to mention dead, but I have always loved him. Probably because I dream one day of somebody saying, 'Nobody leaves Lizzie in the corner.' And of being able to dance without tripping over my feet, falling on my face and/or embarrassing myself.

'Ah, Rex is a cutie,' Viv says, in what might be the second-biggest understatement of the century. 'It's not that different from living with a girl really. Especially as his wardrobe's even bigger than mine and the bathroom is crammed full of his beauty products. What with that and his ten thousand vinyl records, we're quite short on space. We've got a really sweet little flat in the Lanes though, above Roundabout Records. You'll have to come over some time.'

'No way!' I exclaim. 'Roundabout Records is my favourite shop. I go there all the time. I can't believe you live there – that is so cool.'

I try to imagine what this must be like, and I actually can't do it. No more than I can imagine Viv hanging out at Daisy's house with my friends and me, or coming round to my house for dinner with my family. We exist in different universes.

I walk in silence, thinking about this. It's only a ten-minute walk into town. As we get nearer, I realize that my excitement is building. My stomach starts fizzing uncontrollably and I'm not even sure why.

Is it:

a) Pure excitement at skiving off college with my cool new friend Viv.
b) Nervousness as we are getting a bit too near my parents' office and I am skiving off college.
c) A combination of the above.
d) Stop kidding yourself, Lizzie. You are hoping that Viv will take you to Cafe Vinyl again and that you will see her boyfriend. Because, if you hadn't acknowledged it already, you really, really fancy him. You can feel yourself blushing every time his name is mentioned. Yet still you want to bring him up in conversation at every possible lame excuse. Which obviously makes you a terrible person, because Viv is not only the coolest girl you have ever met, but she is your new friend and she is being really lovely to you. So you should feel thoroughly ashamed of yourself and *stop thinking these terrible thoughts.*

For once I'm keeping this little straw poll inside my own head. Daisy and Jake do not need to know about this. It's *c.* I've decided to go with *c.* End of. OK?

'So, where do you fancy going?' Viv asks me.

'Um, I don't know. We could go to Woody's, or go and sit in Pavilion Gardens, maybe. Or . . .'

Not Cafe Vinyl. Anywhere but Cafe Vinyl. Don't say it. Don't be a terrible human being, Lizzie. That is not who you are.

'Hmm, I suppose so,' Viv muses. 'Well, Cafe Vinyl is out, obviously – that lot are so lazy it doesn't even open before mid-morning most days. Rex was still snoring his head off when I left.'

I make an involuntary noise that ironically comes out sounding a bit like a snore.

'Hey,' Viv exclaims, not seeming to notice, 'I know! It's *kind of* sunny – let's head to the beach.'

I never go to the beach. The beach is for tourists, and I like to think I'm cooler than that. But Viv's excitement is infectious. She drags me in the direction of the sea.

It's not *that* sunny, and it's a weekday morning, so the seafront is unusually quiet. I suppose everyone else is at school, or college, or work. I suddenly feel like we're outlaws, skiving off together, and I like it.

I actually like Brighton seafront when it's quiet like this. When my hometown feels like my own again. Viv grabs my hand and drags me down the steep steps on to the beach. There's a strong sea wind and for a second I lose my footing; I nearly fall, until Viv pulls me back up along with her.

'Whoo, we're free!' she screams at the top of her voice, over the wind and the crashing waves. 'I'm so glad we skived off college – I love the sea.'

She spins around in a circle, startling a grumpy seagull. Then she runs out on to the pebbles, staggering on her high heels until she collapses on to her knees, there on the stones, and laughs and laughs.

It's bizarre to see her so excited. I never really think about being by the sea. This is just where I have always lived: my house, my parents, the Lanes, the sea. My parents' friends from London are always visiting and saying how lucky we are, but I've never really thought about it. In between complaining to Daisy and Jake and going to London whenever we get the chance, I don't exactly go around thinking about how lucky I am. Through Viv's eyes this morning, though, the world looks pretty cool. I'm happy to be here and be a part of it.

The sunshine is sparkling on the sea and we can see out for miles, way past the old pier. It occurs to me that it's actually quite beautiful. Here with Viv, like this on a Tuesday morning, I actually feel like I'm on holiday here at home.

I follow behind her more gingerly out on to the stones, even though I'm the one wearing Converse. I've never been a big fan of the stony beach. I've only ever been swimming about three times in all the years I've lived here, and it was never my idea.

'Look, a heart-shaped stone,' Viv says, pulling me down next to her. 'You can keep it. It's good luck – I've decided.'

I take it from her and put it into my coat pocket. It

feels smooth under my fingers, nice to fiddle with. We sit in silence for a moment, staring at the sea.

'So, what's up?' I ask her, shifting to try to get comfortable on the stones, as she is showing no signs of moving any time soon. 'You said you were annoyed about something this morning . . .'

'Long story, babe. I'm feeling better now we've escaped. Thanks for coming with me. Anyway, to cut a long and very boring story short – Jess, she's my bass player, has left the band. Well, if you can even call it a band.'

'What happened?'

'Oh, the usual stuff.' She shrugs. 'Jess and I had an argument. She was being a real idiot actually. She can be a right bitch. But never mind – there's no point me sitting around slagging her off. It's just that I feel like I'm never going to get anywhere with my music. I just want to get things happening.'

'Can't you and Rex just do it on your own?' I ask.

'Well, I suppose we could . . . But I want it to be a real rock 'n' roll band. I don't want it just to be me and Rex and a bloody acoustic guitar, doing Adele cover versions or something. There's just no point doing stuff like that. So we need at least three of us – I'm learning guitar, which means Rex on drums, and we really need a bass player.'

I don't have anything helpful to say. I don't know the first thing about putting together a band. Even Viv's *problems* are cooler than anything that has ever happened to me. *'I've got 99 problems and most of them are total crap I've made up in my own head,'* as Jay-Z didn't exactly say.

'Oh my god!' Viv suddenly exclaims. 'I've just had the greatest idea ever.'

'What?' I reply, startled.

'You're going to be my new bass player.'

'Me?' I actually burst out laughing.

'Yes, you.'

'But I can't even play. In fact, I'm possibly the least—'

'Oh, none of *that* matters,' she interrupts me. 'It's easy. There are only four strings and our songs aren't exactly complicated. Anyone could do it.'

Against my better judgement, I allow myself a second to daydream about the whole thing – being able to play, standing up onstage, an audience of adoring fans. Even just being one of those mysteriously 'other' people I see around town all the time who always have guitars strapped to their backs like the world's coolest rucksacks. It has always seemed like a secret, closed-off world; I never for a moment imagined that could be me. I wish it could be, but the very idea of trying to play a bass guitar is completely beyond me. All that would happen would be I'd embarrass myself – guaranteed.

I suddenly feel panicked. 'No, Viv, really. I couldn't.'

She totally ignores me. 'Don't be silly. You like great music. Rex can teach you to play. I can sort out your image. It's perfect.'

Just for a second I feel a sting like I've been attacked by a wasp that came out of nowhere. I know I'm not as cool as Viv, but hearing her say out loud that my image needs to be 'sorted out' makes me cringe inside. Still, she carries on talking like it's not a big deal and so I try not to dwell on it. Or at least not to burst into tears on the spot.

'I'm just not . . . I can't . . .'

'It's OK,' Viv interrupts me. 'I'll help you with your clothes and stuff. Rex can teach you to play bass, easy. Like I said, he's a musical genius. He's also a really good teacher – he could teach anyone. That boy has the patience of a saint. He can even teach me, and I'm the worst student ever.'

Viv is looking at me with big eyes and an excited expression, willing me to say yes. And I really, really want her to be my friend.

'OK,' I find myself saying, with a vague sense of impending doom. 'I'll do it.'

'Lizzie, that's brilliant!' She throws her arms around me. 'This is going to be so great. You'll be much better than Jess anyway. I can't wait to tell Rex. This is so cool! We're going to be in a band together!'

'We're going to be in a band together,' I echo like an idiot, trying it out for size but failing to wrap my brain around this new turn of events.

'Have you ever been on that roller coaster on the end of the pier?' she asks me.

'Not since I was a little kid, obviously . . .'

'Well, come on – let's go! We're celebrating!'

Reasons why I would be useless at being in a band

- I don't have the right clothes (as Viv pretty much
  said – it only took her two days to notice . . .).
- I know all about music – but I know enough to realize
  that I really, really don't have what it takes.
- I am just not the right type.
- Oh, yeah – and I CAN'T PLAY ANYTHING!

Viv:

UR DOING IT BABE –
NO ARGUMENTS!!! XXX

Viv and Rex's flat reminds me of my nan's house, but if my nan's house was really cool. It's tiny and crammed full of stuff, high up above the Lanes.

'So, we need to come up with a name,' Viv is saying. 'What do you think?'

Viv is showing me her band 'mood board', which takes up an entire wall of her bedroom. It's covered in pictures cut out from magazines, postcards and scrawled notes. She wouldn't let me go back to college at all this afternoon; she said we had to go back to her flat to work on 'band stuff' and break the good news to Rex. Rex isn't here, and we haven't made a lot of progress on the 'band stuff', but I'm having a great time.

'Lizzie, this is going to be great,' Viv says. 'Being in a band together is a big deal. You do realize we're basically sisters now.'

I feign horror. 'Oh no! If that makes us anything like me and my little sister, then we're going to fall out any minute now. Grace is basically Caligula in an Urban Outfitters crop top.'

Viv laughs. 'I'm not sure who Caligula is, but I wish I had a sister. Oh well, I've got you now. This is going to be brilliant, I know it. Anyway, speaking of outfits . . . Now that we're band sisters, you know that means you can share my entire wardrobe, right? Like I said, I can really help you with your image. How we look is just as important as the music – maybe even more so.'

Although this sounds pretty much as terrifying as the Topshop communal changing rooms on a Saturday afternoon, I do feel a pang of clothing greed at the idea of having access to Viv's wardrobe. Looking at her in her patterned Ziggy Stardust jumpsuit and expensive-looking shoes, I can only imagine it as a wonderland of Narnia-like fantasy, like the best of Beyond Retro without the price tags and the smell of mothballs.

Every time I see her, she seems to be rocking a completely different but perfect look, whereas I basically have my Sonic Youth T-shirt, a lot of cardigans and jumpers (I take after my dad – some of them even used to be his) and my one cool vintage dress. If they're in the wash, all I have left that isn't totally lame (i.e. the cast-offs from my emo phase, which I don't like to think about but wasn't actually that long ago) is a few 'fake-vintage'-type Primark dresses and a lot of stripy tops and old jeans. That's basically my entire 'image' – unless we're counting pyjamas, of which I have a lot.

'Go on, help yourself,' Viv says. 'It's really important we have the right look as a band. So you can borrow anything of mine you want.'

I hang back a bit shyly as she moves a few stacks of records out of the way and opens up an entire wall of fitted wardrobes. I actually gasp; if we were in a film, a heavenly light would be coming from the back of the cupboard and some inspiring music would start playing. Like something out of *Lord of the Rings*, only with fewer orcs and more sequins. I just about stop myself from hissing 'my precious' in a creepy voice while I stroke a velvety vintage dress.

It's a total mess – mountains of mismatched shoes all over the floor and stuff chucked into haphazard piles and falling off their hangers – but everything is awesome.

'Rex and I have an arrangement,' Viv says, totally blasé. 'He can have as many records as he likes, but I get first dibs on the wardrobe space. The bathroom's another story – he's always nicking my Liz Earle cleanser and even my Benefit eyeliner. Claims it's a punk thing, but he's the vainest boy I've ever met. He's nearly as bad as me.'

I'm still staring into the wardrobe. Thinking about Rex in a bathroom context is way too much for my brain to cope with, so it's a good thing I'm distracted.

'Anyway,' Viv goes on, 'try on whatever you like. We can do a fashion show. Surprise Rex when he gets home. He'll be back any minute.'

Viv is already peeling out of her jumpsuit and down to a black lacy bra and bright pink knickers. The idea of taking my clothes off – not least when Rex is apparently due back 'any minute' – makes me want to curl up and die. I even go into the bathroom to get changed when I'm round at Daisy's, and I've known her forever. My parents are always walking around half naked – and that's on a prudish day for them – but I'd rather eat glass than do the same in front of them, or particularly Grace.

But for the first time ever in my life my natural caution and anxiety are overridden by something stronger: the weird and irresistible desire to try on Viv's clothes. Like a crazy stalker, but with permission – which is basically what I feel like, here in her flat. We're hanging out together like we're proper friends, but I'm still feeling like a total amateur who's completely blown away by her and her awesomeness.

Viv is already rummaging around and pulling clothes off their hangers – at the rate she's going, we'll be buried alive under an EU stockpile of cool vintage dresses before Rex ever gets home.

'Oh my god, this is going to be so much fun. I love getting dressed up,' she exclaims. 'I'm going to put this on, as I never get the chance to wear it – and some massive heels I could never walk in outside the house. That's why having a bedroom party can be even better than going out sometimes. Especially when you can Instagram it so that everyone can still see you looking amazing. That's my motto: if it's not on the Internet, it didn't happen.'

My heart sinks as conversation invariably goes back to the dreaded Internet – but luckily for me, Viv just carries on talking. 'Like all that weird philosophical stuff about a tree falling down in the woods – if there's no one there to hear it, does it still make a noise? Babe, if it's not on Facebook, I don't even care.'

She's wriggling into a crazy outfit that turns out to be what looks like a vintage cheerleader's uniform. It's got a tiny, flicky skirt in blue-and-yellow pleats, a top with epaulettes on the shoulders, and badges sewn all over it. The name 'Diane' is embroidered over the right boob. I have actually never seen anything like it, but somehow she looks amazing.

'Bonkers, right?' Viv laughs. 'I thought it would be

good to wear onstage one day. I got it on eBay; it's proper, all the way from America.'

While she keeps talking non-stop, Viv puts on tights and enormous heels, fluffing up her hair and pouting at herself in the mirror. This goes on for a while.

Although it's fascinating to watch, she doesn't seem to have registered that I am shivering in my semi-grotty old flesh-coloured bra and my favourite Wonder Woman pants, too shy to help myself to any of Viv's clothes. I hope Viv doesn't notice that I haven't shaved my legs and my rampant bikini line is sprouting out of the sides of my knickers, even though they are quite big 'boy shorts' knickers. I swear it starts at my belly button and practically reaches my knees. This is why I don't like to wear anything other than trousers or thick tights, even in the middle of summer. Ever since we were little kids and she made me hold my forearm up next to hers for comparison, Grace has always commented on how hairy I am, and it's one of the things I'm most self-conscious about. On the extensive list, it's near the top.

Once Viv has checked her hair (on her head, in her case) and put on extra eyeliner in the mirror, eventually she seems to remember I am still here.

'Now we need something for you to wear,' she says, rummaging through the racks of clothing. 'See, this is good practice for being in the band – we need to plan all our onstage looks. That's why I'm always buying all this weird stuff, and it's just going to waste at the moment. It's not like I can wear it to college or whatever in the meantime. Hey, why don't you try this one on?'

She shoves a flimsy piece of fabric at me, so shiny it's almost slippery. It's a black satin minidress, retro-disco style, with a sequinned halter-neck top and the shortest skirt I have ever seen. It's also so tiny that it would be literally obscene on me. Like, I'd probably get arrested – we're talking that tiny. Me, who never even wears shorts except: a) on the beach on holiday, preferably in a foreign country where nobody knows me or will ever see me again; or b) with very thick black tights and a baggy T-shirt, and preferably some sort of oversized novelty knitwear. With my voluminous jumpers and sexlessly cut dresses, even my own mum has been known to accuse me of being a prude.

Still, Viv is looking at me so delightedly, and anything has got to be better than standing about in my underwear any longer.

Anyway, I tell myself, maybe it's about time I became a bit more daring. Maybe some of Viv's magic will transfer to me through wearing her dress. Who knows, I might even discover some sex appeal.

I struggle into the delicate material and, after a couple of false starts with armholes, I manage to manoeuvre my way into the complicated halter neck. It feels too tight, but thankfully the fabric is stretchy and I manage to get the ancient sticky zip done up.

'I got this one in a vintage shop in New York when I was there with my mum last year,' she says, helping me to fasten the hooks at the top of the zip with some difficulty – I can literally feel my back fat bulging out. 'Her family's American, so I've been over there quite a lot. Have you ever been?'

I shake my head. 'I've been to France and Spain on holiday with my parents. That's basically it. Oh, and to Cornwall to see my nan every year. I'm not exactly a seasoned transatlantic traveller.'

'New York's amazing; you'd love it. Williamsburg's kind of like Brighton but even cooler. That's where this dress came from.'

This dress really is far too tight for me. I can just about kid myself that I can squeeze into it, but breathing hurts a little bit.

Viv looks at me straight on for a moment, holding me out at arm's length. She has to look down as she's so much taller than me. She fluffs up my hair with her fingers, and I instantly wish I'd bothered to wash it this morning. I'm worried that Viv's hands are going to come away coated with Batiste. My lank brown bob is shamefully boring – even verging on gross – compared to Viv's perfect bleached-blonde look.

'Well, it's a start,' she says doubtfully. 'Really I suppose you need the whole look, but I'll keep working on you. Don't worry.'

She takes a step back, leaving the mirror free for me to look at myself. I'm unprepared for the wave of miserable disappointment that hits me. If I thought I was magically going to become cool and gorgeous and more like Viv, it's going to take more than borrowing a polyester disco dress. I look dumpy and a bit silly, especially standing next to Viv with her long legs and perfect make-up.

'Hmm, maybe let's try it with some shoes,' Viv suggests. 'Oh no, not those. That's even worse. How about my silver ankle boots?'

They are like clown shoes on me. I am a space clown. Coco the Clown via a galaxy far, far away.

We forget about the shoes. Viv starts rummaging around her dressing table, pulling out pots and brushes and scary-looking industrial eyelash curlers. This gets me almost more excited than the prospect of borrowing her clothes – surely it's the make-up that will make me really, finally pretty. That's what's going to make all the difference. If I could look even forty per cent as pretty as Viv, I'm fairly certain my life would be transformed beyond all recognition – which would, of course, be awesome.

I just hope she doesn't want to tweeze my eyebrows. Hers are very thin – they look like they've been plucked and drawn back on. I'm not very good with pain. I'm always the girl who faints when they do injections at school. It's embarrassing – I even threw up when I finally convinced my parents to let me have my ears pierced when I was twelve, right in the middle of Claire's Accessories. On a crowded Saturday afternoon.

'Close your eyes,' Viv instructs.

She has applied eyeliner to exactly one half of one of my eyes when I hear the unmistakable sound of a key in the front door.

'Oh, that'll be Rex!' Viv exclaims as I freeze in a combination of terror and embarrassment. 'We can tell him the good news about the band. We're in here, babe!'

I quickly grab my tights and start pulling them on, to prevent Rex seeing my pasty, hairy legs in a too-tight dress that barely covers my arse. Trying to kick off the silver boots and pull up the tights in one quick motion, I succeed in getting both feet caught in one leg and losing my balance.

As Rex comes into the messy bedroom, I topple over, tights stuck around my knees, and land at his feet on the worn brown carpet.

'Wow.' He grins. 'I don't usually have this effect on girls. I mean, I know I'm pretty irresistible, but they don't usually *throw* themselves at my feet.'

I'm actually worried I might have hurt myself. I landed really awkwardly and scraped my elbow. But that's the least of my worries as I peel myself off the floor and try to regain some small shred of dignity. Instead, for some reason unknown even to myself, I start babbling uncontrollably.

'I was just . . . um. Well, I have this problem with fainting sometimes. It's something to do with my inner ear. Or low blood pressure or something. Like narcolepsy – sometimes I just keel over on the floor. Like that. Boom.'

What am I even saying? God, Lizzie – just STFU! Even as my brain is thinking this, my mouth just won't seem to listen. I literally cannot stop talking.

Thankfully Viv interrupts and thus saves me from myself. 'Anyway, Lizzie and I have got good news . . .'

'Let me guess.' Rex interrupts her right back.

He looks me up and down – just for a second, but pointedly. Why, I'm not sure, but I wish more than anything that I could just change back into my own clothes. Or at least put my tights back on – after my fall to the ground with them hanging half off, I've had to discreetly kick them away and hope that no one notices. I couldn't exactly hoick them up under my dress with Rex standing there. I'm staring disconsolately at my chipped blue toenail varnish – right up until this very moment it hadn't occurred to me that it makes me look as though I have actually drowned. Without my trusty tights, I feel like a defrocked superhero – not that I was very super or heroic to start with.

It's Rex that finishes off the sentence. 'Don't tell me – Lizzie's going to be in your band. Your new bass player. Right?'

There's a weirdly awkward silence, and I inwardly cringe as I infer that he is not delighted by this news. I guess I'm just not cool enough.

'*Our* band,' Viv says with a tinkly laugh. 'You're going to be in it too, remember?'

'Hmm. What happened to Jess?'

Viv's face darkens. 'I don't want to talk about Jess ever again. Anyway, you're going to teach Lizzie to play bass and it's going to be great.'

'So, Lizzie,' Rex says, 'can you play anything at all, or

is this one of Viviane's harebrained get-famous-or-die-trying crazy schemes?'

'Um. Actually, I'm really not sure this is a good idea. It sounds so cool . . . But, like I said, Viv . . . I really, really can't. I mean, I'd be crap. I can barely play a tambourine.'

'Actually,' Rex says, 'it's a lot harder than you'd think to play a tambourine really well. So I wouldn't go worrying about it too much. I expect Viv's already told you, I'm a bona fide musical genius. Not showing off, just fact. I've also got the patience of a saint. I have to, to live with this one sometimes. No, don't argue, Viv – you know you're a high-maintenance princess. Listen, Lizzie – if you're up for it, I'll have you playing bass like Paul McCartney in no time.'

'Well . . .'

When he puts it like that, how could I possibly refuse? He seems so prepared to believe in me that I find myself trusting him entirely – and even forgetting that I'm so crap it's bound to end in a) at best, total embarrassment; and b) at worst, genuine disaster.

'Who's Paul McCartney?' Viv interrupts before I can answer.

I'm so shocked I can't help giggling. I'm so surprised to hear these words coming out of Viv's mouth. My dad loves the Beatles so much, I can just picture the look on his face if he heard *anyone* say such a thing. I thought Viv was supposed to be into music.

'Viv, it's a good job you're so beautiful.' Rex laughs. 'Have you ever heard of an obscure little band from

Liverpool called the Beatles? *Sergeant Pepper's Lonely Hearts Club Band* and all that?'

'Well, of course I've *heard of* the Beatles,' Viv argues. 'I'm not an idiot. I don't really know any of their songs, but I know the name.'

'We're going to have to do something about this, my little philistine,' Rex says. 'You're missing out.'

He grabs an acoustic guitar that's propped up in the corner and starts playing.

'*Hey, Jude . . .*'

He plays and sings it so perfectly it's like listening to the record – which I have done a hundred times before with my dad. When he gets to the chorus, I can't resist singing along, just really quietly, but it's one of my favourite songs ever and I can't help it.

'Hey,' Rex says as he strums the last few chords and puts the guitar down, 'you've got a really nice voice, Lizzie. And you obviously know the classics. I don't think teaching you is going to be too hard at all.'

'Anyway,' Viv cuts in, 'we've got loads of other stuff to think about. As you can see, I've been working on our image. And we need a name. Oh, and I suppose we need to find Lizzie a bass guitar . . .'

Lizzie:

Is this really happening? Are we *sure* it's a good idea? I can't even play! I'm going to be useless.

Viv:

YES. This is happening. Deal with it, babe. So you have GOT to get hold of a bass. Do whatever it takes! Good luck!

Lizzie:

Well, basically that means asking my dad and not my mum . . . I'll have a go. I'm not promising anything.

Viv:

You've got to! It's for the band – I'm counting on you! Beg, plead, lie and guilt-trip if you have to!

'Hi, Dad.'

'Good god, child! What are you supposed to look like? I sincerely hope that's some sort of early Halloween fancy dress. Honestly, Lizzles, you're supposed to be my sensible firstborn. You look like some sort of demented disco streetwalker. It's enough to give an old man a heart attack.'

I'm not sure whether to be embarrassed or secretly proud – I've never worn an outfit my dad's disapproved of before. What with my usual aversion to showing an inch of flesh, he might as well have Mother Teresa as his teenage daughter. He's certainly never had to worry about boys looking twice at me. I only wore Viv's dress home because I was too embarrassed to ask about where I could get changed with Rex there, so I kept quiet and it just never happened. Viv didn't seem to care when I just bundled my own clothes into my bag and put my leather jacket on over the top. I spent the whole walk home trying to pull the stupid dress down to cover my bum.

'Relax, Dad. The dress belongs to my friend Viv. We were just being silly, trying on clothes.' I suddenly realize I have potentially put my foot in it, and start to panic. 'I mean, I just went round to her flat after college. Just for, like, half an hour. For a cup of tea. I had a free period right at the end of the day, so . . .'

My voice trails off lamely. I suppose if anyone had to be home, I'm lucky it's just my dad. My mum's much sharper than he is; she doesn't miss a trick. Whereas Grace has practically made a criminal career out of pulling the wool over my dad's bemused and usually sleepy eyes. In fact, he's only working at home this afternoon so that he can ferry Grace to and from some acting class.

'Actually, Dad, there was something else I wanted to talk to you about.'

'Oh God, that sounds ominous.' He mock groans, but actually goes a bit pale and starts fidgeting awkwardly, unnecessarily polishing his glasses on his cardigan. 'Are you sure you've selected the correct parent for this? "Talking" is more your mother's forte. If this is about sex, forget it. And actually she knows a lot more about drugs than I do. I smoked a joint once in 1994 and thought my friend Steve was the Antichrist. I've never touched anything but junior aspirin since. True story. And if it's about periods, my ears are closed. Permanently.'

'Dad,' I say gently, 'I swear I never, ever want to talk to you about periods. Or sex. Or drugs. Actually it's about music.'

'Well, that's a whole different story. Well done, eldest daughter. You *did* pick the right parent.' His face actually lights up. Bless my dad. 'Do you want to hear about the time I saw Nirvana on their first and only UK tour when I was a young whippersnapper? Or maybe we could discuss the heated eBay auction that saw me heroically beat off all competition to win a super-duper rare limited-edition Mudhoney EP on vinyl.'

'Dad. Stop. I mean, that sounds really great and all. It's just, the thing is, I've joined this band with my new friend Viv and her boyfriend . . .'

'Lizzie, stop right there. You know I love and cherish and support you in all of your very noble ambitions, don't you?'

'Yeah . . .'

'So it's in a truly loving and supportive way I say this: good grief, do you not remember the violin lessons? You, in a band? *You?*'

'Thanks a lot! Well, it may shock you to know that I'm not actually playing violin in the band. I'm going to play bass. Viv's boyfriend is going to teach me. He says it's easy.' I pause for a second but in the end can't resist adding, 'He's a musical genius.'

'Is he now? Well, as long as you're having fun, I shan't say another word . . .' He pauses and looks uncomfortable again. 'It's just, I'd just hate to think of this being another stick you use to beat yourself up with. So I'm being serious when I say, remember what happened with the violin lessons. And the life-drawing classes. And tennis. I know what you're like, sweetheart. That's all.'

His voice is so gentle, his face so worried, it actually makes me feel terrible. Obviously I'm lucky. Obviously my dad really cares about me. I just wish he didn't have to worry about me so much. I wish I could go back and change that. I kind of don't want to carry on this conversation, but I've started it now.

'Dad, the thing is, I need to get a bass guitar. Rex doesn't have one, but he knows some guys in the big music shop in town, and he can get me a really good deal on a second-hand one.'

'Great idea!' Unfortunately my dad's tone is one that could be filed under 'cheery sarcasm'. 'Maybe you can keep your new bass guitar up in the loft – with your violin. And your tennis racket and your ice skates. Oh, and the tailor's dummy from that time you thought you might become a fashion designer.'

'Oh, Dad – please!' I know I sound like a spoilt, whiny child, but I can't help it – doing this feels really important. 'I've got a bit of money saved up. But to get the cheapest second-hand bass, I still need to borrow about fifty pounds. Obviously I'll pay you back . . . but I could work for it. I'll do anything.'

'I just don't know, Lizzie . . .'

I think of Viv and how she is counting on me. Well, desperate times call for *very* desperate measures. Sometimes in a situation like this – i.e. one that requires manipulation and possible dramatics and all the other things I'm really terrible at – I find it helpful to ask myself a question: what would Grace do?

I steel myself not to look at my dad's crooked glasses or the fact that his hair is nearly all grey at the front now, or anything else that might make me feel bad. Because the answer to WWGD? is always: fight dirty, with underhand tactics and no remorse.

'Well, I don't think I'm really asking for much – considering you must spend that *per week* on Grace's acting lessons and everything else. I'm probably asking for less than her train fare to London for one audition.

And, unlike her, I'll pay you back. I mean, if you're going to be that obvious about who's your favourite . . . Well, then it's no wonder I've got issues.'

It's official. I'm going to hell. I think my dad might start crying.

'Oh, Lizzie.' He takes his glasses off for a second and rubs his cardigan sleeve across his eyes. 'I'm so sorry you feel like that, but of course I'll help you out and support you however I can. I know it must seem like Grace is often the centre of attention, but I promise, you both—'

Oh shit.

'Dad, I'm sorry. It's OK. I didn't mean it. It honestly doesn't matter. Look, I'll work for the money. I could work in the office or clean the house, or . . .'

My dad twigs straight away, now that I'm trying to backtrack. His face has suddenly become a lot more amused now that he's on to me.

'Nice try, kid. Maurice's litter tray.'

'OK.'

'And his food. And grooming. For a month.'

'Deal. Well played.'

We grin at each other; it's kind of a win-win. My dad may be overemotional, but he's not stupid. According to my mum, this is why their company is so successful – my Green-voting, cardigan-wearing dad is the lethal secret weapon.

Maurice is our ancient, flea-bitten ginger tomcat. He was Mum's before I was born, before she even met Dad – that's how old he is. Even though he's technically my mum's, somehow my dad has ended up being in charge of the cat – and the two of them hate each other passionately. I was terrified of Maurice when I was little, and he and Grace have a long-running territorial battle going on. Sometimes I think Maurice might actually be evil.

By this point he's got barely any fur left, he smells terrible and he pees everywhere. My dad takes fifty pounds out of his wallet and kisses the top of my head.

'And, as it's my turn to cook, you might as well make a head start on dinner,' he says before handing over the cash.

AMAZING LADY BASS PLAYERS TO LOOK UP ON YOUTUBE

KIM GORDON - SONIC YOUTH
KIM DEAL - THE PIXIES/THE BREEDERS
  (NB - CONSIDER CHANGING YOUR NAME TO KIM?)
TINA WEYMOUTH - TALKING HEADS
SUZI HORN - PRINZHORN DANCE SCHOOL
MELISSA AUF DER MAUR - HOLE/MADM
D'ARCY WRETZKY - THE SMASHING PUMPKINS
SIMONE MARIE BUTLER - PRIMAL SCREAM

GOOD LUCK, KIDDO! LOVE, DAD X

The big guitar shop is right in the middle of the Lanes, painted bright yellow – you can't possibly miss it – but I've never thought to go inside before. I'm so glad I'm not here on my own.

Even though it's obviously a music shop and we are surrounded by the cacophonous noise of people trying out guitars, it has the hallowed feel of a library. Everyone is taking this *very* seriously. I think Viv and I are the only girls in the place.

Rex isn't with us because he works in the cafe every Saturday, but Viv knows his friends who work in here and she says she can get me a good deal. After all, she comes in here enough to look at her dream guitar – even if she's never spent any money.

'Here it is,' Viv announces, pointing to a pretty turquoise guitar hanging up on the wall. 'Isn't she gorgeous? Courtney Love has one the same. One day that guitar will be mine. Not that I can really play yet, but that doesn't matter. It'll happen. Now we need to find you something just as amazing.'

'With no clue what we're looking for and a budget of less than a hundred pounds,' I remind her, before she can get too carried away.

Some of the prices in here have made my jaw drop. It really is a serious business; people spend tens of thousands of pounds on a guitar, because it's made from a special wood or is exactly the same as one played by some famous old blues musician I've never heard of with a name like 'Blind Billy Bluebeard'. I had no idea.

'Come on. Don't worry – we're going to find you the bass of dreams, I promise.'

I follow Viv up the stairs to the second-hand department, my head already pounding with the sound of yet another teenage boy who wants to be Ed Sheeran but doesn't really have the talent. To be fair, most of them are playing a lot better than I ever could in a million years.

The second-hand section is much smaller, and it's mostly regular six-string guitars – the basses are relegated to one dusty corner. Viv and I stride over there like we know what we're doing. Well, I follow her and do my best to copy her.

I'm scared even to touch anything. And I soon realize, Viv doesn't seem to know much more about this than I do. I find myself wishing Rex was here, then pushing that thought firmly to the back of my mind.

'Right . . .' Viv says, hiding her uncertainty with an impressive flick of her hair, 'I suppose you should try one out.'

'But I don't even know what to do!' I glance around the shop floor – there are clusters of men deep in conversation and the odd person sitting on a stool earnestly trying out an instrument. The air around us is resonant with twanging chords. 'I've never even picked up a bass guitar before – I'll probably try to play it upside down or something.'

'Fake it till you make it, babe!'

Easy for her to say, when she just has to stand there and watch me make a total fool of myself. Still, trying my best to fake it as instructed, we start looking at our options. They are all so big and heavy it's intimidating. I can't even afford most of them anyway.

'Hey, how about this one?' Viv asks. 'It's in our price range and it's awesome.'

'Viv,' I say, looking at the guitar she's holding, 'it's in our price range because it's for a *child*.'

'Don't be unimaginative. I don't think they make bass guitars for children anyway. It's got kind of a Japanese girl-band vibe to it. It's cute. It's quirky. And it's in our price range.'

The guitar she's showing me is small and pink with Hello Kitty on it. Not only is it ridiculous – and I am really not the person to pull that sort of thing off – but, shamefully, my first thought is that a bass that small will make me look like a weird giant. Perspective would not be my friend. I'm so uncool, I know.

'I don't know, Viv . . .'

'Just try it. I think it's cool. It could be part of our image. Hey, we still need a name – how about Viv and the Pussycats?'

'How about no? And if I don't want to be a pussycat, I doubt Rex will go for it.'

I take the guitar from her and try to hold it like I can see other people doing. I strum the strings as if it's my dad's old acoustic guitar, but the four thick strings barely move and make an indistinct, low sludgy noise that sounds all wrong. I don't know what else to do, so I just stand there with it awkwardly half propped on my knee. Even this tiny guitar soon gets really heavy and my arms begin to ache. Viv is snapping photos of me from all angles on her phone.

'How else are we supposed to see if it really suits you?' she says. 'Let's see what the Instagram verdict is.'

Trying out guitars is turning out to be worse than the Topshop changing rooms on a Saturday afternoon – my default interpretation of hell. I'm still awkwardly standing there, Viv snapping away, when a boy approaches us. I instantly become ten times more self-conscious, even though he's about my age and looks much less scary than some of the other guys in here, with a lolloping walk and a curtain of shaggy blond hair. He looks like a Pound Shop version of Kurt Cobain, and as if it's a comparison he's trying his best to encourage, he's wearing a Nirvana T-shirt and a standard-issue grunge checked shirt over it.

'Hey, Dave!' Viv rushes up and hugs him, still snapping pictures on her phone with her other hand. Understandably, his face simultaneously lights up and blushes slightly. I find myself warming to him, even though he's still a scary guitar-shop guy.

'How are you, Viv?' he mumbles shyly, hiding behind his hair.

'You're just the person we wanted to see.' She ignores his question. 'This gorgeous girl here is Lizzie. She's my new bass player. We just need to get her a bass. Then Rex is going to teach her to play it, and soon she's going to be even better than Paul McCarthy.'

Although a brief wave of surprise passes over his face,

I notice that he doesn't correct her. Why would he? Neither do I.

'OK,' he says. 'I can get you a strap and get you plugged into an amp if you like.'

Maybe I'm being paranoid because I have no clue what I'm doing, but he comes off as a bit patronizing. He's obviously annoyed to have to tear his attention away from Viv for a second. He couldn't look less interested in me if he tried. I suppose I'd better get used to it, hanging around with Viv. It's better to be B-list than not on the list at all.

As Dave goes about setting up an amp, I put the atrocious Hello Kitty bass down. Another one catches my eye, mostly because the price tag hanging on its neck indicates it's the only other one in the place I can afford. I really, really don't want a Hello Kitty bass. Even if Viv thinks it's cool. I feel ridiculous enough as it is but I have a feeling that might be something she could never understand.

This other bass is a battered old beast, brown and scuffed, covered in old stickers that are now mostly illegible. Weirdly, I love it. It's so big and heavy I struggle to lift it up at first. But somehow I feel like it suits me.

'I'd like to try this one actually,' I tell Dave, mustering my most decisive tone. And then as an afterthought, remembering my manners, 'Please.'

He fixes a strap on to the guitar, plugs it in and hands it to me. As I pull it over my head like the world's heaviest necklace, it hangs somewhere around my knees.

This time when I tentatively pluck a string, it makes an awesome booming sound that echoes around me like the first menacing note of a cowboy-movie soundtrack.

'That's a Fender Squier jazz bass, sunburst finish – not that you can really tell by this point. Early 90s. It's seen better days, but it's a solid workhorse.' Dave sounds pleased with himself, but he might as well be speaking Russian or Arabic as far as I'm concerned.

'I'll take it.'

Viv stops snapping on her phone for a second.

'Really? You want that one, not the pretty pink one?'

'Sorry, Viv. But I think this one is more me somehow. I don't know why, but it feels right. I'm not sure I'm the pink Hello Kitty type.'

'Do you know what, babe? You're a weirdo, but you might be right. It's better that you have your own different look anyway. As long as it fits with our band image. I've been working on some ideas for you – you've got your own mood board up on the wall now.'

Instead of replying, I follow Dave to the till. I hand over all of my worldly money plus a bit more. Dave, looking at Viv the whole time rather than me, says he'll throw in the strap and a case for nothing. Which is good news, as I'm not likely to ever have any money again. I hope Viv doesn't mind me borrowing more of her clothes, otherwise I have no possible way of conforming to this new 'band look'.

'Cheers, Dave.' Viv winks at him and he blushes again. 'Come on, Lizzie – let's go and get famous.'

She links her arm through mine and leads the way. Suddenly all the money in the world is worth it, as I walk out of there feeling the coolest I have ever felt in my whole life – giggling with Viv, and with a bass guitar strapped to my back. Nobody needs to know I can't play it yet.

'Hang on a sec,' Viv says suddenly. 'I think I left something behind in the shop.'

Before I have time to react, she's darted back inside. I hook my thumbs into the shoulder straps of my new guitar case and do my best to look nonchalant, hanging around on the pavement outside the shop.

Viv reappears with a decidedly naughty smile written all over her face.

'What did you just do?' I ask with an inexplicable feeling of foreboding.

'You are going to kill me!' she sing-songs, and my heart sinks as she links her arm through mine again. 'I gave Dave your phone number and told him that you really fancy him.'

'What?' I exclaim.

'Well, don't you?'

'No! I mean, I haven't even thought about it.'

'So think about it. He's cool, he works in the guitar shop and he's in a really great band. He's just the kind of person you should go out with. He's gorgeous.'

Is he? I honestly didn't notice. I have only a vague impression of a face obscured by a curtain of dirty blond fringe, slightly hunched posture, possibly snobby attitude. Oh, and the fact that he did not pay me even the slightest bit of attention. I somehow don't think that our short, stilted meeting – actually not even a meeting but a business transaction, as presumably he was contractually obliged to talk to me – sparked any amazing sexual chemistry on either side.

'Well, it doesn't even matter, because now he's going to think I'm really desperate. He's obviously never in a million years going to ring me.'

Viv whoops. 'See, I knew it! You do like him.'

Great. Now I seem as if I'm stressing over a boy ringing me, when I genuinely have no interest in him whatsoever. I can't decide whether this is a new low even for me, or if *anything* is better than the total romantic desert that has been my life thus far.

'I don't . . .' My voice trails off. I can't even be bothered to argue, and I suspect that all this over-protesting is making me sound immature. 'Whatever.'

'Don't worry about it, babe. You can thank me later.'

'Yeah, yeah.' I force myself to laugh, outwardly at least. 'You can be bridesmaid at our wedding and godmother to our first child.'

'That's my girl. Hey, I'd better get going. Got to get myself glammed up for tonight. Are you sure you don't want to come to the gig with us? It's going to be insanely brilliant.'

I could actually cry I want to go so badly.

'Sorry, I can't,' I say out loud. 'Like I said, I'm staying

round at my friend Daisy's tonight. I already promised and I can't let her down.'

'Well, you'll be missing out.' She shrugs. 'But don't forget it's our first band practice tomorrow – and I've got a surprise for you.'

'What is it?' I ask.

'It's a surprise, stupid! I could tell you, but then I'd have to kill you. And then I'd have to find another new bass player, which would be annoying. All I'll say is, you're going to love it. I promise.'

Viv:

Lizzeeeeee! Are you absolutely, 100% with a cherry on the top *sure* that you can't come to the gig tonight? It's going to be AMAZING. Everyone is going to be there! You'll love it! PLEEEEEZE?!!!

Lizzie:

I really, really can't but I wish I could!

Viv:

Well, have a brilliant night round at your friend's house! Don't forget our first band practice tomorrow – whoo!

Lizzie:

Have a great time at the gig! See you Sunday.

Viv:

I can't believe you're missing it, it's going to be a legendary night out! I'll send you updates! Gotta go – have fun!!!

'I knew it!' Daisy exclaims, whacking me around the head with a pillow. 'Didn't I tell you? You're going to be off being awesome in your band and forget all about us.'

'Don't be such a pessimist, Daze,' Jake says, not even looking up from the copy of *ID* he's flicking through. 'Think about it. In the highly unlikely event that Lizzie suddenly becomes some kind of quote-unquote "rock star" – and I can't emphasize enough how doubtful that is – then it will be a win for all of us. I believe she'll use her powers for the greater good – like She-Ra. Not even because she's such a nice person, but because she knows I'll kill her if she doesn't.'

'That might be true . . .' Daisy muses, really thinking about it. 'Lizzie, maybe you can introduce me to some guys in bands. I might end up falling in love with a future rock star. That would be a good story.'

'Exactly,' Jake agrees. 'See, Daisy – Lizzie's turning into the Kim Kardashian of the family and you're the funny sister who becomes everyone's favourite in the end.'

Daisy and I both gape at him, not sure which of the two of us should be the most insulted.

'It's true,' he insists, obviously enjoying winding us up. 'Lizzie just needs to have bum implants, a metric arse-load of plastic surgery and make a really boring sex tape. Then we're all going to be stars.'

'Hang on a minute,' I interrupt. 'I have no idea how we went from me joining a band and learning to play bass, to turning into Kim Kardashian and making a sex tape.'

'That's the nature of modern celebrity,' Jake tells me sagely. 'You'd better get used to it. We learned all about it in sociology.'

'How's it going back at West Grove anyway?' I ask, changing the subject. 'What's the gossip?'

It's bizarre how quickly I feel removed from the place. I went to West Grove for five years and not very long ago I could never have imagined being anywhere else. Now I somehow have a hard time even picturing it.

Of course, now Daisy and Jake, along with all the others, have moved to the sixth-form block, so I can't even accurately picture where they are any more. I tell myself it's impossible that I can really have changed so much in such a short space of time – in this case it's like the past is not so much another country as a parallel universe.

'So, come on – spill. Are Cameron Taylor and Ashley Freeman still joined at the lip? Has Tiffany Smith's hair got any bigger? Is Ms Pring still secretly in love with Mr Gillespie?' Even as I say it, I am forcing myself to try and care – it feels a bit like trying to run backwards.

Luckily Jake and Daisy are both easily distracted. They start chatting about all the old school gossip and don't seem to notice that I'm only half listening.

Staying over at Daisy's is great, but my mind is already on tomorrow's band practice. I'm going to get up early and take the bus home first thing in the morning, then go round to Viv and Rex's flat in the afternoon. I've already decided on my outfit and – more importantly – I have been spending every free minute googling facts about bass guitars and famous bassists. It's all a bit beyond me at the moment, so I hope I don't seem too clueless when Rex attempts to teach me to actually *play*. My beast of an instrument is propped up in one corner of my room, and I have so little idea of what to do with it I'm almost scared to go near it.

'Lizzie, are you listening to me?'

I come back down to earth – or more accurately under a blanket on Daisy's sofa – to find that both of my friends are staring at me.

'What were we talking about just now?' Jake demands.

'Um . . . Sorry, I was miles away. You know me, away with the fairies and all that.'

'Well, this is important stuff,' Jake goes on with a roll of his eyes. 'I'm debating dyeing my hair black, and Daisy might be in love with Noah from Year Thirteen. You remember, the one with the teeth? Everyone used to call him Dracula, but he's had braces and now he's quite fit.'

'Oh yeah, I remember,' I murmur.

I'm surprised at how hard it is to concentrate on what is actually happening here with my friends. As well as panicking about my first time playing in a band tomorrow, I can't help wondering what's happening at the gig and what Viv is up to. I'm worried this makes me a terrible, fickle person, and do my best to pay attention.

'Hey, is anyone else hungry?' I ask, aiming for neutral territory – and counting on the fact that Daisy is *always* hungry.

'Ooh, could you make us those Nutella toasties again?' she responds instantly. 'They were amazing.'

'Coming right up . . .'

Just for a second my brain flips back to Rex and his love of flapjacks and all things baked. Then I pull myself together, grin at my friends and head into the kitchen – if making a mess at Daisy's parents' pristine Aga is what it takes to make them happy, I'm more than willing to oblige.

Lizzie:

Sorry I had to sneak out – didn't want to wake you guys up, you both looked so sweet! Daze, I did the washing-up as the kitchen was such a mess!! Have to get back for Family Sunday stuff. See you soon! xxxx

Jake:

And you've got 'band practice' today, right?

Lizzie:

Yeah, but that's later on. Wish me luck?!

Jake:

Break a leg!!!

'I feel as if we've barely seen you this weekend, Lizzles.'

My dad flips another pancake on to my plate. His Sunday brunches are legendary. They might be anything from waffles to breakfast burritos, but they are always something exciting. My parents are fairly relaxed, but one of the rules is that Grace and I have to be home for Sunday brunch, so that we're guaranteed at least one 'family' meal every week.

My dad always cooks, invariably while listening to Radio 4 and wearing this old apron he has with a picture of a lobster on the front. My mum drinks coffee and reads the *Observer*. Grace generally complains. Given the food and the fact that I don't usually have anything better to do, I don't exactly consider it a great hardship.

'That's because we *haven't* seen her all weekend, Nick,' my mum agrees, barely looking up from her newspaper.

I concentrate on slicing a banana on to the pancake that I've just coated in Nutella *and* peanut butter. It's a topping combination that my dad and I came up with and agree is unsurpassed – we call it 'The Elvis'. I will probably resemble Elvis in his latter years quite soon, if my Nutella consumption this weekend is anything to go by.

'Big wow.' Grace rolls her eyes. 'Now that Lizzie has one new friend, she actually goes out at the weekend.'

'Unnecessary, Gracey.' Again my mum doesn't look up.

'So, what's going on today, Lizzie?' my dad soldiers on.

'Um. It's our first band practice. This afternoon.

Round at Viv and Rex's flat. In the Lanes. I'll be back this evening.'

'Band? Seriously?' Grace doesn't even laugh as she says it, as I might have expected. She looks genuinely disgusted. In fact she even puts down her fork and stops eating. 'I've had enough. I'm going upstairs to . . . I don't know, do something else.'

I can't help noticing, as she slinks out of the room, that Grace somehow looks vaguely glamorous even before she's cleaned her teeth on a Sunday morning, in holey leggings and a baggy T-shirt, her hair sticking up in every possible direction. I wish I could put my finger on what exactly it is that people like her and Viv possess, what it is that separates them from mere mortals like me. If I knew, maybe I could try to recreate it – but it's impossible.

'Now, about this *rock-band* business . . .' my mum begins, putting down her newspaper and propping her reading glasses on top of her head.

'Yes, Mum – I *know*!' I explode before she's even finished her sentence, which I don't think I have ever done before in my life. 'And yes, I do remember the bloody violin lessons.'

As both of my parents look on in utter shock, it occurs to me that maybe I'm a bit more stressed about my first band practice than I realized. I would never usually speak to my parents like this, let alone raise my voice. I'm supposed to be the good girl of the family; I'm usually the peacemaker.

'Sorry,' I mutter, feeling embarrassed about my little outburst.

'All I was actually going to *say*,' my mum goes on pointedly, 'is that your dad and I are going to be in town this afternoon so we could pick you up from your friends' house later if you wanted.'

'We're going to the museum,' my dad chips in, 'to see that new Grayson Perry exhibition. We might go for ramen after. If you're interested.'

'Thanks, guys. I'm not actually sure what time I'll finish, so don't worry about it. Really, thank you though.'

'That's the other thing actually,' Mum goes on. 'It *is* a Sunday. You've got college tomorrow. We need to know what time you'll be home.'

'Oh . . .' I am genuinely taken aback. 'Sorry, I hadn't really thought about it. I'm not sure.'

The idea of having to tell Viv I have a curfew is already embarrassing me. I am such a *child* compared to her. She might as well be my babysitter at this rate.

'We've never made Lizzie have these sorts of rules before,' my dad says, reading my mind and earning himself a sharp look from my mother.

'Well, it's never been an issue before,' she replies. 'We'll expect you home by nine, Lizzie. At the latest. I expect you still have homework to do, and stuff to get ready for Monday morning. I think that's pretty reasonable for a Sunday night, don't you?'

My dad opens his mouth and then closes it again, clearly thinking better of it. I do the same. Sadly I am not Grace – or anything like her.

'Fine,' I say. 'See you later. Have fun at the museum. And I'm sorry I was snappy earlier – I guess I'm just a tiny bit nervous.'

'Well, I don't suppose you've got anything to feel nervous about,' my mum says briskly. 'They know you aren't going to be any good. I mean, you've told them you can't actually play anything.'

'Yeah . . .'

I go to leave the kitchen, feeling weirdly deflated.

'Lizzie?' I turn to see what my dad wants now. 'Knock 'em dead!'

Lizzie:

I know you're both already bored of me going on about it . . . But you guys, I'm really nervous! Walking into town for my first band practice (aka bass lesson). Any advice???

Jake:

Don't eat yellow snow . . . That's what my dad always tells me.

Lizzie:

Helpful, J. Thx

Lizzie:

Daze???

Daisy:

Don't worry about it. I'm sure you'll be fine. Good luck!

Lizzie:

Thanks?!

Daisy:

I'm embroiled in English coursework hell and my mum's hidden the biscuits, so I can't manage any more words of wisdom for now. Soz. Speak later, K.

I'm standing outside Viv and Rex's front door, with my bass strapped to my back and my hair going flatter than ever in the rain.

I've been standing outside the building, pressing the buzzer, for over five minutes. Six minutes and four seconds, to be more precise. Maybe Viv's in the loo or something. Maybe I got the time wrong. Maybe she changed her mind. I'm too nervous to keep pressing the buzzer, in case I'm just being an annoyance.

Just as I'm contemplating trudging back home in the rain and the embarrassment of having to tell my family I've been stood up by my new friends, the door opens. Rex is suddenly right there, with bare feet and damp (still perfect) hair, pulling on a stripy T-shirt. I concentrate on the floor. He smells of mint and grapefruit.

'Lizzie! Have you been standing out here for aeons? I heard the buzzer but I was in the bathroom.'

'Sorry. I mean, Viv said to come over. You know? For the first band practice? I can just go, if it's not really a good time . . .'

'Oh, don't take it personally. Viv is so scatty she forgets everything. I hardly ever get to see her myself. Come in. We can get a head start. Viv should be back soon anyway.'

I follow Rex indoors and up the stairs, acutely conscious of the fact that the rain has made my hair both lank and frizzy. Worse than that, I can smell something musty and vaguely unpleasant – I'm not sure if it's the threadbare carpet of this communal hallway or if it's me. I've got my favourite bright green ballet pumps on. You know that smell of well-worn ballet pumps if they get soaked in the rain? Yeah. That.

'Should I take my shoes off?' I ask as I enter the upstairs flat.

'Whatever you like. Come and sit down. We might as well get started on our first lesson. Actually it's probably no bad thing that Viv isn't here. She'd only distract us. She's got the attention span of a three-year-old.'

'I could do with the distraction,' I admit. 'This is going to be so embarrassing. I know I'm going to be crap. Everyone keeps reminding me of my disastrous violin lessons when I was ten.'

'Well, you didn't have me as a teacher then. Ye of little faith and all that. So . . . what kind of music are you into?'

It's the worst kind of question. So many things I want to say, but my brain goes instantly blank. I make a noise that sounds like a cat dying, already knowing that I'll think of loads of great bands to casually reel off the second it's too late.

'Come on,' Rex insists. 'You know all the words to the Beatles. Plus you're wearing a Sonic Youth T-shirt, and I can't believe you're one of those deeply irritating people who wears the shirt but has no idea about the band. If you are, I'll have to ask you to leave now, I'm afraid.'

'No way! Those people annoy me too – all those Ramones T-shirts. I *do* like Sonic Youth. I like lots of retro stuff like that – you know, Nirvana, the Smiths, David Bowie. I'm really into Courtney Barnett at the moment . . . And I like Joanna Newsom and Feels and Wolf Alice and stuff like that. Sorry, I'm banging on.'

'No, don't be silly – by the sound of it, I'm going to be wanting to borrow records from your collection.'

'Well, actually I *do* have an old Dansette turntable and loads of boxes of vinyl,' I say, neglecting to mention that it's one my dad had that migrated up to my bedroom when he upgraded.

'Sweet. Now I've made a playlist of the best bass lines of all time, in my humble opinion. Only on Spotify unfortunately – not original vinyl. You sit there; I'm going to get us coffee and cake.'

Rex cues up his laptop. As he disappears into the kitchen, 'Come As You Are' by Nirvana echoes around the flat.

'You'll be playing this in no time,' he insists as he comes back. 'I made a carrot cake this morning. Here you go – you'll be needing it, with the graft we're going to put in at the musical coalface.'

I know you're not supposed to talk with your mouth full, but as I raise one forkful to my lips I immediately cannot help it.

'Holy Christmas, that's bloody amazing! Did you really make this yourself?'

'Well, it's not rocket science, but it is my own recipe. Pretty good, yeah? I put in some maple syrup and buttermilk to make it extra-moist, and a few other tricks that I can't possibly divulge. Now let's get cracking. We're starting with Nirvana.'

As Rex sits down on the floor next to me, my hands

start to feel like shovels – huge and clumsy and totally useless for these purposes. Even more so as he moves close enough so that he can angle my fingers on the neck of the guitar.

He shows me what to do, playing along on his own guitar so I can copy him, and scribbles it all down for me.

'This is your homework – so you can keep practising by yourself,' he says, drawing out sketches of the strings.

It's not long before I'm too engrossed even to be embarrassed. (Like, can he hear me chewing and swallowing the carrot cake; did I remember to put on deodorant this morning; can he see into my ear from this angle and when was the last time I went at my earholes with a cotton bud?) All the internal voices that are usually clamouring for my attention and hardly letting me hear myself think pretty much shut up. Not totally, but mostly.

We keep 'Come As You Are' on a loop and soon I am playing along with the bass line and Rex is strumming out the melody on his acoustic guitar. I am a bit slow and clunky, so I miss the odd note, but I basically get it. We keep playing it over and over again, and I can actually feel myself getting better each time around.

I'm listening so intently and concentrating so hard on my fingers, which are starting to ache, that I don't even hear Viv when she comes in.

'Hey, guess what?' Rex announces as she comes into the room, still in her leopard-print coat and pointy ankle boots, looking untouched by the rain. 'The girl's a natural. This plan of yours might actually work. Where have you been by the way? Poor Lizzie was standing out on the doorstep in the rain for hours because I was in the bathroom and didn't hear the buzzer.'

'Well, then maybe you shouldn't take so long doing your hair. I forgot what the time was. You don't mind – do you, Lizzie?'

'No, of course not,' I find myself saying. 'Not at all.'

'See?' Viv sticks her tongue out at Rex. 'Lizzie doesn't mind. Anyway, it looks like you two have been busy.'

'Yep, thanks to my masterly teaching and Lizzie's raw talent, we've got the hang of Nirvana and we're starting on the White Stripes next. 'Seven Nation Army' – one of the best bass lines of all time.'

'That's quite funny,' I chip in. 'The White Stripes having one of the best bass lines of all time, when they didn't even have a bass player, did they?'

'Hey, you're right!' Rex exclaims. 'I never even thought about it. One of life's great ironies. OK, let's have a break before we tackle the next one. We've earned it. Can I get you two ladies some coffee and cake?'

'No, thanks,' Viv replies quickly. 'I'm watching my figure. I think it's important for the band's image.'

I feel as if she's looking right at me as she says it. Viv's basically got a perfect figure, so I dread to think what she must think of mine.

'Lizzie?' Rex asks.

I think longingly of that dreamy cake.

'No, thank you. Um, I'm quite full.'

Rex rolls his eyes and disappears into the kitchen.

'Actually, guys,' Viv says, 'your next masterpiece might have to wait. Lizzie and I have more important band business to attend to. Rex, would you mind leaving us alone for a bit?'

'What, like play guitar in the bedroom while you have a quick chat? Or banished from my own home for the rest of the afternoon?' He sighs like he already knows the answer and he's used to it.

'The second one actually – if you don't mind, babe. If you could just go out for a while. It's important, I promise. What time do you have to go home, Lizzie?'

'Um, whenever. I shouldn't be too late getting back, I suppose . . .'

'OK. Rex, don't come back for two hours minimum. OK? Prepare to be wowed.'

'I'd better be,' he grumbles good-naturedly as he shrugs into his leather jacket. 'Is it still raining outside?'

'Hardly at all. Honest. Oh, don't make that face – go and mooch around your boring old record shops for the afternoon. Lizzie and I have girl things to do – trust me, you're better off out of here.'

Rex leaves us alone in the flat, whistling as he closes the front door behind him. Viv turns to me, eyes shining.

'You know I told you I had a big surprise for you . . . ?' She disappears into the bedroom and returns with several bulging carrier bags. 'Look!'

'Um . . .'

'We're going to give you a makeover!'

Am I going to look like . . .

a) A slightly better version of my boring old self?

b) My same boring old self in terrible fancy dress?

c) A complete stranger who I hardly recognize when I look in the mirror?

Viv won't let me look in the mirror. She is hovering around me, chattering and fidgeting with me non-stop.

'Trust me,' she says. 'I'm brilliant at this stuff.'

I can't believe the effort she's gone to, all for me. She has picked out piles of clothes from her own wardrobe. But I recoil in horror when she produces a pair of scarily professional-looking scissors and a pack of hair dye.

'I used to have a Saturday job in a hairdresser's,' she assures me, seeing the look on my face. 'I've cut *loads* of my friends' hair. Rex even lets me do his and he's the vainest man on the planet – he's obsessed with his hair. I cut my own fringe all the time. And obviously I dye it myself every two weeks.'

I can't argue with Viv and her perfect hair. She won't let me near the bathroom mirror in case I get freaked out, so she makes me sit down on the floor with a bin bag under me and another wrapped around my shoulders, and puts the TV on to distract me.

'Ooh, I love this!' she exclaims as she flicks through the channels until she finds an old episode of the Kardashians.

This is somehow unexpected, but to my total surprise and a bit of delight, we end up chatting enthusiastically about the Kardashians for a good half-hour. Although I love a bit of trashy reality TV, I somehow assumed that Viv would be too cool for that kind of thing – thankfully not.

All of this means that I barely even notice her busily combing and snipping and spraying around me, until two episodes have passed and I realize that I seem to be sitting on what looks like a thick rug of my own boring brown hair. I suddenly want to be sick, and not just because it looks really ratty and gross. I blame Kim and Kanye for this. I raise a hand up to my head to feel the damage, but Viv grabs it.

'Seriously, Lizzie – don't. I promise when you see the full effect you'll be blown away.'

Yeah, blown away like a war casualty. Still, I have to admit that a small bit of me likes the attention. I sit there like a puppy at the grooming parlour, while Viv uses her full arsenal of make-up, industrial strength hairdryer and straighteners on me.

When she's finished she hands me a scrap of black material that is so tiny it weighs almost nothing.

'Now, don't freak out,' she says. 'You're going to love it. Don't worry – that dress is really stretchy.'

I bite the bullet and squeeze myself into the painfully tight body-con dress. Luckily Viv is right and it is stretchy, but it still takes a lot of manoeuvring and I'm really not sure that every fibre of the fabric is supposed to be at full stretch. I glance wistfully at my nice comfy cardigan in a discarded pile on the floor – I don't know how Viv does this every day. It's barbaric – I feel like a girl in a Victorian film being kept down by both corsetry and patriarchy. I'm going to need a nice sit-down once I've wrestled myself into this Lycra nightmare.

Once I'm in, doing my best to pull the dress down to cover my bum, Viv chucks me a pair of ridiculously high heels.

'They buckle up at the back and you can adjust them, so they should fit,' she explains. 'See, I've thought of everything! It's almost time for the big unveiling . . .'

Viv is poised in front of me as if she's a Z-list celebrity and I'm the ribbon she's about to cut in a supermarket opening. Then the front door opens. Rex comes in and stops in his tracks when he sees me. I can't read the look on his face at all, so that doesn't exactly help. It just makes me feel more nervous and self-conscious.

'So, here we have it,' Viv announces. 'The result of all my hard work – the new and improved Elizabeth Brown!'

She pushes me in front of the mirror and for a second I am speechless. The reflection is not my own. I'm so shocked I can barely breathe, let alone speak – I was not in a million years expecting the shock to be so big. Viv has changed me beyond all recognition.

Standing in front of me is a girl with short black hair, cut into a tufty crop with a brutal fringe – not as short as Grace's but not far off. Her eyes, wide with surprise, are ringed with perfectly swooping black eyeliner – to match the sexy black outfit that I would never in a million years have chosen myself. I cannot believe it, so much so that I actually have to stop myself from putting out a hand to touch my own reflection just to check this is real, like some sort of idiot. I smile cautiously, and the wide red mouth of the girl in the mirror smiles back at me.

Just for a second, it feels fantastic to look like someone else entirely. Not to recognize myself. Looking like a whole different person, I can imagine just for a second that I really am someone else – a break from my own neuroses and beating myself up and feeling wrong in my own skin so much of the time. From a distance, I look brilliant. Not as good as Viv, but like a person who I might think was cool if I saw her walking around the Lanes. Someone better than me, probably.

But it only lasts for a second. As the shock wears off and my eyes come back into proper focus . . . of course, it's just me. It's always still just me. There's nothing that can be done about that. The make-up and the black hair and the short haircut might be a temporary distraction, but all of my flaws come back into sharper focus than ever. My forehead suddenly looks very big underneath the fringe, and the longer I look at it, the less sure I am that this haircut suits me at all.

'So, do you love it?' Viv grins at me.

I can't speak. I catch sight of Rex's face, backwards, in the mirror. Strangely, his expression looks just like mine.

'Doesn't she look awesome?' prompts Viv.

'You look lovely, Lizzie,' he says dutifully.

'She looks better than *lovely*,' Viv cuts in. 'With that amazing new haircut, she looks like a retro pin-up model. A bit like Louise Brooks, or Bettie Page. Actually, that reminds me of something I was thinking about the other day . . .'

'What?'

'Well, Lizzie Brown doesn't exactly sound like the name of a famous rock star. No offence – I mean, you've said so yourself loads of times. So, Lizzie is short for

Elizabeth – and so is Betty! Betty Brown the bass player – it sounds really cool. Anyway, I think it suits you. I'm going to start calling you Betty.'

'But that's not her name,' Rex says. 'You can't just change someone's name, Viv.'

'I'm not changing her name, *Rex*. It's just a different nickname. It's cool. You don't mind – do you, Betty?'

'Um, no . . .'

Betty Brown. A new name to go with my new look. I don't hate, it but I'm not sure it feels like me. Maybe that's a good thing.

While I'm pondering this idea, I catch sight of the clock and realize that I'm going to be late home if I don't hurry up.

Then another thought simultaneously comes into my head. I glance nervously between the clock and the mirror: I have no choice but to take my new image home with me. This isn't confined to some fantasy world in Viv's flat; yep, my parents are going to go ballistic when they see me. Or rather, when they see Betty.

Lizzie:

Guys . . . Photo attached.
What do you think??!

Daisy:

Who is this person and what has
she done with my friend Lizzie?

Lizzie:

Srsly, what do you think?

Jake:

It's . . . different.

'You look like you have a melted record on your head!'

'No, it looks more like she cut her hair with a pair of garden shears and then poured paint all over it.'

My mum looks disapproving but my dad is laughing his head off. This is really not the reaction I was expecting.

'You look like a goth Lena Dunham,' Grace pronounces. 'It's actually not a bad look. I kind of like it.'

'I'm going to my room, to practise,' I call over my shoulder as I stomp up the stairs, hauling my giant bass guitar. 'If that's not too hilarious to you all.'

Well, I thought I might be in trouble, so I try to tell myself that at least ridicule is preferable. Just forget it, calm down – stop dwelling on things so much, you idiot. You're sixteen years old, practically an adult, and it's just a new haircut. It was time to get rid of the boring brown bob anyway. Think like Viv – as if she would care about any of this.

With that in mind, I settle cross-legged on my bed and pull my bass out of its carry bag. I don't have an amp or anything at home, but Rex gave me a few plectrums and told me I'd be able to practise fine without any of the other stuff. In fact, he sent me home with all sorts of things, which I take out of my bass bag and spread around me on the bed: a teach-yourself-bass book (it was his when he was younger and he says it's really lame but ought to do the job), all his handwritten notes and diagrams, and a mix CD he burned specially with some easy bass lines for me to play along with.

'Let's meet up again next week – and by then I reckon

you'll be up to speed on all of them,' he said.

I'm determined to prove him right. For some reason, I don't want to let him down. Especially when I start going through all of his 'homework' notes and instructions – and I see that he has scribbled little messages in the margins, like 'Lizzie Brown – bass-playing super-heroine!' along with a cartoon picture of me wearing a Wonder Woman costume and playing my bass. It's actually a really good picture and I wonder if there is no end to his talents.

I slot the CD in and get to work. I'm soon surprisingly engrossed and, with the help of Rex's instructions and liberal use of the pause button, I play along with the whole thing. OK, badly, but I keep at it. When it finishes I put it on again from the beginning and laboriously play along with every note one more time, pausing it to go over the more challenging bits. I repeat this process on autopilot, until I realize that hours have passed – and I'm actually getting better.

I've never concentrated so hard on music before. It sounds stupid, but even though I've always really loved music, I've never really listened to it that closely. For me it has always been about gut feeling. If I feel happy, I blast out some cheesy Taylor Swift or 80s Madonna; if I'm sad, I play my dad's old Joni Mitchell records and sing along badly; sometimes I lie on my bed and close my eyes and put the Velvet Underground on – and I actually feel like it's the 60s and I'm possibly on drugs. That's the power of music and its effect on my mood. But like my dad, I'm just a fan – that's always been as far as it goes.

I've always spent all my spare money on records – just as likely to be from the charity shop, such is the beauty of old-school vinyl – and now I am the one telling my dad about new bands, generally discovered via music blogs and getting lost in black holes of YouTube videos.

But this is the first time I've concentrated on all the different layers – I don't think I ever used to really notice the bass line in a song, but now I'm tuned into it I can feel it automatically in everything I hear. It's like Rex has got me listening to music on a different level. It's really cool. It even makes me feel like maybe I can do this.

As I keep playing and playing, it occurs to me that I always thought actually making music was for *other people*. Other people, who know more than me and are cooler and better at things. But why not me? I love music, and Rex thinks I can do it. And I've got Viv to make me cool. Between them, it's like they can turn me into a whole new, better person.

My playing is suddenly interrupted by the sound of my phone. I consider ignoring it, as I don't want to stop, but then I recognize the song my phone is playing. It's long been a joke that my music geekery even extends to my phone ringtone – I always carefully choose a matching song for each of the friends in my address book. 'Dancing Queen' by his beloved Abba for my dad; 'Maneater' for Daisy; 'Cold As Ice' for Grace. Much to his consternation, Jake's is 'Addicted to Love' by Robert Palmer – as Daisy and I have never let him forget that famous fortnight last year when he took to wearing a single glove 'to look like Michael Jackson' and refused to take it off until we sang, 'You're gonna have to face it, you're a dick with a glove,' at him every time we saw him.

I don't feel much like talking to anyone – especially Daisy or Jake, who are basically the only people who ever ring me. Even though I was with them last night I feel a bit guilty, like I've been neglecting them lately or leaving them out or something. I don't really know what to do about it. They're my friends and I love them, but I'm finding it harder and harder to keep up with their lives now I'm not at school with them every day, and I've noticed that they seem annoyed that I'm doing my own thing. I can't help feeling bad about it whatever I do. I don't want to fall out with them, but I can't deal with them right now – which is probably very immature of me, I know.

But as I listen to the ringtone, I realize that it's not actually Daisy or Jake. Instead I hear the opening bars to 'One Way or Another'. Knowing this means it must be Viv, I make a flying leap for it across the bed. I haven't assigned Rex a ringtone yet, even though he's given me his number – I guess 'Ever Fallen in Love (With Someone You Shouldn't've)' by the Buzzcocks would be a bit melodramatic.

'Viv? I mean, hi!'

'Hey, Betty.' I'd forgotten about my new nickname; it kind of surprises me that she uses it so automatically. 'Babe, I've got amazing news.'

'What?' My head is so full of bass lines and ambitions, I assume it must be about the band.

'Well, you remember Dave, from the guitar shop . . .'

My heart sinks. 'Oh god, what?'

'Don't be like that. I said this is good news, remember? Well, what are you doing tomorrow after college?'

'I . . . I don't know.' I stammer awkwardly. 'I mean, I'm not really supposed to—'

'We're going on a double date. That's what you're doing after college tomorrow. You and Dave, me and Rex. This is happening. It's going to be brilliant.'

Viv takes my silence for agreement, as she talks about what we're going to do and how great it's going to be. We're all meeting at Cafe Vinyl, and Viv gives me detailed instructions on which of her dresses I'm supposed to wear for the occasion. She's got it all figured out.

'I think you should start using an eyeliner pencil and wearing it smudgy, because – no offence, babe – you're not great at drawing a cat's eye. And wear high heels, not your Converse, OK? Trust me – guys love heels.'

Yeah, I think, because then you can't run away. I don't say this out loud, because I think Viv is probably right. Maybe my life will be improved if I can finally figure out how to walk in heels without looking like Bambi on ice. I make a mental note to practise around the house. Maybe if I can master playing bass and wearing high heels both at once, I can kill two birds with one stone.

'Anyway,' Viv goes on, 'it's going to be great. Don't worry – you'll have a really good time. Dave's a good person to know, so it will be useful for the band too.'

By the time she finishes talking, her excitement has almost rubbed off on me. She's that kind of person, totally contagious. If she thinks it's a good idea, it probably is – her own perfect style/boyfriend/life prove it.

Anyway, let's face it, I'd probably go out with Charles Manson if it meant I got to hang out with Viv. And I can't wait to tell Rex about the progress I've made on the bass.

'I've been practising my bass all evening,' I start to tell Viv as soon as there's a gap for me to speak.

She cuts me off before I have time to elaborate. 'That's so great, babe. Keep it up! Listen, I've got to go. Like I said, it's going to be capital A-mazing. I'd better leave you to get your beauty sleep. If you're not too excited. Catch you on the flip side.'

As Viv hangs up, her comment about beauty sleep makes me wonder how late it is. I have been so engrossed I have no idea how much time has passed. I am shocked but somehow pleased when I look at my phone and see that it's nearly midnight.

Even though I've got college in the morning and I should really go to sleep, I put Rex's mix CD on from the beginning again, playing along with every bass note until my fingers have blisters and I fall asleep in my clothes.

Things to try to talk to Dave about on our (ick) 'date'

- Music – he works in the guitar shop so hopefully he likes good music. Tips on playing bass – too tragic?
- Is he from Brighton?
- Has he watched any good films lately? (Urgh, kill me now.)
- What is his favourite book? (WHAT IS WRONG WITH ME?)
- Maybe we should just talk about Viv, because that's all he's interested in and he would rather not be stuck going out with me at all. Based on these thrilling conversational ideas, who can blame him?

It's ironic. Tonight's so-called 'date' is the first development in my new college life that Daisy would actually get properly, genuinely excited about. Yet I haven't told her about it. Given the climate that seems to have been developing between me and my friends, I wasn't quite sure how to go about it.

Usually at this point I would be frantically texting to gauge Daisy and Jake's opinions on everything from my outfit to the topics of conversation to whether it's better to arrive fashionably late or not. In fact, that is what I would like to do right now more than anything. I feel lost by myself, and too embarrassed to ask Viv half of the things that I really want to – it's great that she seems to assume I'm as cool and confident as she is, but I don't want to shatter her illusions by allowing myself to sound like a total imbecile in front of her.

I just don't know what Daisy's reaction would be. She's been so weird with me lately. I really want to talk to her about all this, but I can't stand the idea that she might think I'm showing off or, worse, trying to rub it in that all this is suddenly happening to me.

So the safest thing seemed to be just to leave it. Maybe that makes me a coward, but somehow that's marginally more appealing than being a bitch – accidentally or not.

This means I'm left to my own devices. Which I'm sure is a very, very bad idea. As I walk to the cafe, I can't even decide whether I'm nervous or not. I'm so stunted, and I have never wanted to put myself out there in the scary world of boys and relationships, so I suppose this technically counts as my first date. It's almost comical that, after all this time, it's with someone I'm not even particularly enthused about.

I'm much more excited about telling Viv and Rex about my bass-playing progress – I even got up early this morning to do an hour's practice before college – than I am about seeing Dave again.

It's weird though. Despite all this, I'm realize I am still nervous. I might not like Dave that much, but I'm obscurely terrified that he won't like me at all. The whole thing will be a complete embarrassment.

At least Viv will be there to keep the conversation going, as she's so much better at that sort of thing than I am. Even so, I'm sure her presence will make me look like even more of an inferior second-rate choice.

On a very shallow level, I have a big problem – my hair. Without Viv's styling expertise, my new short haircut has gone what I can only describe as a bit 'mushroomy'. I tried my best with the hairdryer, and even sneaked into Grace's room to borrow her straighteners after she left for school this morning, but despite my lame attempts, the result is decidedly fungal.

'Betty!'

I don't recognize my new name until I see Viv waving at me from a booth in the corner. I'm still not used to it.

As I head towards her table, I make a secret bet with myself, as I so often do: if I can walk in a completely straight line through the cafe without tripping, it will be an OK evening; if I trip over or bump into a chair, it will all end badly; if I . . .

'Of course, you remember my friend Betty,' Viv says to Dave as I sit down awkwardly in the seat next to him.

'Hi,' Dave says, not looking at me.

'Hey,' Rex says. 'How's the star pupil getting on?'

'Actually I really think you might be pleased with how I'm doing,' I tell him, and hold up a newly calloused hand across the table as proof. 'I've been practising loads, and I can pretty much play everything on the CD you made me. So maybe when we have our next band meeting on Sunday, we can do some new ones.'

'Wow, definitely. Look at those blisters – you really have been working hard.' Maybe he's just being polite, but I'm pleased to note that Rex looks genuinely impressed. 'If you've picked up the basics that easily – like I could tell you would – maybe we can start playing some originals soon.'

'So, Dave,' Viv interrupts, 'Betty is the bass player in my band. It's really going to be awesome. You should come and see us when we start doing gigs – hopefully it will be really soon.'

'Yeah, sure,' Dave mumbles, gazing across the table at her like a love-struck puppy, as if he thinks that his long fringe will mean that we all don't notice.

'We won't be playing gigs any time soon if you don't start practising guitar a bit more,' Rex tells Viv. 'We're nowhere near good enough.'

Viv laughs this off with a wave of her hand. 'You've

already got loads of songs written; we've got Betty now – it's going to be great,' she says.

'I've had the total of one bass lesson so far!' I protest. 'Let's not get carried away.'

'How's *your* band going, Dave?' Viv changes the subject. 'If you've got any gigs coming up, Betty and I would love to come along.'

Dave proceeds to tell us at boring length about his band, Breakfast of Champions, and their upcoming gigs. Viv appears really interested in hearing about his band though. Watching her in case I can pick up any tips, I notice that she listens with wide eyes as he mumbles on and on about an argument with his drummer over a pedal that is ridiculously called a 'Superfuzz Bigmuff'. He noticeably blushes when Viv starts cracking up at this, and even I can't suppress an embarrassed giggle.

'So, Lizzie . . .' Rex begins, and gets a death stare from Viv. 'Sorry, I mean, Betty. I was thinking for our next bass lesson we could—'

Viv interrupts. '*Anyway*. Dave, Betty – we'll leave you to chat and get to know each other. That's the point of this, after all. Rex, come on, let's go . . . somewhere else.'

I actually want to curl up and die. Left alone, I have no idea what to do. Dave picks up a sugar dispenser and starts fiddling with it. He's so incredibly awkward I start to think that maybe we are kind of similar and he might even be really nice if we could just find a way to get talking. Then he starts licking grains of sugar off his fingers, as if he doesn't care that I'm there at all, and I'm suddenly not so sure. He's so clearly not interested in me.

I have a go anyway. It's got to be better than sitting here in a quicksand of painful silence – right?

'So, what kind of music do you like?' I ask.

My heart sinks as he not only still doesn't look up, he actually *groans*.

'Urgh, please. I get so bored of talking about music in the guitar shop all day. Seriously, man. I can't take it. I don't even listen to music any more, except my own.'

I have literally no idea what to say to this.

'So,' he asks eventually, with another big sigh, 'do you, um, have any brothers and sisters?'

'Um, just one sister. She's called Grace and she's an evil genius. She's also an actress.'

'That's a coincidence.' My dying hopes flicker into life for a second, as I think we might actually have something in common. 'Because I love watching TV.' My hopes die. 'Lot of actresses on TV. Is she pretty?'

'Yeah. Really pretty. Um . . . Do you have any brothers and sisters?'

'Nah. Only child.'

'Oh.'

I can feel the panic rising in me as we lapse once again into silence. I want to be anywhere but here. Dave's practically straining his neck trying to see where the others have gone.

I keep reminding myself that I don't even like him. But that doesn't matter – it's still one more failure, one more total embarrassment.

Viv is nowhere to be seen. I try to think what she would do, but my mind is completely blank. I have no moves, literally none. I can't even pretend. I'm not like Viv; I can't do it.

'So,' Dave says glumly, 'got any pets? I've got a dog called Chester. He's a Labrador.'

Lizzie:

So . . . I went on a *kind of* date last night?! I mean, it was a total disaster and the poor guy clearly wanted to kill himself rather than hang out with me (spoiler alert: he was forced into it by friends). But, you know, progress . . . right?! Literally NOTHING will come of this, but you know – news! Just wanted to let you know.

Jake:

WTAF? What is going ON? Who is this guy? Just: what???????

Daisy:

I can't believe you are only telling us about this AFTERWARDS. Priorities, woman.

Lizzie:

Guys, it's honestly not that big a deal. I maybe made it sound like more than it actually was. Sorry. It's just a funny story. Remind me to tell you next time I see you.

Jake:

NOTED.

My disastrous not-really-a-date almost – *almost* – seems funny now it's over. Now I'm sitting in Rex and Viv's flat with a cup of tea to hand and my bass in my lap and I'm turning the whole thing into a hilarious story. Our band practice is involving more chatting than practising right now, but my playing has been going so well that I'm not feeling terrible about myself for once – so the whole disaster with Dave doesn't seem to matter so much any more.

'He couldn't have been less interested in me if he tried – and I don't even particularly *like* him!'

'Well, what happened when he walked you home?' Viv asks.

I'm embarrassed even to talk about it, but I keep the smile glued to my face. It was Viv who insisted I couldn't possibly walk home alone and mentioned that Dave lived near me – well, vaguely in the same direction and not too far out of his way. Even when I kept saying I could get the bus. She was trying so hard to do me a favour.

'What do you *think* happened?' I force a casual tone. 'We walked home in awkward silence . . . and then he half-heartedly tried to snog me outside my house.'

What I don't mention is how panicky and slightly repulsed I felt when, without warning, he lunged at me with his mouth open. At the same time I felt weirdly curious and ended up kissing him back in a way that I know I really shouldn't have done. Even as it was happening, it was like I was watching myself. Still, at least now I've kissed *someone* other than my drunk gay best friend. It feels like progress. At least it's one box ticked that makes me slightly less of a loser. I can almost see why Daisy is so desperate to ditch her virginity.

'You kissed him, I knew it!' Viv exclaims. 'Go, Betty!'

In spite of myself, I grin. It's funny – sometimes even though I feel so awkward about things, a bit of me enjoys the attention. For once it's me who has a story. Something happened to me.

'Well, anyway . . .' Viv goes on, 'I'm glad you, ahem, got on so well with Dave in the end. Because I have important band news.'

'What's she going to spring on us now?' Rex wonders out loud and makes a face at me. 'Band uniforms? Ukulele solos? Choreographed dance routines?'

'Hey, those are all quite good ideas,' Viv says, so straight-faced I can't actually tell if she's joking, 'but this is much more exciting . . .'

'What is it?' I ask.

'I've entered us into a Battle of the Bands!'

Rex opens his mouth but Viv keeps talking over him.

'And so I've asked Dave to be our drummer!'

Rex and I utter one syllable in unison: 'What?'

'The Battle of the Bands,' Viv repeats calmly as if we didn't hear her the first time. 'I spoke to the promoter and we're on the bill. The prize is a recording session in a studio with some famous producer.'

'How long have we got?' I ask.

'Um . . . Two and a bit weeks before the first round.'

I am nearly sick in my mouth, but fortunately I manage

to swallow it back just in time. Well done, me.

'Hang on a minute,' I manage to say. 'What about the other bit? Dave's going to be in the band?'

'We're not ready to play a gig,' Rex says at the same time. 'We haven't even had a proper rehearsal yet.'

'You're always saying that, Rex,' Viv explains patiently. 'That's why I've asked Dave to join. We can't hang around forever, and I'm getting nowhere fast with the guitar. Sorry, Betty – I may have had slightly ulterior motives for trying to get you together with Dave, but I'm sure you'll agree it's for the greater good of the band.'

'Pimping Lizzie out because you can't be bothered to practise,' Rex mutters, but she ignores him.

'Rex, if Dave plays drums, then you can play guitar. This way I can concentrate on singing and Betty can play bass. She's doing so well at it. See? Sorted!'

'Sounds like you've got it all worked out,' Rex says. 'I've got to get to work. See you later.'

He walks out of the room, leaving Viv and me alone.

'Are you OK, Betty?' she asks me, laying a hand on my arm. 'This really is going to be great, I promise.'

'Viv, I'm really not sure about this . . .'

'What's the matter, Betty?' she asks, genuinely baffled. 'Rex says you're doing really well on the bass. Honestly, I'm the one who should be nervous. As the lead singer, most of the attention will be on me.'

'But, Viv, it's just . . .'

I get a sudden flashback to when I was five and refused to go onstage in the school nativity play because I was too scared. I didn't even have any lines. I was never the type to get to play the Virgin Mary. I had the glittering role of Star Number Seven. All I had to do was stand there and sing 'Little Donkey' along with thirty other kids. And still I threw a massive wobbler. In the end my mum had to bribe me with chocolate buttons and I was still too frightened to join in the singing. I just stood there. Like a lemon. I always was a weird kid. Still am, really.

I am not cut out for attention or ambition . . . or stress. I am not the right type for this.

'Come on, tell me what's bothering you,' she says. 'You can talk to me.'

'The thing is . . .'

Suddenly I want to tell Viv everything. I've never spoken about this to anyone, ever. Well, not really. It's not like I deliberately set out to act like it never happened, but even with Daisy and Jake it seems to have slipped between the cracks of conversation and fallen into the category of Things We Don't Talk About.

'I've kind of had problems in the past with . . . stress. I don't always deal with things very well.'

'Join the club, babe.' Viv laughs. 'Sorry, sorry – this is obviously serious. Go on.'

'Last year, during GCSEs, I basically had a breakdown. The stress really got to me, I became really obsessive and, well, everything started to go wrong.'

'How do you mean?'

'I wasn't sleeping. I couldn't eat. I started doing . . . weird things. The irony is, I didn't even do well in the exams. I became obsessed with all these rituals that took up so much time it stopped me from actually getting any work done. Like, if I can stay up all night and walk down the stairs with my eyes closed and not fall over, I'll do well in my exams. I even started thinking that if I didn't pass, my family would all die or the world would end or something. Losing the plot, basically.'

'So, what happened?'

'By the time I got to the last couple of papers, I was exhausted. I don't even remember it happening, but in my maths exam I started crying and I couldn't stop. I tried to get up and leave, but I passed out before I even made it out of the school hall. The teacher who was invigilating the exam called an ambulance, there was this whole fuss, I . . . Well, I ended up spending the first week of the summer holidays on a teenage mental-health unit.'

'Shit, Betty.'

I've never said any of this out loud before. Now I've started I can't seem to stop.

'It was really scary. Thankfully it's all a bit of a blur. I was diagnosed with generalized anxiety and mild OCD. Almost worse than that was all the fuss. Everyone who was in that exam had to get "special consideration" from the exam board because of me and all the disruption I'd caused. It was the first time anyone at school had ever even paid any attention to me, and suddenly it was because I was a total freak. Well, that's what it felt like anyway.'

I haven't even told her some of the worst bits.

I don't want to say them out loud.

'That's why I don't go on Facebook any more – everyone was talking about me on there. I didn't go to the results-day party with my friends . . .'

'You're not really the sort of person who likes attention, are you?' Viv says. 'I know what it's like to feel like a freak. I was dreading going to college until I met you. After the disaster at my last school, and my crazy family . . . I know I seem confident, but I'm not. Not always. Nobody is. Fake it till you make it, babe.'

I take a deep breath. I don't want to intrude by asking personal questions, but she's mentioned it a couple of times now so I guess it's OK.

'What do you mean about your last school and your crazy family?'

Maybe we are more alike than I realized – maybe that's why Viv seems to like me and I feel as if we could actually be proper friends.

'Well . . . it's a long story. I guess my parents are pretty useless. I've always had to fend for myself and pick things up as I go along. That's probably why I seem old for my age. I mean, I know I'm eighteen, but it's a bit weird to be doing my A levels while I'm already living in my own flat, right? My dad doesn't want to know; he just chucks money at me – hence this place. Poor little rich girl – what a cliché!'

She gives a brittle laugh, obviously trying to put a brave face on it all. I think of my own dad and how much he worries about me, and I feel unbearably sad for her.

'I mean, I know I'm "difficult",' she goes on. 'My parents are very conservative; they didn't know what to do with me. I was always rebelling, trying to get attention. On the plus side, it's made me really want to make something of myself. My parents, all those bitches back at St Catherine's – I'll show them all.'

'And it's so great that you've got Rex,' I say tentatively. 'I mean, a boyfriend who loves you, who you live with – it must be . . . amazing.'

My voice trails off and I realize I was daydreaming and getting carried away. I hope I haven't embarrassed myself, because Viv just laughs again.

'Rex?' she says. 'Yeah, he's all right.'

There are a million words that I could think of to describe Rex, and none of them are quite so tepid as that. I'm ashamed to note that her total nonchalance reflexively made a tiny little spark of 'what if. . . ?' rise up in my chest. Just for a second. I swallow it back down and tell myself off. I turn my mind back to my friend, and our band.

'We can do this, right?' I say tentatively. 'I really want to, but I'm seriously worried I'm going to mess everything up and have a meltdown again.'

'Stick with me, Betty. It'll be fine – I promise. Trust me.'

To my own surprise, I'm glad I've talked to Viv about this. I actually feel better. I believe her.

Rehearsal Schedule

- Practise three times per week until Battle of the Bands.
- Win Battle of the Bands.
- Recording?
- World domination?
- 'Hello, Wembley!'

OK? It's going to be great!

Love, Viv x

I've never been in a rehearsal studio before. This one is called the Black Bunker and it is just as dingy as you would imagine from its name. We are in a tiny, too-hot basement room with no windows; the walls are painted black and are visibly, unpleasantly damp. The floor is sticky with chewing gum, layers and layers of ancient spilled beer and, hopefully, the inspiring sweat of future rock stars. It's kind of cool.

I may not be an expert player yet, but I must admit I enjoyed walking into town after college with my bass. Just on my way to band practice, like you do. You know, whatever. Even if Rex had to help me plug into the amp, as I had no clue how to do it myself.

It's the first time we've all been in a room together to have a real band practice. We're running through the songs that Rex has written, and the whole thing is not as scary as I thought it would be. He's kept the bass lines really simple and written it all down for me to practise at home, so I pretty much know them by now. Dave's a good drummer, but Rex is the one holding it all together. The songs he's written are great – the sort of stuff I can really imagine hearing on the radio.

Viv definitely has a good voice, as I heard that day in the college toilets. But I can tell she's nervous, which I really didn't expect. Her timing isn't great, and she keeps messing up the same bits – she's obviously losing patience. This is so different to singing along with the radio or doing karaoke. I'm glad I've got my bass to hide behind and I'm not the one up there at the front singing. I feel for Viv.

'I don't know what to do with my hands,' she complains, after standing there awkwardly and fluffing yet another line.

'So learn to play guitar,' I hear Rex mutter under his breath, before saying more loudly, 'OK, let's try it again.'

'Five, six, seven, eight . . .' Dave counts us in, clicking his drumsticks in the air, which inexplicably makes me want to laugh – I suppose it's how it really works, but it seems like such a weird cliché, like something out of *Spinal Tap*. Which obviously my dad and I have watched about a hundred times.

I concentrate as hard as I can, counting in my head as I play along. I've kind of got my part figured out – I have to admit it's sounding pretty good.

Yet again we get to the point when the vocals should start – and nothing happens. Viv misses her cue and then makes a frustrated noise into the microphone. We all stop playing.

I feel weirdly disappointed. I should probably be glad that I'm holding up my end OK, but I feel acutely embarrassed for Viv as I watch her visibly struggle. I try my best not to think the traitorous thought that sneaks into my head: maybe just looking great and wanting to be famous might not automatically make Viv a brilliant front-woman without working at it a bit harder. It's never occurred to me before, and I feel mean for even thinking it. After all, she's the cool one and this is *her* band.

'Sorry,' she says. 'I missed my cue again, didn't I?'

'Don't worry about it,' Rex says, taking a deep breath. 'We'll get there. It's only our first proper rehearsal; it's fine.'

Viv glares at him, even though – or perhaps because – he's trying to be so nice.

'Yeah, yeah,' she mutters. 'Whatever.'

He sighs, as if sensing trouble ahead. 'Look, do you want to leave it there for now? We've nearly finished our two hours anyway.'

'Oh, just shut up, Rex,' Viv replies impatiently. 'Let's try again while we still have time. Who knows, I might even manage to get through one whole song without screwing it up. If we're really lucky.'

'OK, Viv, I just meant—'

'Seriously. Just. Don't. And, Betty, you can stop looking at me like that as well. Right. Dave, let's go. Come on, count us in.'

In fact I'm doing my best just to look at the floor. I can see Dave is doing the same, and for a second I feel quite close to him in a funny sort of a way. This is odd, as we haven't spoken to each other or even made eye contact since we arrived at the studio. My hands feel a bit shaky and clumsy, just as it takes Dave a second to pull himself together and get on the beat.

'Five, six, seven, eight . . .'

I hold my breath as I try my best to concentrate on playing my own part.

'Girl on fire, in the rain . . .' she sings, coming in perfectly at last.

She sounds great. We all play on, and I'm listening avidly to all the separate parts making up the whole. I try so hard to keep up the momentum and not mess this up. Just for a few moments, in that dingy rehearsal room, I feel inspired by how amazing this could be.

This time Viv gets halfway through the second verse before the timing goes wrong and she stumbles over a line. I keep playing on, hoping we can get back on track – after all, most of my bass practice so far has revolved around me trying to keep going, even while I'm messing up – until I realize that everyone else has stopped and my bass is the only sound left.

Viv throws her microphone down on the grubby concrete floor, where it drops with an ominous clunk and then gives a horrible scream of feedback. She's already halfway out of the room, so Rex is the one to pick it up and switch it off. By the time he has done that, Viv has slammed the door behind her and he has to run after her.

Dave and I are left, in a room buzzing with silence. It is not a room that was designed to be silent; it is supposed to absorb noise. I'm still standing there with my bass round my neck.

'Shit,' Dave says eventually.

'Yeah,' I agree.

There's a bang on the door and the slightly scary guy from the front desk appears. He looks like a cross between Russell Brand and Boy George – with neon dreadlocks piled up under a ratty top hat.

'Time's up,' he yells as he shambles into the doorway,

his voice reverberating around the empty space. 'Blimey – quiet in here, isn't it? I'm used to having to shout over all sorts of racket. Never come in to silence before. Gave me a fright, that did. Right, kids – that's your lot. Your two hours is up, and I've got a jazz-funk goth six-piece cluttering up the corridor. Clear out, time to go home.'

So, my first official band practice is unceremoniously over. I think it's safe to say it was a disaster. Still, I have the sneaking suspicion that I did a respectable job of holding up my end.

In spite of everything else, I'm starting to get the feeling that I might finally be finding my thing.

VIVIANE

Viviane has arrived.

She's a femme fatale with a gypsy spirit and a don't-care attitude. Steeped in rock 'n' roll glamour and an art-school sensibility. She's a punk nightmare dressed up as a blonde dream.

Most importantly: that voice. She comes from the tradition of big voices, blues and soul, but with a poetic style that is all her own.

Now based in Brighton, where she lives in the Lanes and makes music deep into the night, Viv Weldon has travelled the world and experienced sights way beyond her young age. She's now ready to take the music scene by storm.

Prepare to fall in love.

Lead vocals: Viv Weldon
Guitar: Rex Matthews
Bass: Betty Brown
Drums: Dave O'Connor

I suppose it should be a relief. Viv is acting like our disastrous rehearsal never happened. She texts me with instructions to skip college and come straight round to hers first thing in the morning.

So I do. I walk right past college and carry on going. Viv is at home in an empty flat, drinking coffee, dancing around to 'Be My Baby' by the Ronettes, wearing sparkly hotpants and an equally sparkly grin.

'Hey, girl!' she greets me. 'Rex is at work so I'm raiding his record collection. He's always saying I should educate myself. This one's pretty cool – they're called the Ronettes. I don't know if they're a new band – they sound quite retro, like Amy Winehouse.'

For a second I have to bite back annoyance. I'm the one who knows that the Ronettes are a famous New York girl group from the 1960s who were produced by Phil Spector and recorded loads of classics that I know off by heart – but because Viv's so pretty, she's automatically considered the cool one?

She grins at me and does a little shimmy, and of course it's not her fault. I'm the one being grumpy and mean-spirited, even if it's only in my head. I definitely got out on the bitchy side of the bed this morning. I don't know what's the matter with me.

'That's cool. I really like the Ronettes,' is all I say, and she doesn't ask me for any more of my fascinating opinions on the matter. 'Shall we walk into college together?' I ask. 'We should probably get going.'

'Well, we *could* just skip our first class.' She catches

sight of my face. 'Oh, come on, Betty – I've got something important to show you.'

Before I know it, I'm sitting on the sofa with Viv, shoes off, cup of tea at hand and both of us huddled around her laptop.

Viv has made a website. Like we're a real band.

Then I look more closely, and scroll through the text to page after page of selfies of Viv. It occurs to me that this doesn't actually make us look that much like a band at all.

'Viv, this is . . . great. Really professional,' I say. 'But did you, um, ask the others about the band name?'

It's weird. I get so panicky about being on the Internet; when Viv asked me to join the band in the first place, one of my first thoughts was that I just wanted to remain anonymous. I was actually relieved at the idea of having my new name to hide behind, so I should be relieved that I'm almost invisible on our new 'band' website.

But then when I see the website and that it's all about Viv, I don't even want to admit it, but I am surprised to find that I do kind of mind. I'm working harder than she is, Rex writes all the songs – being relegated to her backing band feels a bit wrong. But I don't feel like I get a say – if I said anything, it would make me look really petty and egotistical. Besides – who am I kidding? Nobody's going to turn up to look at me playing. Viv's the star; that was always the deal. I never even wanted to be in a band until now – it was all her idea, and none of this would be happening without her.

Viv shrugs. 'We needed a name, and no one else has come up with anything.'

'Well, I don't know if you meant it to come across like this . . . but it kind of sounds like you're a solo artist and we're just your backing band.'

'No, it doesn't! It's not my fault. It's my name – I can't help that, can I? What are you saying?'

She sounds absolutely outraged – and I am such a coward.

'Sorry, Viv. I didn't mean it like that. Of course I don't mind. I'm just the bass player.'

Viv puts the laptop down. She pats my knee and looks at me kindly. I feel the same slight dread in my stomach that I did when Dave kissed me.

'Look, Betty, I know it's difficult. Band politics and all that. I guess we have to be prepared for it. I kind of thought this might happen.' She sighs. 'As the lead singer, I'm probably going to get a lot of the attention. I'm not trying to be horrible; it's just how it is. I know it must be hard for you. I mean, it happened to Debbie Harry, Gwen Stefani . . . Let's be real, all the pretty blonde singers. You mustn't feel bad about yourself.'

'But I didn't mean . . .' I stop mid-sentence; there's no point arguing. 'It's fine.'

'Cool. I mean, the website is just a start for now, really. We can put some pictures of you up there if you like. You can have your own page.'

'No, no! Honestly. I didn't mean that.'

'Oh, by the way,' Viv says casually, 'we've got an interview lined up.'

'What do you mean, an *interview*?'

'Well, the Brighton student newspaper is covering the Battle of the Bands contest. They're interviewing all the bands who are entering. It turns out there are only six bands in the contest, and three will go through to the final . . . So I reckon we've got a really good chance of making it into the final at least. And then who knows what might happen?!'

'So when's this interview? What do we have to do?'

'We're meeting up on Saturday at the cafe. It's a girl with a weird name – she's called Wednesday or something, like the Addams family. I guess maybe her parents were goths. She's a first-year student, but she's already the music editor of the student paper. She sent me an email; she sounds pretty cool. Can you believe it? Our first interview already! I told you, Betty – it's all going to start happening for me. I mean, for us.'

Betty Brown's Media Training Notes

1. Be cool.
2. Shut up and let Viv and Rex do the talking.
3. Try not to fall over at least.
4. Do not, under any circumstances, do anything stupid like 'be yourself'.

We've all turned up early at Cafe Vinyl, early for the interview and in our best outfits like the keenest kids in school. Viv looks beautiful, the obvious star. The two boys have made a real effort to look extra cool; in their skinny jeans and leather jackets, there is no doubt that they are in a band.

So I suppose that just leaves me. I wonder if people would look at our little group and wonder how I fit in – eyeliner a bit wonky, not quite cool enough.

Even though we're not actually practising today, I've come with my bass strapped on my back to give me confidence. It reminds me that I am actually in a band now; I am A Bass Player.

I immediately regret this decision. Today my bass is not making me feel powerful. It is making me feel very clumsy. I hadn't realized how annoying it would be in a small, crowded cafe on a Saturday. I have already elicited countless tuts as I excuse myself and try to squeeze past people, and I had to apologize in profuse embarrassment when I accidentally whacked a lady round the head with it.

For someone who is allegedly supposed to be interviewed today, I definitely don't want to draw any extra attention to myself. I am hoping just to disappear into my Sonic Youth T-shirt and let the others do the talking. I have a feeling this won't be a problem at all. I can't imagine this music editor is going to want to talk much to me as long as Viv is around.

'Hi, are you guys Viviane? The band? I'm Tuesday

Cooper – yes, that's my real name – from the uni magazine.'

The girl standing by our table and grinning is not what I expected. For some reason I pictured a girl who looked like a model but in thick-framed glasses, older than me and intent on being a Serious Music Journalist, only into the coolest new bands and scathing about everything else. In short: absolutely terrifying.

This girl is ordinary and smiley, not intimidating at all. She seems genuinely enthused to meet us. She's wearing a dress printed with pictures of sausage dogs, with gold high-top trainers and a bright red Adidas tracksuit jacket.

When I met Viv, I was instantly struck by her perfection. This girl is somehow the opposite of that, but she is just as cool in a different way. It's her imperfections that seem to come together and make her interesting. I don't have that sense of 'I want to *be* her', just that I would love to be her friend. She looks happy and interesting and like she'd be loads of fun to hang out with.

I happen to be nearest to her when she sticks out a hand with multicoloured painted nails, so I shake it.

'Thanks for meeting me. You guys must be the most mysterious bunch in the Battle of the Bands, so I'm intrigued. I can get the first scoop!'

Tuesday squeezes into the seat next to me. Viv starts fluffing up her hair and trying to get her attention.

'Hi, I'm Viviane. Viv.'

'Cool, pleased to meet you, Viv. And the rest of you – who's who?'

'This is Rex, Dave and Betty. My band.'

There is a slightly awkward pause.

'Those flapjacks look amazing,' Tuesday says. 'Can I have one? And I could murder a hot chocolate.'

'Your wish is my command,' Rex says. 'Whipped cream and marshmallows?'

'Of course. I'm not stupid.'

'Rex works here,' Viv explains. 'If you let him, he'll spend the next hour boring you with the finer details of his flapjack recipe.'

'Shame I don't work for *Flapjack Monthly* then – that sounds great.' Tuesday rummages around in her rucksack and gets out a notebook and her phone. 'So, I'm interviewing all the acts who have entered. Most of them so far have been pretty standard – it's all boys from the music college. I mean, no offence – some of them are very sweet guys – but I must admit I was pleased when I saw you lot had put in your entry. You're kind of the wild cards of the contest; it's pretty cool. Oh, thanks very much.'

Rex brings Tuesday a gigantic hot chocolate and she immediately starts dunking bits of flapjack into the mountain of whipped cream.

'Wow, this is heaven on a stick. Sorry, I'm getting distracted. Great plan, by the way, to ply the journalist with baked goods. So, nobody's heard any of your material yet . . .'

'We're brand new,' Viv says proudly. 'I've been singing for years and I play a bit of guitar, but we only got together as a band quite recently. I just needed to find the right line-up.'

'So, what's your sound like?'

Viv continues. 'It's . . . It's like nothing you've ever heard before. It's going to be amazing. Kind of a bit retro but really modern. It's just . . . really cool.'

I want to step in, but don't have the nerve. Viv sounds like she doesn't know what she's talking about, just grabbing at random words.

Tuesday tries a different tack. 'What are your influences?'

Luckily Rex steps in. 'Like Viv said, it's a real mixture. But we all love classic stuff like Nirvana and David Bowie . . . I love anything weird and post-punk – from Joy Division to Gang of Four to the Fall. Dave's more into hardcore old-school stuff. Betty's got great taste in music – she's a big Sonic Youth fan, as you can see.'

'Yeah, I noticed your T-shirt,' Tuesday says to me. 'It's amazing.'

'Thanks. My dad is really into music so I ended up with all his old band T-shirts. That probably sounds a bit weird. And not very cool. Definitely not interesting enough to go into the article. So never mind. Sorry.'

Tuesday laughs, but kindly. 'Relax, Betty. I think that's really cool. You're lucky. My mum's awesome, but she loves 5 Seconds of Summer a bit too much. It's slightly worrying in a middle-aged woman. She's way more of a trendy teenager than I am.'

'My mum's a bit like that.' I laugh too. 'She won't admit

it, but she secretly loves Jackson Griffith. You know, from Sour Apple. She sings along in the car when she thinks no one's listening. She's so excited that he has a new album out and he's touring again.'

Viv interrupts, changing the subject. 'I've always dreamed of being a star. When I was a little kid I used to sing into my hairbrush. I'd put on shows and make my mum video me. All those old clichés.'

Exactly, I can't help thinking – they're clichés because *everyone* does that. Everyone. It's like writers saying they've been making up stories for 'as long as they can remember'. All kids make up stories and stupid dances and sing songs and show off. Some of them become writers and actors and pop stars, and some of them don't. Nobody is born special. Or maybe Viv was – maybe being that pretty makes a difference.

I catch myself thinking these thoughts that are verging on bitchy, and I'm a bit shocked at myself. As she carries on talking, I can feel myself getting irritated. I'm not even sure why. Maybe I'm just jealous.

I force myself to tune out of the conversation, not even trying to join in while Viv keeps talking and the two boys chip in with their own comments. Instead I look down and start counting the tiles on the cafe floor.

'Betty!'

I literally jerk to attention as Viv kicks me under the table. How horribly embarrassing.

'Sorry,' I mumble. 'I was miles away.'

Viv laughs, with a slight edge to her voice, and I hope

she's not annoyed with me. 'That's our Betty. Such an eccentric.'

Eccentric leaves a nasty taste in my mouth. I guess Viv felt she had to say something; I just wish it didn't have to be that. Let's face it – that's only half a step away from 'mental'.

I'm actually relieved when there is a diversion.

'Rex!' Lauren – the waitress-slash-photographer – comes over, looking harassed. 'Listen, I hate to ask, but it's rammed in here and we're short-staffed. I know your shift isn't supposed to start until this afternoon – but you couldn't give us a hand, could you?'

'Of course, if you guys need the help. I don't think I'm really necessary for this interview anyway. I'm not exactly some Keith Richards-style raconteur.'

'You've all been great, thanks. I've got enough for my piece anyway,' Tuesday assures him. 'I can't wait to hear you guys in the first round of the contest next week. Oh, and thanks for the flapjack – if you ever end up on *Celebrity MasterChef* in years to come, you've got my vote.'

Rex wipes his hand on his MC5 T-shirt before shaking hands with Tuesday and running off.

Dave glances at his watch and leaps out of his seat. 'Crap, I'd better get back to work too, or I'll be in trouble.'

He waves and shuffles out of the cafe.

'They seem like nice guys,' Tuesday comments once they're both out of earshot. 'Boys in bands can be such dicks, but they're sweet. That's even without the flapjack factor.'

'The Flapjack Factor,' I say, laughing to myself even though it's not particularly funny. 'That's a cooking show I would totally watch.'

I'm kind of surprised that Viv doesn't say anything – now would be the perfect opportunity to mention that he's her boyfriend. If I was her, I'd probably want to shout it across the rooftops of Brighton (and Hove as well). Then again, she also hasn't mentioned that it's Rex who has single-handedly written all the band's songs and taught them to the rest of us.

'Must just nip to the loo.' Viv excuses herself. I suspect she actually wants to check her lipstick.

Tuesday and I are left alone. She is still dipping pieces of flapjack in the dregs of her hot chocolate. She has a slight chocolate moustache – I am too shy to point it out to her, and I have a feeling that she wouldn't be particularly bothered even if I did.

'So is this the first band you've been in?' she asks me.

I nod.

'Wow, first band *and* first gig coming up. Don't worry, I'm sure this whole Battle of the Bands thing will be fun, nothing too serious.'

'I hope so,' I say, suddenly nervous and wishing I could talk to her about it.

'Well, that's how the magic happens, right?' she says. 'You've got to get out there and give it a go. Just be yourself and do your own thing, and I'm sure you'll be fine.'

Looking at her sincere face – with eyeliner that might

actually be wonkier than mine – I wish that I could talk to her about . . . well, everything.

'Everything all right?' Viv asks as she reappears.

'Great, thanks,' Tuesday says. 'You guys have all been brilliant. I can't wait for the gig.'

'Maybe you can do another article on us after you've seen us play?' Viv suggests.

'Let's see what happens at the gig. Of course we'll be doing a whole feature on the winners. I'll see you there anyway. Thanks again. See you, Viv. Bye, Betty.'

As soon as Tuesday leaves, Viv turns to me. 'We have *got* to win that competition.'

Viv's Perfect Master Plan for World Domination!

Schedule:

- For the next week, practise every minute that we can!!!
- Viv: work on outfits for the gig.
- PLAY A GREAT GIG AND GET THROUGH THE FIRST ROUND!
- Then practise extra hard for the final, which we have GOT to be in.
- WIN THE WHOLE THING!
- Become Tuesday Cooper's favourite new band so she writes a glowing article about us.
- More gigs.
- Publicity!
- WORLDWIDE FAME!
- Maybe a reality TV show, fashion/make-up contract, acting career . . .
- FORTUNE!
- EVERYTHING WE'VE EVER DREAMED OF!!!

Lizzie:

Hi, guys! Just wanted to check in as it's been a while. How's things? What you up to for half-term?

Jake:

Not much. Same old, same old. Etcetera . . .

Lizzie:

Oh, OK. Cool. What's up with Daisy? I haven't heard from her in ages.

Jake:

Don't stress about it, she's gone to Cornwall with her parents for the week. I'm sure that's what it is. I haven't spoken to her that much either. Prob no signal or sth.

Lizzie:

OK. Thx. Well, see you soon?

Viv is a girl on a mission. She's obsessed. All she cares about now is winning.

I really want to support her. After all, as I keep telling myself, this is her dream and I'm just along for the ride. It's funny though. The closer the contest gets, the more I am realizing the difference between us. And that maybe it's not just her dream now.

As I keep practising bass and working hard, it's becoming more and more obvious: for the first time in my life, I'm doing something I think I could really love.

Viv is obsessed with us winning because it's her path to possible fame and fortune – well, at least a start. I was never particularly interested in fame and fortune before, and Viv's attitude is making me realize that even more.

I've always loved to listen to music for its own sake, but now I love it on a whole new level. Playing bass, even if it's just by myself in my bedroom, is the only thing I want to do. This feeling that I'm constantly getting better – that I might even be good at something – is totally new to me, and it's addictive.

All I want is for the effort to pay off and for us to do a great gig when we get up there next week. Just not embarrassing myself would be a really good start.

I am genuinely getting better and better the more I practise, and it's a brilliant feeling. I'm starting to have my own ideas and suggest bass lines. Viv's preparation for the gig seems to consist solely of trying on outfits, and I've started to notice that she's pretty good at making herself scarce while the background work is going on.

Dave is often playing with his other band or working in the guitar shop; he only comes along to 'official' practices at the Black Bunker. He's a good drummer and a surprisingly nice guy to have in the band. He's so chilled out he's practically horizontal at all times – plus he barely speaks, which kind of suits me as we have never had a whole conversation since the night he half-heartedly snogged me. Generally we just nod at each other when required.

So Rex and I have been spending a lot of time together on our own in the flat, working on ideas and running through the songs again and again.

'Rex, I've been doing this new thing in 'Last Call' – when you do your solo during the middle eight, if I slow down and play half-time, it could sound quite cool. Shall we try it?'

'Yeah, I know what you mean,' he says straight away. 'Kind of a trippy underwater feeling. Let's give it a go.'

We play it through a couple of times, trying out different timings, before Viv appears from the bedroom. She's wearing the tiniest dress I've ever seen, adorned with fringing and sequins, and over-the-knee boots.

Rex takes one look at her, bursts out laughing and then starts playing 'These Boots Were Made for Walking', singing in an exaggerated American accent. I can't help giggling, but Viv just rolls her eyes.

'Never mind,' Rex says, shrugging. 'Viv, we need you for some more serious business anyway. We've been reworking the middle eight for 'Last Call'. Do you want to give it a run-through with us?'

'I don't have time, sorry.' She doesn't sound particularly sorry. 'I've got to go into town to pick up these new shoes I've ordered. See you later. Are you coming, Betty? We need to decide on your outfit for the gig.'

That's when it hits me. At the start, the main point of this whole exercise for me was hanging out with my cool new friend Viv. Not to mention borrowing her clothes. Trying to be more like her.

Now I see that something has changed, without me even realizing it.

'Actually, we're making pretty good progress,' I say. 'I think I should stay here and keep working on this song. Are you sure you don't want to stay and practise with us? We could all really do with it . . .'

I'm aware my voice sounds slightly pathetic – Viv's lack of interest in the nuts-and-bolts business of the band has been starting to trouble me more and more, but I don't feel it's my place to tell her what to do.

'Rex,' she says, 'could you leave Betty and me alone for a minute?'

'Sure, I'll go and make a cup of tea . . .'

He smiles at me kind of sympathetically as he walks out of the room, leaving me alone with Viv.

'Betty,' she says with an edge to her voice, 'I really don't need *you* of all people telling me what to do, OK? I get enough of that from Rex, and at least he knows a bit more about it than you do.'

'Sorry,' I mumble, feeling like I've been slapped round

the face and wishing I had never opened my big, stupid mouth. 'Viv, is everything OK?'

'What do you mean?'

'You just seem kind of . . . stressed.'

'Yeah, of course I'm stressed. The gig is coming up and Rex is doing my head in. Honestly, I know you think he's great, but he's a nightmare. If it wasn't for the . . . oh, never mind. I've got to go,' Viv says. 'See ya.'

'OK, see you later then.'

Viv chucks on a jacket, then she turns around and looks at me. I can't believe she's got the balls to leave the house in that outfit, just to go to the shops in the middle of the afternoon – I thought she was wearing it because she was trying on clothes for the gig. I guess she's really going for the image – she wants to look like a star at all times.

It's as if she reads my mind.

'Betty, I know you and Rex are just here practising this afternoon, but I'd really rethink that jumper if I were you – it's a bit . . . supply teacher. No offence, but you know what I mean?'

Before I can say a word, she turns on her heel and leaves. When he hears the door slam behind her, Rex emerges from the kitchen.

'Are you all right?' he asks me. 'You look like you're going to cry.'

'I'm fine,' I say quickly, automatically rubbing a hand across my eyes, smearing my eyeliner and no doubt making me look even worse. I wipe my smudgy hand on the side of my frumpy 'supply teacher' jumper.

'No, really – what did she say to you?'

'Oh, nothing much. I mean, nothing. I think she's just stressed, that's all.'

'I dunno . . . She's always been pretty moody. But she seems worse than ever lately.' Rex shakes his head in bemusement. 'Don't take it personally anyway. I don't know what's up with her at the moment. Let's face it, she can be kind of a bitch at times.'

'Well, I'm sure she has her reasons,' I mumble awkwardly, not quite sure what to say to this.

That tiny, disloyal feeling bubbles up again – only this time, with Rex in the same room standing right in front of me, I suddenly blush bright red for no apparent reason. I can feel my cheeks turning hot and I stare resolutely at the carpet.

'Let's have a quick break before we get back to it,' Rex suggests, to my relief. 'My brain is absolutely fried. Not to mention we've been playing for so long I can't feel the fingers in my left hand any more.'

'Hey, me too!' I exclaim, trying and failing to make a fist. 'I hadn't even noticed!'

He yawns and stretches. I see a strip of flesh above his waistband and hastily look away.

'I'm starving,' he says, strolling back into the kitchen. 'Have you eaten?'

'Um, no . . .'

We've been working solidly, so I hadn't realized it's getting late and I'm starving too. I haven't eaten since breakfast. I really should have been home ages ago.

'Stay there and I'll make us something,' he calls out, heading back into the kitchen.

I feel suddenly panicked at the idea of eating in close proximity to Rex. We've been spending pretty much all our time together poring over our guitars and song lyrics. But for some reason the idea of eating in front of him – *masticating* – makes me feel distinctly uncomfortable.

What an idiot, I tell myself. I *am* starving. We've become friends. He definitely sees me as 'one of the lads'. What's my problem? I can't believe I'm still thinking like this. It's not just pathetic, it's morally wrong. He's my best friend's boyfriend, and clearly I'm only acting like an idiot around him like this because he's the most beautiful boy I've ever seen. I don't want to admit it, even to myself, but it's true. Not only that, but he is nice and funny and talented, and . . .

And Viv doesn't even seem to like him much anyway. No, Lizzie. Don't be a bitch. Just . . . no.

I can hear him whistling and talking to himself, and the odd crash comes from the kitchen. When he eventually emerges, I fiddle with my bass, pretending that's what I've been doing the whole time rather than listening to what he's doing.

'Hey, I've made us the ideal working snack,' he announces, handing me a plate. 'It's always a good time for an all-day breakfast.'

We sit on the floor with our plates on our laps, still surrounded by music equipment and pages of lyrics.

'Rex, these scrambled eggs are amazing.'

'Thanks – another of my special secret recipes. Actually, not so secret – everyone knows the key to scrambled eggs is a low heat, constant stirring and a dollop of double cream. Ain't nothing to it.'

'Easy to say when you're good at *everything*,' I can't resist saying, then bite my tongue and try not to blush, mentally rolling my eyes at myself.

He chuckles. 'You flatter me. I'm rubbish at maths, and it took me four goes to pass my driving test. Oh, and I'm sure Viv could give you a whole list of things I'm really disappointingly crap at around the house.'

'Seriously, you know that's not what I meant. You're amazing at cooking and, as we're always saying, you're a musical genius. You're a great teacher too – you must be, to teach me! And your drawings are really good . . .'

I trail off, feeling like I'm starting to get too gushy and embarrass myself. Not to mention that Rex looks pretty embarrassed as well.

'I think that's my problem,' he says. 'Not to show off, but I think I'm *quite* good at loads of things. I like playing guitar, but I also like making flapjacks. I loved art at school, but I've ended up studying English literature. It would be so much easier if I had a great passion for one thing. I don't just want to play music and nothing else, the way Dave does. I'm not interested in trying to *make it* as a musician. I just do it because I really enjoy it. It's fun.'

I don't mention that he's practically reading my mind. This is exactly what I've been thinking – that talent and passion are what's important, and doing something for its own sake. Probably my own guilty conscience, but I feel like I ought to bring the conversation back to Viv.

'You and Viv doing the band together though – that's so cool,' I say.

'Well, Viv just wants to be famous,' Rex says. 'That's not what I'm interested in. One day I want to move to the country and open my own cafe. Now *that* would be cool. I could make all my own cakes and put on live music nights . . .'

'Really?'

'I'm serious. It would be great. Imagine, I could play music, decorate the place, make flapjacks all day and put on bands at night. That's the dream.'

'That actually sounds amazing. If a place like that existed, I'd definitely hang out there all the time.'

'It won't be in Brighton though. Once I've graduated, I'd love to move to Devon. That's where my granny lives and it's my favourite place in the world.'

'I'm kind of surprised,' I say. 'But that's a great dream. You should do it. I bet you will. Maybe one day you and Viv could move to the country together—'

Rex snorts through a mouthful of scrambled eggs. 'Are you joking? Can you actually imagine Viv in the countryside, running a cafe?'

OK, I realize that's an unlikely image. But for some reason I don't want to say that. It feels like it would be a betrayal – almost like slagging her off behind her back, even though I'm not saying anything horrible.

'I don't know,' is all I say, shrugging.

'Come on, Lizzie. I'm not stupid,' Rex says. 'Viv and I aren't going to end up together. I know she's just using me. She wants to be a singer; she's never going to learn to play guitar, she just likes to pose with one. She might get lucky, or in the end she might become one of those girls – you know the type, really hot and a tiny bit talented, bitter that they never became a big star.'

'What? That's harsh.' I bristle.

'Is it? I'm just being honest. Either way, she's going to leave me behind, that's for sure. She wants to take over Brighton and then move to some cool flat in east London after she's finished her A levels. Next stop: the world.'

'Well, maybe you could do both. You know, you're so talented. You could do the band, and travel, and then one day—'

'Lizzie, don't worry about me. This isn't *Romeo and Juliet*. We both know the score. I'm just a music geek; she's the kind of girl that wouldn't have looked twice at me at school.'

'But that's so sad . . .'

It's actually so depressing I want to cry. But maybe I just don't have a clue.

'Let's not talk about Viv any more,' Rex says. 'It's not fair, me banging on at you about all my problems just because things aren't going well. What about you?'

'What *about* me?'

'Well, I dunno. We hang out together loads but never really talk about stuff. I'm interested.'

'I'm the most boring person in the world, remember? Nobody wants to talk about me. Especially me.'

'Hey, you're always saying that, but I don't think it's true. You're really cool, you're great to hang out with. I know you've only been playing bass for about five minutes, but look how good you are already, and you're so *nice*. And pretty.'

'Ha!' I scoff awkwardly, secretly delighted on the inside but at the same time wanting to chew my arm off with embarrassment at the idea of the word 'pretty' being used about me.

'Seriously. I mean it.'

He looks at me intently with those wide green eyes and it feels like my heart literally stops for a second. When I see the look on his face, I believe him. It's like when he said he'd be able to teach me to play bass and he did. I trust him.

We just stare at each other for a moment. I'm actually relieved when he speaks, breaking the tension that seems to be building in the room.

'Hey, have you ever heard any Billie Holiday?'

I shake my head. 'No, I've heard of her – my dad says she's one of the greats. But I don't think I've ever heard any of her songs.'

He grins at me. 'At least you've got the balls to admit it when you don't know something. When I asked Viv that once, she said, "I love him."'

I suppress a laugh and resolutely push the 'Paul McCarthy' incident out of my head. This conversation feels strangely dangerous all of a sudden. I don't want to flatter myself, but all this talk is not a million miles away from 'my girlfriend doesn't understand me' kind of stuff.

I can't help thinking that Rex and I have so much more in common than he and Viv do. Still, that doesn't change anything – she's the pretty one and that's why Rex is her boyfriend. But for someone who said, 'Let's not talk about Viv any more,' only a few seconds ago, he's managed to bring her up again pretty quickly. He obviously can't help himself. Who can blame him?

He opens up Spotify on his laptop.

'So, here's Billie Holiday. You'll love her. This song would be one of my *Desert Island Discs*. We should really be listening to this on vinyl on your turntable, but I'm not as cool as you . . .'

He hits play and I can scarcely believe the sound that comes out. It really is incredible, beautiful and dark and like nothing I have ever heard before. I close my eyes without even realizing I'm doing it. Before long, I forget everything. I forget where I am entirely.

When the song comes to an end, I breathe out very, very slowly. I feel as though I have had an out-of-body experience.

As my eyes open, Rex is staring at me. He is leaning over, only inches from my face. Somehow – and I'm honestly not sure how it happened – we are holding hands.

'You liked it?' he whispers, as if speaking any louder would break the spell. 'I knew you would.'

I can't speak. I must leave. I don't want to move. I feel like I can't move. I genuinely feel like a million volts of electricity go shooting through me as he reaches out and touches the side of my face. When I dare to look at him, he is staring at me with those green eyes.

'You're not like Viv at all, are you?' he murmurs.

Before I can decide if this is supposed to be a compliment, he kisses me. For a moment it's like magic. It's like everything I ever dreamed. I find myself kissing him back and I never, ever want it to end.

Then the real world comes crashing back in and I realize what I am doing. I awkwardly break away, stumble to my feet and bang into the door frame in my haste to get out of there.

'Betty . . . I mean, Lizzie . . . Wait—'

'Rex, I'm sorry, I've got to go.'

What to do about this situation

• I don't know.

• I have no idea.

• I have literally no idea.

NOTE TO SELF: THERE IS NO POINT EVEN TRYING TO
MAKE A LIST WHEN ALL YOU CAN REALLY THINK
ABOUT IS REX.

REX REX REX.

REXREXREXREXREXREXREXREXREXREXREX.

Lizzie Brown, you are a horrible human being.

It's our last proper band practice before the Battle of the Bands.

We've been locked down in the Black Bunker for the last two hours; our time is up. We should be at our best by now, feeling reassured that we can do this. We have one day until the gig.

This would probably be OK – if it wasn't for me. I'm ruining everything, in every possible way.

It isn't just that I'm not on my game. I've lost it completely. I didn't sleep last night. I didn't cry all night or anything dramatic like that. I lay there, rigid and unable to close my eyes, staring at the ceiling – on high alert, waiting for something to happen . . . Nothing happened. My phone didn't ring. The house was silent all night and then it got light and it was morning.

I'm on autopilot, functioning like a zombie. My fingers won't work, but it's not only that – my brain and my hands are not connected in any way. I can't hear the music; it's like I don't remember any of the songs. I feel as if I am watching the world from behind a pane of glass.

Everyone else seems to have upped their game, in excitement about the gig tomorrow night. They'd be better off if I just switched off my amp and stood there doing nothing. I'm useless. Worse than useless – I'm dragging them all down.

'Earth to Betty: come in, Betty!' Viv intones through her microphone, laughing as the sound echoes around the otherwise quiet room.

I busy myself with fiddling with my bass, unplugging

from the amp and sorting the leads away.

'Our time's up,' I say robotically. 'We should go. Sorry I was so crap, everyone. Sorry I wasted our last rehearsal. I'll try my best not to screw up the gig.'

I struggle with wrestling my bass into its cover, my hands still not working properly. It's all too much, and the desperate urge to get out of there quickly is making it even worse.

These guys have become my closest friends over the past few weeks, the people I have spent more time with than anyone else. We are all in this together, on the final stretch before our first gig as a band.

Now there is literally nobody in this room who I can look in the eye any more. The idea makes me so sad I can hardly see straight to get out of the door. This chance I always wanted, and I have blown it. I wanted to become cooler and make new friends – not become the worst person on the face of the planet.

'Seriously, Betty,' Viv goes on. 'Get it together! You're OK, right?'

I open my mouth and then close it again. Before I get round to trying to formulate a response, she's turned her back and started packing up her microphone. I guess it was a rhetorical question.

Inadvertently I look over to Rex. Only to find that he is staring at me. I can't read his expression. Our eyes meet and neither of us looks away. This can only last for a second, but it feels like forever. I can feel the colour mounting in my cheeks and I suddenly feel paranoid that the whole thing is horribly obvious. How can it not be?

I wish I knew what he was thinking . . . He looks away before I do.

'Hey, it's just last-minute nerves,' Rex says. 'They affect everyone in different ways. Don't worry about it. I've played enough gigs in my time to know that you'll be OK when you get up there. It's like a marathon, and you've done the training for it. You've worked hard, we all know that, and you'll be fine.'

His voice sounds slightly weird, like he's trying too hard to be normal. Apparently I'm the only one to notice this, as the others don't seem to react in any noticeable way. I suppose there is the chance that I need to chill the hell out, but that is impossible.

'Yeah, Rex is right,' Dave chips in. 'Don't worry, dude. You're a trooper.'

'Thanks,' I mutter.

As there seems to be nothing else left to do, I reluctantly start to put on my jacket and strap my bass to my back. I don't know what I'm hanging around or hoping for. I wish I could talk to Rex on his own, but obviously that is impossible. Conversely I also wish I could talk honestly to Viv – I can't deal with being this horrible person with such an awful secret – but I haven't even begun to figure out the best way to do that. So I guess I'm stuck in this limbo of being eaten up from the inside for the foreseeable future.

Rex's words are still reverberating around my head:

'You're not like Viv at all, are you?' I wish I could be more like her – maybe then I wouldn't feel as wretched as I do. Maybe I wouldn't care.

'Well, I suppose I'll see you all tomorrow . . .' I say, reluctantly backing out of the room. 'Again, sorry I was so rubbish today. Bye.'

I trudge out of the studio and I am nearly out on the street when I hear footsteps behind me. Involuntarily, my heart leaps for joy at the thought that it might be Rex.

'Hang on, Betty, wait!'

I freeze as my eyes meet Viv's. She's left the boys behind and she's got her fluffy leopard-print coat on.

'I'm walking home with you,' she tells me.

I carry on walking and stare at the pavement. It's the only way I can keep functioning. I nearly didn't come to band practice today – I only got myself to the studio by counting every footstep on my way there and trying to avoid every crack in the pavement, keeping a running commentary going in my head.

I can feel myself unravelling, and it feels dangerously like what happened last year. I have no idea how I got myself into this situation – but I know it's all my own fault.

'So, Betty . . . It's not just nerves, is it?'

The physical symptoms of anxiety take hold with full force. The blood is rushing in my ears and my legs have gone numb. I somehow keep walking automatically, trying to look normal while fearing I might actually pass out.

I'm struggling to breathe and I don't know how I'll get the words out. But I have to tell her. I have to. I can't be the sort of person who doesn't – I won't be able to live with myself.

'Viv, the thing is . . . I have to . . . There's something . . .'

Her voice is hard. 'Betty, you are going to be able to play the gig tomorrow night, aren't you?'

'Um, yeah, but—'

'That's all that matters right now, OK? Listen to me, Betty. We've got to get through tomorrow night. I don't care about anything else.'

'OK,' I say, letting out a long breath. 'OK. I know how important this is to you. Of course I'll do it. But, Viv, there's something else I need to—'

'Betty. Stop. I don't want to hear it. We just need to get through the gig.'

'But—'

'I'm not trying to be a bitch here. Honestly I'm not. But until this gig is out of the way, keep whatever it is to yourself. Got it? I just need to know you can do the gig.'

I am defeated. The moment has passed. Kissing Viv's boyfriend is bad enough; I'm not going to ruin her big gig now on top of everything else. Suddenly it strikes me that honesty might not always be the best policy. Maybe I'm being a better friend by keeping it to myself until the time is right, uncomfortable as that might make me feel. Perhaps that should be part of my punishment for what I have done.

'Yeah,' I agree softly. 'We'll get the gig out of the way and talk after that.'

'Cool. Whatever it is, it can wait.'

We walk along in silence for a minute, me still glumly staring at my plimsolls.

'I've got my own stuff to deal with, you know,' Viv says, looking at me sideways. 'Me and Rex, everything – I've got to get it figured out, but after this gig. Work out what I'm doing with my life. Onwards and upwards, yeah?'

I don't dare to say anything out loud. I hold my breath and tell myself not to get my hopes up. After the gig, maybe things are going to change for all of us.

Lizzie:

Rex, I don't know if texting you is a terrible idea.
I just couldn't stand it any more. Can we talk?

Rex:

Hey, sorry for late reply.
Defo talk soon, yeah? R x

When I get home, all I want in the whole world is to shut myself away in the safety of my bedroom and not have to speak to another human being all night.

Alas, in my house that is never, ever going to happen.

'Lizzles! Long time, no see. How art thou, daughter of mine?'

'Fine, thanks,' I mutter, trying my best to summon a smile and avoid a worried interrogation.

'Your mother is still at the office, on a conference call with New York. I'm making my famous Thai green curry if you're interested.'

'Oh, I already ate. Thanks, Dad.'

My dad looks at me slightly suspiciously. I really wish I could tell him everything that is going on in my life. I'm sure there was a time not very long ago at all when I used to do exactly that; we'd talk all the time. So much has happened that the idea of doing that now seems impossible.

Obviously he knows about the band, and thankfully the violin comments have died down. I'm now really not sure why I haven't mentioned the Battle of the Bands thing. I didn't want to invite any more mockery, and I didn't want my parents to worry about the additional 'pressure' on me. Then I kind of let it slide until it felt like it was too late.

It's actually been fairly easy because I've barely seen either of my parents lately, but seeing my dad now makes me feel not only guilty but sad. I've missed him. I suddenly feel very lonely. I'm worried I might start crying. I've got myself into such a mess and I can't even talk to him about it.

'Actually, Dad, I'm really tired. I think I'm just going to go upstairs and get on with my college work. I've got a lot to do.'

'Eyes on the prize, kiddo. It's half-term next week. Party time for all you crazy kids, right? Maybe we could hang out a bit too – I know there's been this big project on at work, but we seem to be like ships in the night these days.'

'Yeah,' I say. 'That would be really nice.'

I'm halfway up the stairs when there is a knock on the front door. My dad glances at his watch and ambles over in his stripy socks to see who it is. I hang back in the hallway, frozen with apprehension while at the same time having to hold back the crazed idea that it might be Rex. These days I always have the crazed idea that it might be Rex.

'Hmm, has the fair Annabel forgotten her keys again? She's made it back in time for my famous . . . Oh, hello, Daisy. You're in luck – the prodigal's just got home. How are you?'

'Fine, thanks,' I hear Daisy say from the front doorstep.

I haven't spoken to her in so long another wave of guilt threatens to engulf me as I go over to the doorway, both of us not quite looking at each other. My dad doesn't pick up on the vibes and insists on hovering around us.

'Have you eaten, Daisy?' he asks. 'Would you like some Thai green curry? I can't seem to tempt anybody else around here.'

'Thanks, but I've already had dinner. I just needed to talk to Lizzie about something, if that's OK.'

'No problem. I'll leave you girls to it then. Nice to see you, Daisy – it's been a while.'

My dad disappears into the kitchen, where he has his curry bubbling away on the hob and Blur playing on the stereo.

'Um, shall we go upstairs?' I ask Daisy.

She shrugs and follows me silently, until we're safely in my bedroom with the door closed behind us and she doesn't have to keep up the polite pretence any more.

'Lizzie, why didn't you *tell* me?'

I feel even worse that I don't know exactly what she means. It could be any one of a few things.

1. That I've kissed TWO different boys since I last spoke to her.
2. One of them is my best friend's boyfriend.
3. Which means that my best friend is sort of not really her any more.
4. And I haven't actually told her any of the above.

'Um, tell you what?' I am forced to ask, cringing as I do so. All I can think about is the situation with Rex, but how could Daisy possibly know about that?

'Don't you even *know*?'

This is ridiculous and apparently could go on for a while. Are we just going to keep asking each other questions, on a loop, forever? Are we? Are we really?

What do you mean, 'really'?

Luckily the loop is broken as Daisy takes something out of her pink satchel and chucks it on to my bed. It's one of those free listings magazines they give out everywhere in Brighton, with music reviews and club-night previews and gig listings. It's definitely not something she'd usually be interested in.

'Frankie Elliot gave it to me at school today and said, "Isn't this that girl you *used to* hang around with?"' she explains with an understandable sneer in her voice. 'I don't even know how he knew. I guess rumours have been going round about you, again. I would hardly even have recognized you from the picture. And of course it says your name is *Betty*, so . . .'

I literally flinch like I've been slapped. The venom with which she said 'Betty' is so strong and so uncharacteristic, it slays me. There is so much pent-up resentment in those two syllables, I can hardly believe it.

It's starting to feel as if 'Betty' is my evil twin. She's running around doing all these things Lizzie would never, ever do. Maybe it's Betty who is a terrible person and the worst friend ever, not me.

'But, Daisy, I haven't told anyone. Not even my parents.'

She thinks about this carefully for a moment before she explodes. 'That doesn't make it OK! Teenagers aren't *supposed* to tell their parents everything. But ditching your friends because you suddenly think you're too cool for them is a whole different thing. It's not OK.'

'But that's not what I'm doing!'

'Oh, come on, Lizzie – sorry, I mean, *Betty*. Yes, it is. It's exactly what you're doing. Since when did you want to play bass in a band? It's ridiculous, let's face it. You wouldn't be doing any of this if it wasn't for that girl Viv. You just want to impress her, so you've joined this band and changed your name and you're even dressing just like her. Look at you – it's pathetic!'

Painfully I can see that's exactly what it must look like. I don't want to argue and say that I'm actually doing something I really enjoy. I'm too tired.

'I've been feeling really stressed,' I say instead. 'I'm sorry I didn't tell you. I just wanted to get this gig out of the way. I've made a complete mess of it all. As usual. I'm sorry.'

Daisy makes a tiny frustrated noise in the back of her throat. 'No, Lizzie! You are not going to make me feel bad about this! This is about *you* ditching *me*. Not about your "mental-health issues". I know you struggle with things, but not everything is about you. Not everyone is paying attention to *you* all the time.'

Wow. I am actually floored. There is nothing I can say to that. I can't come up with another word to argue about this. I'm suddenly so tired I can't function. I curl up in a ball on the bed, facing the wall, and wait for Daisy to let herself out.

'Jake didn't even want to talk to you,' she says before she leaves, but it sounds like it's coming from a long way away. 'Good luck with your fabulous band and your big gig, *Betty*.'

Battle for Brighton's Best Band!
By Tuesday Cooper

This Saturday will see the first round of contenders for the title of Brighton's best new band. Here's a rundown of the city's newest and hippest young gunslingers from roving writer-around-town Tuesday Cooper . . .

Skyfall
Classic pub rock in Adidas trainers. They belt out the tunes and like to rhyme 'sky' with 'high' whenever they can. An Oasis for the Instagram generation. Just don't ask them what a Wonderwall actually *is*. (Editor's note: What actually *is* a Wonderwall?)

East Street
Indie with a twist of rap, from the mean streets of Hove. Just when things might be getting a bit too predictable with the 4/4 timing and anthemic melodies, MC Bellow (real name Atticus St John Hancock) spits some rhymes to mix things up.

Gypsy Death Curse
Layered soundscapes consisting of 'found beats', toy instruments, laptops and an absence of vocals are likely to make this one of the more challenging acts of the evening. The band perform wearing balaclavas, as a comment on 'the modern culture of fame'.

Dream Genies

Wearing their David Bowie fan-club badges on their catsuit lapels, this trio of glam-rock art students just want to party like it's 1979. And there's nothing wrong with that, especially not when there's such a high ratio of fun and feather boas involved. Bonus points for the Ramones style band names: here we've got Tommy Genie, Oli Genie and Sanjay Genie.

Viviane

The contest's most mysterious bunch, at the time of going to press they don't even have a Soundcloud! What they do have instead is chutzpah by the bucketload and a glamorous blonde bombshell in the form of their eponymous lead singer. Bass lines come courtesy of Betty Brown, in the tradition of classic lady bass players Kim Gordon and Kim Deal (not just a lazy gender-based comparison: she has a new-wave vibe and an encyclopaedic knowledge of music that qualifies her to wear her vintage Sonic Youth T-shirt with pride). All will be revealed on Saturday night – their first-ever live performance.

Dirty Harriet

It might be a cliché to pitch this as 'the battle of the blondes' but Dirty Harriet definitely have the peroxide, the pizzazz (a word that's not used nearly enough) and the pop hooks to give Viviane a run for their money. Riot grrrl-influenced, but with sneaky pop sensibilities and pretty three-part harmonies, the trio are all seasoned musicians who have been in bands before, but have teamed up specifically to make an all-girl supergroup. World domination awaits.

While we get ready for the gig, Viv is even crosser about the write-up than Daisy was.

'It doesn't mean anything – don't worry about it,' Rex says, and gets an evil death stare for his trouble.

'I think it's pretty cool actually,' Dave ventures. 'If you really go through it, I think she's put them in reverse order of who she likes best. She clearly can't stand Skyfall; they're the kind of landfill indie she was yawning about when we met her. Obviously the last two bands are her favourites – us and that other one get much more space than everyone else.'

'Yes, exactly!' Viv hisses. 'Us *and that other one*. She clearly prefers them. They sound like a better, more professional version of us. Who the hell are Dirty Harriet anyway? I've never even heard of them. Now I'm supposed to get up and perform on the bill with them, when I'm obviously the shit runner-up.'

It's the first time I've ever heard Viv sounding anything other than the most confident girl in the world. I don't like it.

'Well, you know what they say,' I chip in, trying to help. 'Comparison is the thief of joy. I'm not sure *who* said it. A dead American president maybe. I probably saw it on Tumblr.'

'Oh shut up, Betty, you're not exactly helping.'

Viv shoots me such a withering glare that I wish I had never opened my mouth.

'And I don't know what that writer Tuesday What's-her-stupid-name thinks she was playing at,' she goes on, getting to the real point, which I have been trying *not* to think about. 'My band is called Viviane. I'm the lead singer. Of all the photos on our website, why would they use that one of *Betty*?'

I can totally understand why Viv is so upset, and I feel weirdly guilty. I don't know why they used that picture; I can only think there must have been some sort of mistake. Of all the dozens of selfies of Viv to choose from, they have instead chosen one of the few of me with my bass, wearing my Sonic Youth T-shirt, swiped from Viv's Instagram.

'Sorry,' I say feebly.

This is the last thing we need when we're getting ready for the gig. We're literally on the final countdown now. I'm feeling uncomfortable enough already, squeezed into one of Viv's dresses. When she helped me do my hair, she burned my scalp with her straighteners. It reminded me of being wrestled into getting ready in the mornings by my mum when I was little.

I keep telling myself that the only important thing is to do my best and get through the gig. I just need to focus on playing, get myself into that groove where the music fills my brain and nothing else matters. I can think about everything else afterwards.

'So get out there and show them then,' Rex says to Viv. 'You know you can do it. Go out there and smash it.'

The look that passes between them stabs me through the heart. Whatever Rex might have said about them having problems or being incompatible, he knew exactly what to say to her. For a second they are a little team of two and I am on the outside. He glances over at me and I have to look away. I can't bear it.

It's clearly done the trick. The old Viv sparkle is back, instantly.

'Let's do this,' she says.

The venue is a dark and dingy basement bar in the Lanes. It already seems packed when we arrive, and it isn't even open yet. We're here early for our soundcheck; the only people here are the other bands, the bar staff and various hangers-on.

The stage seems to loom over me, casting a shadow over the whole of one side of the room. It's not even that big a deal in reality – it's really just a raised wooden platform. Never mind Wembley, this isn't exactly Brixton Academy. But it's still a stage.

For now I'm more nervous about sound-checking in front of the other bands than anything else. Suddenly doing our first gig so publicly seems like the world's stupidest plan. They all look so at home, so blasé, so professional. Not like us.

The bands are each huddled in their own corner, guarding their equipment like their lives depend on it. The atmosphere is not quite one of animosity, but the air is crackling with the electricity of competition, even though everyone has an air of deliberate casualness.

Still, I can't help smiling to myself when I think of Tuesday Cooper's article profiling the bands. She totally nailed all of them. It's immediately obvious which band is which. I guess that means everyone knows exactly who we are too.

Skyfall and East Street are on opposite sides of the room, self-consciously sizing each other up. Two gangs of 'lads', all tracksuit tops and brand-new trainers, drinking beers and messing about. Only the indie haircuts versus baseball caps make it possible to tell them apart.

Dream Genies must be the guys in long scarves and velvet jackets, propping up the bar, laughing and chatting loudly among themselves. They look like art students. One of them is wearing a big floppy hat. They seem to be having the most fun of everybody here. I envy them.

Although they are not yet wearing the promised balaclavas, Gypsy Death Curse must be the very serious-looking lot currently on the stage and immersed in a very involved and technical soundcheck. Looking at them, I am ashamed to note that my first mean thought is: no wonder they wear balaclavas onstage. It's not that they're even ugly; they just look so very ordinary, like computer programmers or trainee teachers or something. Even given the number of boys in here in Ted Baker and trainers, they are by far the least stylish people in the room. No wonder they want to do something to make them seem a bit more mysterious. The sound emanating from their equipment sounds like a sickening combination of bass sludge and nails on a giant blackboard.

'I think it needs more treble, Noah,' one says.

A harassed-looking man with dreadlocks and a beard

adjusts some leads and then gives them a nod.

'OK, guys, that should be it . . . Your levels are fine. We only have a ten-minute slot for each band to soundcheck, OK?'

They totally ignore him and carry on playing and talking among themselves. Every time they make an adjustment, it sounds worse than ever – yet they seem very pleased with themselves. If anyone complains about the noise, they roll their eyes like 'you just don't get it'.

I've listened to music weirder than this with my dad. He's been known to make us listen to Captain Beefheart, who is as 'difficult' to get as his crazy name suggests, over Sunday brunch, even when Grace claimed it made her feel too sick to eat – so I know what's good-weird and what's just pretentious rubbish. This is not good-weird.

'We might be here for a while . . .' Rex mutters.

In a way, this charmless cacophony should make me feel better – like these chancers shouldn't be any sort of competition. But they do go to the music college and are so confident. I try to tune out and not think about what anyone else is doing. Just concentrate on keeping calm. As I said to Viv, comparison is the thief of joy.

We find a table with a long bench and extra seats, tucked away from the others, and commandeer it as our band camp. With the four of us and all our stuff, we take up quite a lot of room. As well as our instruments and equipment, Viv's actually brought a giant suitcase on wheels filled with extra clothes, make-up and her hair straighteners. As far as she's concerned, it's the most important bit of kit we've got.

Viv is sitting around looking as beautiful as ever, but she seems jumpy. Her eyes are out on stalks and I know exactly who she's looking out for. Dirty Harriet are the only band not here yet. Somehow their dramatic late entrance makes them seem even more intimidating, but I suppose there's always a chance they might not show up. If we're really lucky.

'Hey, doll . . .'

A beautiful guy with long black hair, smudged eyeliner and an impossibly skinny bottle-green velvet suit sits down next to Viv.

'Hi, I'm Sanjay Genie,' he says. 'Can I get you a drink? Although I must admit that is a less altruistic offer than it sounds, as the beer is free for bands. I'm guessing *you* have got to be either Viviane or Harriet.'

I half expect her to tell him to get lost. Instead she bats her eyelashes and turns on the charm.

'I'm Viviane – the original and the best rock 'n' roll blonde in town.'

'Pleased to meet you, Viviane. How about that drink?'

'Well, if the beer's free,' she says, 'then the least you can do is buy me something different. I'm not in the habit of accepting free drinks from strange men. But if you pay for it, that's a different matter. I'll have a glass of wine.'

He raises his eyebrows and laughs.

'Touché, Mademoiselle Pussy Cat.'

Then his eyes swivel to the other side of the room, as the door opens. It's like something out of a film as a force field of energy suddenly grabs everyone's attention. It's as if the temperature of the room changes within a split second.

'Sorry, haven't you heard all musicians are broke?' Sanjay says as he abandons Viv and scuttles away; like everyone else, he stares at the group of girls who have just entered the room.

Unlike everyone else, I don't take my eyes off Viv's face for a second. As she watches Dirty Harriet come in, I'm suddenly reminded with full force of the day when I first saw Viv; when she walked into the hall and she didn't even see me. I can still remember so strongly that feeling of wondering what it must be like to be such a magnificent creature, a different species from me, what it must be like to *be* someone like that. To be that perfect, to have that perfect life.

As I watch Viv's face, I realize for the first time that it's all relative. Viv's face right now looks just like mine did back then.

This girl seems to represent everything Viv is jealous of. Yes, Viv in her slinky black satin dress, with her perfectly straight platinum hair and cut-glass fringe, her high, high boots and her swoops of eyeliner, all her glitter and glamour. In that second, Viv's face looks just like mine. Prettier, maybe, but no better.

From a distance, the girl she is staring at looks like Viv, but drawn with a brighter pen. She's got the blonde hair and the confidence that makes heads turn. You can tell just by looking at her that she is a genuine star.

But if you really look at her properly, it's easy to see that they have a lot more differences than similarities. This girl is a lot scruffier than Viv. Her hair is bleached blonde too, but hers is a don't-care tangle tied up with beads and ribbons. She's wearing a glamorous party dress, but with hobnail boots that make her look tough. This girl is definitely not trying to be sexy; she's way too cool for that. When she shrugs out of her long coat, she has a huge tattoo that snakes around her shoulder and disappears underneath her dress. She looks like nobody I have ever seen. Where Viv is perfect, this girl looks like she is daring you to see her imperfections. And she looks so amazing that she can pull off this flawed, crazy look.

The two girls that come in behind her look just as cool and badass, while appearing not to care at all. One is also tall and blonde, the other small and dark; all of them scruffy and a bit weird-looking. It shouldn't work, but it does. They shouldn't be cool, but they are. They're grungy and punk, but they're laughing together and apparently having a great time. Not for them the air of studied indifference cultivated by everyone else; they don't need to. They just *are*. They obviously know what they're doing and don't need to prove themselves.

They troop in like all the rest of us did and dump their gear down near us. Then I watch, transfixed, as they walk directly towards us.

'Hey, Viv,' says this girl who must be the lead singer. 'I thought "Viviane" must be you. Look, I don't want there to be any weirdness so I'm just coming over to say hi. Good luck, yeah?'

Viv looks suddenly, inexplicably furious. I do my best not to stare while I try to figure out what's going on.

'Hi, Viv,' says one of the other girls, hanging back behind her – the one with the dark hair, who right now looks like she wants the earth to swallow her up. 'How are you?'

Viv looks her up and down with the bitchiest look on her face I have ever seen in my life.

'Jess . . . Oh, and it's Harry and Lola too. So, you three are Dirty Harriet,' she says dismissively. 'Well, this is just like a school reunion. How cosy. Glad to see you're still the total freak of the class, Harry. Still shopping at Top Goth, are we?'

The members of Dirty Harriet all gawp at Viv and I realize I'm doing the same thing. Jess looks like she might burst into tears, so Harry hustles her out of the way and takes a step closer to Viv.

'I thought you might have grown up a bit since you left St Catherine's,' she says quietly. 'Obviously not. You're still a bully. You've always been a big fish in a small pond, but karma will bite you in the end. Good luck tonight, Viv – you'll need it.'

Harry turns on her heel before Viv can reply. Which is probably a good thing because Viv looks ready to kill somebody.

Fortunately Dirty Harriet are being summoned by the harassed sound man, even while he is still trying to hustle

Gypsy Death Curse reluctantly off the stage.

I am just standing there like a total idiot, trying to put all the pieces into place.

'Wasn't that Jess?' Rex says to her. 'Your mate who you wanted to play bass with us before? What's she doing here?'

'Don't even ask,' Viv seethes. 'I should have known she'd have something to do with this. Those losers were all in my class back at St Catherine's. What a bunch of sad sacks. They're ugly weirdos, especially bloody Harry Jackson. Their band's going to be crap. I—'

Her rant is cut short by a loud screech of feedback from the stage.

'Attention, please!'

At the microphone is a small guy with spiky hair and loads of crackling energy. He's wearing a kilt, a woolly hat and a Sex Pistols T-shirt.

'That's Mad Jack McKray,' says Rex. 'He's the promoter – and the guy to impress tonight. He's in charge of the competition and the main judge.'

'Why's he called Mad Jack?' I ask.

'Because he's mad apparently. He used to be in a punk band called Slutz – with a z – in the 80s. They were known for being pretty bonkers.'

'Come on, come on, let's be having you,' he says in a sharp, nasal voice that captures the attention of the whole room and makes it fall instantly silent – I wonder if that's an old punk trick. 'Right, you 'orrible lot. I'm in charge tonight. You young whippersnappers had better be bloody good. Me and my mate Keith are the two judges of this competition. Keith and me used to be in a band together, called Slutz – with a *z* – back in the good old days. Keith is now the head honcho of his own record label, you might have heard of it, called Pop Boutique. If you catch our attention, who knows what will happen? So break a leg – and don't come bothering us with any demo tapes or any of that crap. If we think you're any good, we'll tell you. If not, leave us alone. No one likes a pest. Now . . . the running order for tonight was picked at random, so no arguments: Dream Genies, East Street, Gypsy Death Curse, Skyfall, Dirty Harriet, Viviane. Got it? Good.'

A vague muttering goes around the room in response to the running order – a lot of people aren't happy.

Jack goes on, to further muttering from the bands. 'Bad luck for some of you, but we've only got time for one more band to soundcheck before we get on with the show. Not my fault – those techy idiots took up three times as long as they were supposed to, so don't complain to me. See ya.'

He shambles off the stage, leaving everyone slightly dumbfounded. Dirty Harriet proceed to get on with their soundcheck. They are setting up on the stage like pros, and I am torn between wanting to watch them avidly to see how it's done, and tearing myself away before I get any more depressed.

'We're not going to get a soundcheck,' Dave says in dismay, his face looking like he's been slapped.

Rex shrugs. 'We'll just have to wing it, I suppose.' But he sounds doubtful.

'It's not fair,' Viv says. 'It's a fix. That freak Harry Jackson has copied me and stolen my old bass player and now she's stopped us from having a soundcheck. I'm going to complain.'

'Viv, calm down. Seriously,' Rex says. 'You heard Mad Jack McKray. Complaining isn't going to get you anywhere. Half the bands here haven't had a soundcheck; it happens sometimes; it's always chaos before a gig like this. We're on last, the headline slot. Think of those poor guys going on first – we got lucky.'

He might think it's lucky, and Viv looks mollified by this, but to me it sounds pretty torturous. OK, going on first isn't exactly ideal, but to me neither is last. Somewhere in the middle would have been nice – safe, anonymous – but maybe that's just me. Going on last means I have even longer to get nervous. Our set seems a very, very long way off.

'Sod this. I might as well go and get a drink then,' says Dave, disappearing towards the bar.

'That's the best idea I've heard all day,' Viv agrees emphatically, following close behind him.

This is what I've been hoping for and dreading with equal measure – Rex and I are left alone together. Finally. The moment I have been waiting for all this time, while quietly going out of my mind – and now I have no idea what I am supposed to do.

I feel like all of the air has suddenly been sucked out

of the room. I feel like I'm standing all wrong; I don't know what to do with my hands. My lips feel dry and I'm too self-conscious to lick them and this brings back an involuntary memory of him kissing me on the carpet while Billie Holiday played.

What can I do?

a. Keep quiet and see what he says. This would be the sensible thing to do, I am sure.
b. CONFRONT HIM. Maybe I have the right to be angry – or maybe I don't? I have no idea – that's the whole problem.
c. Tell him I've been in love with him since basically the first time I met him.

I just stand there, feeling an unbearable tension mounting and trying not to spontaneously combust on the spot. I find that I can't even look at him.

Then he reaches out and puts his hand on my arm. My heart does that thing and I swear I might actually collapse to the floor in some manner of Victorian swoon. Our eyes meet and I hold my breath in anticipation of what he is going to say.

'Look, I'm really sorry.'

'What?' I ask stupidly.

'I'm sorry. About what happened. I mean, I know it was just a kiss, but you were obviously upset and then you ran off, and . . . I know I messed up. I think you're really sweet. And cool. And we get on so well . . .'

It's like a slap in the face. He's sorry about what happened and it was *just a kiss*? I hadn't realized how high I'd let my hopes get, until he smashed them. I know I should try to be cool, laugh it off like I don't care – sound like this is no big deal to me and I go around kissing guys all the time. I just can't bring myself to do it. I am sick and tired of pretending to be cool when I'm not.

'Are you OK?' Rex asks.

'No, Rex,' I say. 'I am very much not OK.'

I am in danger of having a full-on panic attack. Or bursting into tears. Or punching someone. I have literally no idea. I can't breathe.

All I know is I have to get out of here. Right now.

Viv:

Betty, where are you???

Viv:

Seriously – WTF?

Viv:

Call me ASAP!

Viv:

Where are you?????????

Rex:

Are you OK?

I run out of the venue as fast as I can. I leave my bass, my bag, my coat – everything. I just turn on my heel and run, leaving Rex standing there.

I do what everyone in Brighton does when they have nowhere else to go – I run to the beach, in Viv's tight dress and the stupid high heels that I was forced into wearing.

Looking out to sea and breathing deeply, I try to make the chattering voices in my head shut up for long enough to let me think straight. Even out here it's not working. The voices are telling me I'm evil, horrible, a terrible friend, an even worse bass player, crap at everything, not even pretty, definitely not clever. The list goes on and on and on, until I just have to close my eyes and give in to it. There is no point trying to fight it.

I should never have done any of this. I was never the sort of person to be in a band. I'm not cool enough. I am hopelessly unmusical. *Remember those violin lessons, Lizzie?* This was always a bad idea.

Betty is not me. Betty doesn't even exist. The whole problem is that I've been trying to be something I'm not. Trying to live a double life. I'm not cut out for that sort of thing. I can't cope with life at the best of times.

I just want to be at home, wearing my favourite cardigan – the neon-blue patterned charity-shop one that Viv wouldn't let me wear because it 'didn't suit our image' – hanging out with my family, listening to records at the kitchen table and eating my dad's macaroni cheese.

That's what I'll do. I'll go home. I'll tell my dad everything. I'll put on my pyjamas and watch the

Kardashians and make toast. I can't think of anything nicer in the whole world. I don't even like going out.

I'm so close to doing it. I could get up now and walk home. Leave all my stuff back at the venue, forget about everyone – just go home.

I would be letting everyone down, but maybe that's not so bad. Maybe they'd be better off without me. Maybe I'd be doing us all a favour. It's not like we're going to win anyway – let's face it.

Then I think of my bass guitar, back there at the venue. All the hours I've put into learning, playing on my own in my bedroom – the feeling that I might actually be good at something. That I might finally have found my thing. Despite everything else, the idea of leaving that behind physically hurts.

Who am I trying to kid? Going home might be the cosy option, but missing this gig after everything we've worked for – no matter what happens afterwards – is unthinkable. I couldn't make myself do it even if I wanted to. I've come this far.

I'm not giving up playing bass. That's the one bit that makes me feel like myself. In a good way for once. More like myself than I ever have before.

After this gig I might end up playing back in my bedroom by myself, but that's OK. I'll have played this one gig, done what I said I'd do and proved that I can. Showed myself how far I've come since the summer – boring Lizzie Brown, then mad Lizzie Brown, not knowing which was worse but not wanting to be either one.

I'm just going to go back there and play this gig as Lizzie Brown.

I stand up, brush myself off and walk back towards the Lanes.

Remember

1. You can do this! (Can I? Can I *actually*?)
2. The show must go on! (Really?)
3. What can possibly go wrong? (Right . . . ?)

[end]

By the time I get back to the venue, there is a crowd outside. I have to push past people to get to the entrance. I can hear a bass rumble emanating from the basement and wonder how much I've missed.

It's only when I see the doorman checking tickets and ID on the door that I realize this is a queue to get into the gig. That's what all these people are here for. I'm under no illusion they've come here especially to see me play or anything, but it still feels pretty weird to think that they *will* all be seeing me play tonight. Whether they like it or not.

As I push my way to the front and stride up to the doorman, who let me pass earlier, it occurs to me that I no longer have the armour of my bass strapped to my back, or a whole band to back me up.

'Excuse me,' I say hesitantly, squeezing past people who look much cooler and older than I do. 'I'm in one of the bands. Viviane. I'm the bass player.'

'Yeah, right,' the girl at the front of the queue sneers. 'Bit late, aren't you? If you're the bass player, I'm the castanet player. Will you let me in for free too, pretty please?'

She simultaneously bats her eyelashes at the bouncer and gives me world-class evils.

'You're lucky I recognize you from earlier,' the bouncer says to me. 'You're in the band with that pretty blonde girl. Make sure you get your hand stamped this time, or I won't let you in again. You'd better get a move on.'

The place is now absolutely heaving. It's standing

room only. The mass of people has raised the temperature of the damp basement, and you can practically see the sweat dripping down the walls. I can feel my eyeliner melting and my hair beginning to kink, and I haven't even been anywhere near the stage yet. Fortunately I don't particularly care any more.

Skyfall are in full flow. That means I've already missed the first three bands; next is Dirty Harriet, then us. Skyfall are OK: nothing particularly original, but they're perfect for all the drunk boys in the crowd – who are swaying with their pints of beer and singing along, guessing the repetitive words and usually getting them right. The music sounds so familiar, I'm not even quite sure if they're playing covers or original songs.

Just as earlier I could instantly tell which band was which, it's easy to spot each band's supporters in the crowd. The flamboyant art-college types must be here for Dream Genies, and the ones looking all serious and disapproving are definitely with Gypsy Death Curse. I'm just not sure who's here to see us, if anyone.

'Oh my god, there you are!' a voice shouts over the music as a hand grabs my arm. 'We've all been wigging out! Thought you'd done a Richey Edwards . . . sorry, bad joke. But thank god you're back!'

It's Tuesday Cooper, looking rather startling in a bright orange playsuit, with stripy tights and a rucksack in the shape of a teddy bear.

'I just . . . went to get some fresh air,' I tell her, not wanting to get into it.

'Some fresh air – you've been gone ages! Never mind, come with me.'

She drags me behind her through the crowd.

'Here she is!' she announces proudly.

The rest of the band are still sitting at the same table, surrounded by stuff, not even watching what's happening on the stage. Given Tuesday's triumphant presentation, none of them look quite as pleased to see me as she might have thought.

'So nice you've decided to grace us with your presence,' Viv says. 'We'd given you up for dead. Were you having another one of your crazy episodes, or what?'

OK, I guess she has the right to be annoyed that I disappeared. But I'm still utterly shocked at the way she's speaking to me.

Then I notice that there are quite a lot of empty glasses on the table in front of her. As she looks at me with glittery eyes and a punchy attitude, I realize she's drunk. Really drunk. No wonder Dave is sitting there with his head in his hands and Rex looks so worried. A missing bass player and a drunk lead singer – not exactly the winning formula we'd all hoped for.

I have this sudden flash that Viv knows the gig is going to go badly and there is no future for the band, so she doesn't see the point in being nice to me any more. She only likes people who are some use to her. Drunk or not, I can see no other reason right now for the way she's looking at me with open annoyance and so casually using my secrets against me.

It's a good thing I'm doing this for me now, not for her – because she's really not making me want to do her any favours.

'The show must go on, right?' Rex says with an awkward laugh. 'At least we're all here. We can't pull out now.'

I realize the music from the stage has stopped, and then the noise of the crowd starts up again with a vengeance. They're really excited all of a sudden.

'All right, you reprobates,' Mad Jack shouts from the stage. 'Without further ado, I give you our penultimate band of the night . . . Dirty Harriet!'

The crowd quite literally goes wild, drowning out Viv's bitter, drunken heckling from the corner. It's clear that a lot of people are here especially for this set. As I turn, I find myself caught up in the tide and propelled towards the stage. I just go with it. I'm too curious not to. What's the harm?

Dirty Harriet stride out on to the stage. From the second they start playing it's obvious they're special. They've got a proper rock 'n' roll energy and their sound is genuinely unusual, but the songs are really catchy. Harry's voice isn't as good as Viv's, but it's much more distinctive – and you can't take your eyes off her. She plays guitar as well as sings, and she's actually a better guitar player than she is singer. She's proper; you can tell. All three of the band sing, joining in harmonies that sound like they've been singing together all their lives.

Best of all, their songs are witty – the lyrics are full of

puns and about real-life topics, instead of all the usual generic stuff. There's no interest in boys or romance here. Some of it is even a bit political – one of their songs is called 'Don't Call Me a Bad Feminist', and it namechecks everyone from Courtney Love to Theresa May.

I've never heard anything like it. One minute Harry is screaming, and the next they've all launched into a chorus of 50s girl-band doo-wops and handclaps. I don't even know what style of music to call it. Just when it sounds for a minute like normal punky indie, a reggae beat or a cheesy disco section will come in.

I've never been so inspired. This is the best thing I've ever seen. These girls are making me want to be like them, but only in as much as they are making me want to be my best self and do my own thing. I feel transformed by the experience, and it's only halfway through. I've basically forgotten I have to stand up and play my own set straight after them. I'm swept away, just happy to be a part of this crowd.

'We're Dirty Harriet and this is a brand-new song called "Your Friends All Hate You and So Do I" . . .' Harry says into the microphone. 'Thanks for coming out to see us tonight.'

I'm energized and hypnotized all at once. On the stage, all three of them are playing so unselfconsciously, like nobody is watching, I find myself doing the same and dancing along, not caring how I might look. Harry is singing, dancing and shredding her guitar all at once, conveying the music through every means possible.

I look around at the audience, conscious that we're all sharing an amazing communal experience. The drunk lads who had been bellowing along to Skyfall have retreated, although I can see a few of them further back dancing along – it's impossible not to dance, the beat is quite tribal and the music so joyous and emotive. It's all girls at the front, some singing along, all dancing crazily, some with their eyes closed. The effect is incredible.

I make out two girls in a dark corner, who have obviously blagged their way in somehow as they are definitely younger than me. They must have done it especially because they love this band; they are dancing so intently together. They are obviously a couple and both love the music equally; when the song finishes, they stop dancing for a moment and kiss.

Then one of them looks right at me. I can't believe they saw me staring at them like some sort of weird pervert. I didn't mean to. I'm about to look away apologetically. Then when I catch her eye, I realize that one of the girls looks very familiar.

'Grace!' I say out loud, but nobody hears me because the band have started up again.

This is their last song. It's a crowd pleaser and an absolute belter. Loads of the people around me seem to know the words. A girl behind me even gets some of her friends to help her up to try and crowd-surf. She kicks me in the head by accident, but I hardly even notice, and not only because luckily she has Converse on as opposed to DMs.

I lose track of Grace in the crowd; she has disappeared entirely. Before I know it, the song is over.

'We're Dirty Harriet, and you've been absolutely awesome,' Harry says, grinning out at the room and swiping her sweaty hair out of her eyes.

She pauses for a moment, just gazing out at the crowd, and for a second I swear I know exactly what she is thinking. She is savouring the moment, making the most of it all before she has to get off the stage and go back to normal life – whatever her normal life is. This is what she wants to do, she loves it, and she has connected with the audience in a way that was special for everyone.

The three members of Dirty Harriet all look at each other for a second and break into huge grins. Harry beckons the other two to the front of the stage; the three of them clasp hands, bow very briefly and run off the stage in a blaze of absolute triumph while the crowd is still roaring in appreciation.

And I suddenly remember that I'm going on straight after them. Dave is already heading on to the stage from the wings, setting up his drums and adjusting everything. I still feel shell-shocked and have to force myself back to the here and now.

I push my way through the dense crowd to go and grab my bass, running into Viv and Rex on my way. Viv is swaying on the spot and looks green.

'There's no point even bothering,' she says. 'I can't go on after that. We are totally screwed.'

'Come on.' Rex grabs her hand and drags her in the

direction of the stage. 'We're doing this.'

I follow behind them, as if I am hypnotized into some kind of a trance. I can hardly believe it's happening as I step on to the stage and take my place, plugging in my bass as I've learned how to – for a second my mind flips back to that first day in the guitar shop when I didn't have a clue, and I think how far I've come since then.

Somehow we all assemble in the vague formation of the band. The lights go back down, and thankfully this means that I can't make out anyone's actual face beyond the front row, only sense the heat and energy and chattering noise of the crowd. It's better than being able to see them all in too much intimidating detail anyway.

Rex looks around at each of us in turn and then nods at the sound guy. Mad Jack bounds on to the stage and I guess this means it's really happening.

This. Is. Really. Happening.

'Well, I certainly wouldn't want to go on after Dirty Harriet, would you?' Mad Jack cackles. 'Now, this lot here are Viviane, and my sources tell me this is their first-ever gig. So they're either mad . . . or on drugs. Who knows? They're our last band of the evening and they are virgins at the altar of music, so let's hear it for Viviane!'

Maybe they're all still pumped up from Dirty Harriet's set, or maybe they're just all drunk by now, but the crowd gives a huge cheer.

'Five, six, seven, eight . . .' Dave clicks his drumsticks together and we are off.

At first I am almost surprised to find that playing in

front of an audience is just like playing on my own, only even better. I go into my own space, despite the audience. The songs are so familiar to me by now, it's like my fingers are working on their own and my body is automatically responding to the music, but with a crackling electricity that makes it even more exciting. My heart is racing and my head is spinning, but in a good way.

Rex, Dave and I are solid, and just for a minute it feels brilliant. Then Viv misses her first cue to come in, just standing there clutching the microphone, doing nothing. My heart goes out to her, but I also want to shake her. I silently will her to get a grip – you've got this, Viv, come on.

I plough on, but I can feel us all falter as nothing happens where the vocals are supposed to kick in. We all keep going, playing the bars over again until we get back to the same point. This time Viv gets it.

'Last night, you said . . .'

But her voice sounds weaker than usual, not quite in time and too hesitant; it's obvious the nerves have got to her – not to mention the alcohol. I can feel that we're losing the audience. We haven't grabbed them. I understand instantly that we only have a tiny window before they start talking among themselves and drifting off to the bar or the toilets. Up here onstage, you can feel the mood of the crowd like a palpable force. I'm tuned in to it.

I think of Dirty Harriet and how I felt when they played and I disappear into the music and let it take me, my hands moving automatically and my body doing a weird dance I've never done before – I don't care whether a whole massive packed roomful of people is watching or not. It's the only way to do this; if you thought too hard about people watching you, you couldn't do it at all – I couldn't anyway.

It's bizarre how all of this seems perfectly natural and logical to me – the girl who can barely even walk down the street without tripping over and getting embarrassed about it. For some reason, this other extreme is somehow preferable. That's me, I'm starting to realize – I can't seem to cope with normal daily life, but I can do the crazy stuff just fine.

I'm so focused on the music, the song passes in a blur. I'm barely conscious of being here on the stage. Something strange happens to time, in just the same way it does when I'm on my own in my room practising.

As we keep going, it dawns on me that this is going pretty well, considering. I'm holding my end up perfectly respectably, and Rex and Dave are solid. Viv is doing just about OK, keeping her head above water. Although you can kind of see her legs kicking beneath the surface to keep herself afloat.

The crowd aren't exactly ecstatic, but they're not against us either. Considering the start this gig got off to, this is a win as far as I am concerned. People are generally nodding their heads rather than dancing with abandonment the way they did for Dirty Harriet, but they haven't drifted off completely. Most importantly, there has been no heckling or jeering – seriously, when Viv missed that first cue, I thought it might come down to worst-case scenario.

The whole thing goes by in a flash. We're OK. The end is in sight.

'This is supposed to be our last song,' Viv says before I know it.

Hang on. Supposed to be? I stand there and stare at her dumbly, not quite sure what I'm meant to do now. The two boys are doing the same. Although she's just about managed to coast through the set list, being onstage doesn't seem to have sobered Viv up at all. If anything, she looks even more drunk than she did when we started. She seems barely conscious of where she is, like she's finally hit the wall.

'We're Viviane,' she slurs, unsteady on her feet now, 'me and these losers. Obviously we're not going to win, not after Dirty Harriet – who, by the way, are a bunch of total freaks who nobody liked at school. And they nicked my bass player. So I found our new bass player, Betty, instead. You might recognize her from her picture. Take a bow, Betty.'

I have an unbelievably bad feeling about this, but I don't know what to do, so I give a sort of awkward nod.

'Betty had never even picked up a bass until about six weeks ago. Hasn't she done well? She also used to be a social outcast who had no life and was desperate for friends.'

I want to speak up, say that's not strictly true, but

I'm frozen to the spot. Everyone in the place seems to be similarly hypnotized by this weird spectacle that's happening here.

Viv begins to sway, her face turning more poisonous. Rex steps towards her, holding a hand out to touch her arm.

'Let me finish.' She wrestles her arm away from him and raises her voice, as if she's becoming aware that her time is limited and she wants to get it all out. 'So, it's all thanks to me that Betty is standing here in front of you. Oh, and to my boyfriend Rex, who's *such* a good teacher. Betty is so pathetic she's madly in love with him and thinks I haven't noticed. Probably because she's not only a loser but apparently she's "mentally ill".' She makes exaggerated air quotes with her fingers. 'Yeah, I don't seem to have very good luck with bass players. This one's bat-shit crazy. If she was any sort of a threat, I'd probably have more of a problem with her running after my boyfriend. But I don't care. It's made me realize I'm bigger than this band. This is our first and last gig. It's over.'

I can't take it any more.

Barely aware of what I'm doing, I take a running leap towards Viv and push her out of the way. I was only trying to get her away from the microphone, but I'm angry and she's drunk – we're both so unsteady on our feet that we go flying. I pull myself up and grab the microphone.

'*My name is Lizzie!*' I shout with all my might.

I push the microphone stand over and wince at the

screech of feedback that fills the room.

I pull my bass strap over my head and chuck the guitar down on to the ground. I jump off the stage and shove my way through the crowd. There are so many people I can't find my way out; I've lost my bearings. Total panic is setting in and I can hardly see straight.

I spot a sign for the toilets and run for it, slamming the door behind me.

Reasons to come out of this disgusting toilet cubicle
None.

Literally none.

The banging on the toilet door is incessant but I am not budging.

'Go away, please,' I shout yet again. 'I'm not coming out.'

The volume is only for audibility; I say it quite calmly by now. As if I have decided to live here forever and it is perfectly normal that I will never come out again. I will stay here until I grow old and eventually die. That's my plan.

In fact, being in here has worked out for the best in so many ways. After I'd been in here for a while, I thought I might as well actually use the toilet. That's when I realized that, just to add insult to injury, my period has started with no prior warning and wreaked havoc on my favourite lucky Wonder Woman knickers. Like this night can get any worse. At least I'm in the right place. Even if there is no loo roll.

I don't know how long I've been huddling in this disgusting toilet cubicle. I've mostly just been grateful that a lynch mob led by Viv didn't come straight in after me. At least I've been able to sit here and panic by myself and quietly cry my eyes out – and cry every last smudge of my stupid eyeliner off – in peace. I've ignored all the banging on the door, and people have eventually gone away, so it's worked out fine.

The toilet doors are so thick and heavy that the noise from outside in the venue is muffled. It has been hard to hear what's been going on. There hasn't been any more music and it seems to have quietened down now, so I guess everyone's leaving. I've no idea what the time is.

Eventually there is a more purposeful knock on the door, breaking the silence.

'Betty, um, Lizzie – it's Tuesday. The bar's closing; we have to go. Are you OK? I'll wait for you if you like . . .'

'No, no – I'm fine, thanks,' I shout back as brightly as I can.

'Well, I got your bass and things for you – they're just here, outside. I hope you're all right . . .'

I feel touched that she's been so nice when I barely know her, obviously because she feels sorry for me, but I'm too embarrassed to face her. I wait until she's gone before I force myself to get up from my awkward hunched position on the loo. My legs have gone numb.

Outside the toilets, the venue is pretty much deserted. The chairs are stacked up on the tables, and a girl is wiping the bar with a dishcloth.

I sigh and strap my bass wearily to my back, wondering if I'll ever play outside my bedroom again. As I walk out, I pass Mad Jack sitting at a table counting money out of a cash box.

'Bad luck, darling,' he calls out to me. 'Great night, yeah?'

I smile at him ruefully as I exit the building, aware that I have eyeliner streaked down my face and a general air of defeat.

I walk home by myself, knowing that it's a stupid thing to do and that I only have myself to blame if I am horribly murdered. It would be no less than I deserve.

By the time I get home, it's nearly two in the morning. I was really hoping for lights out and quiet, so I could creep inside and fall into bed. It looks like it is not to be – there are definitely lights on and I can hear voices coming from indoors. My parents might even be having one of their famous Saturday-night kitchen discos. Hopefully this means I can sneak past them and up the stairs while they dance to Prince and PJ Harvey in the sitting room.

I take a deep breath as I put my key in the front door. My best hope is that my mum has had one too many glasses of wine and my dad is regaling her with his 'legendary' DJ skills, playing a rare disco bootleg from the Paradise Garage circa 1979 or similar.

So I'm surprised and a bit worried when I open the door and don't hear any music playing. There are voices coming from the kitchen, but it doesn't sound like the usual jolly Saturday night chez Brown. I hope everything's OK. I suddenly feel panicky, like something bad might have happened.

'Lizzie? Is that you?' my mum calls out sharply.

I step into the kitchen. My parents are sitting at the table. There's a half-drunk bottle of red wine between them, but they really don't look like they're having any fun. Disaster, death and divorce instantly come into my mind. Why else would they be up at this time?

'Hi,' I say in a slightly strangled voice. 'Is everything OK?'

'No, not really,' my mum says. 'No, everything is not OK.'

My dad doesn't say a word. It's never a good sign when my mum does the talking. This usually means she has banned my dad from opening his mouth. It means it's a situation that requires the Bad Cop.

Still, it would be ironic if my parents found out about my 'big gig' now that it's over. I just wanted to save them from worrying about me. I don't suppose Grace has had the chance to grass on me yet, but I don't know how else they would know. It's not really Grace's style though – she's such an evil genius, I'm pretty sure she'd try blackmailing me first.

'Sit down,' my mum says. 'Is there anything you want to tell us, Elizabeth?'

Shit. She's good. I suppose the only thing left to do is be honest.

'Look, I only didn't tell you because I thought it would worry you . . .'

'Oh, Lizzie,' my dad says sadly, and my mum quiets him with a warning look.

'I'm really sorry . . . I guess you know all about the Battle of the Bands contest. The first round was tonight. I know I should have told you.'

'Battle of the Bands . . . What? With your band? Did you get through?' my dad asks.

'Nick! That is hardly the point.' My mum looks at him in utter exasperation. 'I have no idea why you're telling us all this now. I expect we ought to discuss the fact that you've been lying to us, sneaking out and going to nightclubs . . . But what does this have to do with you

233

being thrown out of college?'

It's like the floor has fallen away from me. The shock feels physical.

'Lizzie, are you OK?' my dad asks, immediately jumping up from the table.

'Nick, sit down!' my mum thunders.

'Annabel, look at her – she's had a shock; she obviously didn't know. You know she doesn't deal well with stress . . . We don't want . . .'

His voice tails off and it's like he can't even bring himself to say some of the words – the things we don't talk about.

I can't believe I've made things so much worse than I even realized and now my parents are arguing over me. I can't take it.

'Thrown out?' is all I can manage to say. 'But . . .'

'But what, Lizzie?' My mum suddenly sounds very tired and like she would rather be doing anything but having this conversation, which makes me feel even worse. 'Your attendance is less than fifty per cent. You missed a controlled assessment last week that would have contributed to your exam grade. Your sixth-form tutor says she's barely even met you since you started. I could go on, if you like.'

'But I didn't know any of this – no one told me!'

'That's the point, Lizzie,' my mum says witheringly. 'You're at college now, not at school. If you're being treated as an adult, you're supposed to act like one. I had my concerns that you wouldn't be able to cope, but I gave you the benefit of the doubt. I never dreamed you would let things get as bad as this without talking to us. What have you been *doing* all this time?'

I open my mouth to reply. I think back to that first day, when I was crying in the toilet until Viv came along.

'It was a rhetorical question,' my mum goes on before I can say a word. 'It's pretty obvious what you've been spending your time doing. I just don't know how you expected to get away with it. Did you really think you wouldn't get found out? The college sent your half-term report, along with a letter saying that you might as well not bother going back.'

'I'm so sorry . . .'

'We're all tired,' my dad says. 'I think perhaps we should get some sleep, talk about this in the morning.'

I expect Mum to argue with him, but she nods gratefully. They both look exhausted.

'Go to bed, Lizzie,' Dad says.

'I'm just so disappointed in you,' says my mum.

'I'm sorry,' I whisper.

I don't want to leave it like this, but neither of them says another word and I don't know what I can say.

I pick up my bass and trudge upstairs with it. I've been kicked out of my band and out of college, all in one day. I have no idea what I'm going to do.

Battle of the Blondes

Last night's Battle of the Bands contest in Brighton ended in a bang when one of the losing bands instigated an onstage brawl.

Viviane Weldon, of the eponymously named band Viviane, launched into a drunken public tirade against fellow (winning) competitors Dirty Harriet and unceremoniously sacked her own bass player.

The audience was left shocked and Viviane were ejected from the competition. Dirty Harriet – lead singer Harriet 'Harry' Jackson, formerly of several well-known local bands – are favourites to win the overall contest and will be competing against Skyfall and the Dream Genies. The prize is a recording session with 'Mad' Jack McKray, of controversial 80s punk band Slutz, now talent spotter for the Pop Boutique record label.

The final takes place next Saturday night – watch this space for more divas and dramas . . .

SEE MORE: Drunk onstage rant by Brighton singer Viviane – watch the video here!

<u>Comments</u>
Dirty Harriet are an amazing band – this girl Viviane is such a try-hard. She's obviously just desperate for the attention. Harry FTW!
Brighton_girl

Look at that bass player's face – she looks like she's about to burst into tears and/or piss herself. Hilarious!

Indiekid101

I was there. It was actually embarrassing. The bass player locked herself in the toilets crying and that girl Viviane had to be carried off the stage, she was a right mess. I guess she knew she wasn't going to win and so thought 'screw it'. Her band were actually OK, but Dirty Harriet deserved to win. They were properly brilliant.

Princessmononoke

You've got to watch the video just to see the bass player go mental at 02:37 . . . she pushes the singer over and then legs it out of there . . . Bat-shit crazy girl fight! I'm going to watch this in slow motion every time I need cheering up on a Monday morning. (Plus that singer is fit.) Classic!

Skyfall_Fan

Who are these people? Who cares???!

Anonymous

I was at school with Lizzie Brown (bass player). Can't believe she managed to get in a band as she was a bit of a nobody back then. But she was always a bit spooky. She left school after she totally lost it during one of her GCSE exams. I wasn't actually there but I heard it was mental. She left school and obviously changed her name, but it's definitely her. So she always had ISSUES. Obviously now she can add anger management to the list lol.

BrightonBelle

When I wake up in the morning, the sunlight streaming through the crack in my curtains, it takes me a second to remember everything that happened last night. Just for a moment, it's blissful. Life is normal and OK. These days, I'd take OK.

Then the sleep fug wears off and I come crashing back down to earth with a bang. I've been kicked out of the band. I've been kicked out of college. Viv hates me. My parents are angry with me. Daisy and Jake aren't even speaking to me. Oh, and to add to the mini-dramas, Grace is: a) probably gay; and b) probably not speaking to me either.

I am filled with dread as I get out of bed. I need to go downstairs and face the music.

I can hear the noises of Sunday morning around the house. Grace is taking one of her hour-long showers, where she uses all the hot water and ignores anyone else banging on the bathroom door, no matter how urgent. At least she came home after her secret nocturnal adventures, I suppose. Bumping into her last night has made me realize I know literally nothing about her life.

It occurs to me that maybe that's how my mum and dad feel about me this morning. I can hear the radio on in the kitchen, so they're up. I know they suggested last night that we sleep on it and then talk about the whole thing this morning, but I can't think of anything else I can say. *I'm sorry, I messed up, I had no idea.* No wonder they're so disappointed in me – they're right to be. So am I. I'm a disappointment. But what did any of us expect?

I put my onesie on, for comfort – and to hide in, if necessary – and go down the stairs. My dad is in the kitchen making omelettes and my mum is drinking coffee. The *Observer* has been delivered, but nobody's looked at it yet.

'Hi,' I say, standing hesitantly in the doorway.

'Morning,' my dad says. 'Fancy an omelette? Cheese, mushroom and spinach?'

He sounds suspiciously friendly. I should be pleased, but I am shocked when my mum stands up and hugs me. I even have a horrible feeling she's close to tears. I don't like it.

'Don't worry,' she says tremulously. 'We'll work this out. OK? Let's sit down and have breakfast and talk about it.'

'OK . . .'

'I don't expect Grace will be up for a while yet, so we should be safe.' She half smiles.

'She's having one of her epic showers,' I say. 'She'll be ages.'

'Good grief – expect severe water shortages in the greater Brighton area . . . The rest of us will be using the water butt in the garden for the foreseeable future, I expect,' says my dad.

He tips the omelette out on to a plate and puts it in front of me. He switches off the radio, tops up my mum's coffee and joins us at the table. This suddenly all feels very official.

'Have you been so unhappy again, sweetheart?' my

dad says straight away. 'Why didn't you talk to us about it?'

My mum puts her hand over his on the table, as if to tell him to calm down.

'It's just really important we figure this out,' she says. 'This has all come as a big shock to us, and we were tired last night. We need to talk about this properly. We thought you seemed so much better, but you obviously aren't. We're worried about you, Lizzie.'

I have a flash of things getting as bad as they were a few months ago, and I know I have to convince them that I'm OK at all costs. I *am* OK.

'The thing is . . .' I begin.

Then Grace walks into the kitchen. She's wearing only a long vest top and knickers; her hair is wet from the shower and sticking up in fierce spikes.

'What's for breakfast? I'm starving.'

'Gracey, we need to talk to your sister in private,' my mum says. 'Do you want to take something to eat upstairs?'

'Suits me.' She shrugs. 'You're the ones who usually insist on that whole tedious Sunday-brunch-together thing. Can you give me that fifty pounds, please? Then I'll go.'

'Excuse me, young lady?'

'Yeah. Fifty quid. For that long fringy dress in Urban Outfitters. Because I got straight *A*s in my half-term report. Dad said.'

'Oh dear. I did, didn't I?' Dad agrees sheepishly.

He hands over the cash and Grace vanishes. Not before she smirks at me on her way out. I can tell she thinks I'm in trouble for last night – if only she knew the half of it. I can't even be bothered to throw her under the bus with me.

'Lizzie,' Mum says as soon as the kitchen door has closed behind her, 'can you tell us what's been going on? Have you been unhappy at college?'

'It's not that,' I say. 'Honestly. I haven't been unhappy. Not like before. I'm OK. It's just been . . . a bit of a culture shock, I suppose. It's my fault. I've had other things going on. I'm sorry.'

'This is our fault. We should have kept a closer eye on you.' My mum sighs. 'This new image you've been doing and everything . . . I suppose it should have been a warning sign. But I actually thought you seemed happier.'

'Is this anything to do with your band and all that, and your new friend Viv?' Dad asks.

'We're not friends any more. And I've been kicked out of the band. God, kicked out of college *and* the band. I'm a washed-up dropout has-been at the age of sixteen.'

'Maybe it's for the best,' Mum says. 'This Viv girl obviously hasn't been a good influence. The whole "band" business has clearly been a distraction. It's not as if you've ever shown any particular musical talent in the past; it was probably very stressful for you. I know you said you didn't get through the first round of this contest you entered. I just wish you'd told us you had all this going on. It's so unlike you.'

'I just didn't want you to worry about me.'

'I understand that,' my mum agrees. 'But it's all over now, isn't it? If you're not in the band any more, and you aren't friends with this girl, everything can just go back to normal. Back to how things were. We can forget the whole thing.'

I think of playing bass, and how it's all I want to do now. I guess I can still just play in my bedroom. A nice little distracting hobby. I'm never going to be in a band again.

'Yeah,' I say. 'I suppose you're right. It's over.'

'Good,' my mum says decisively, as if that's that.

'Are you sure you're OK?' my dad asks, looking at me intently.

I nod and force a weak smile.

'I'm going to make an appointment to speak to Ms Wilding, back at West Grove. It's only been half a term. I'm sure if I explain, she'll let you go back. It might take some negotiating on my part, but I think it would be for the best, don't you?'

My heart sinks. It would be such a backwards step. I try to imagine myself going back there after all this and I just can't picture it.

But I don't know what else to do. There are no other options. I've got myself into this mess and my parents are worried about me all over again and are trying to fix it. So I just go along with it and agree. And really, really wish I didn't have to.

*

It's the first time in weeks that I've been a whole day without playing my bass. It's there, propped up in the corner of my bedroom; I keep looking at it, but I don't want to pick it up again yet.

Even though it's only been a matter of weeks, it was becoming a part of my identity and now I've got to get used to not being in a band again. Just playing by myself, without any purpose.

Just going back to being boring old Lizzie Brown, rather than Betty the cool new bass player. I know it all went wrong, but it's the loss of potential that's hardest to take – at least before, there were new possibilities. I need to work out how I can be myself again without going backwards. Lizzie Brown, but a new improved version, who might even have learned some stuff and got tougher and changed a bit. Trying to reinvent myself didn't work, so I suppose I've just got to be who I really am.

So of course I've just spent the whole afternoon lying around in my bedroom, wearing my onesie and watching crap on YouTube. Kind of like I used to before I started spending all my time playing bass, but now it feels a bit weird. A bit pointless, like I should be doing something else.

When there's a knock on my bedroom door, halfway through a video of an otter wearing sunglasses, I presume it's my dad bringing me tea and toast, which is his way of showing love.

'Come in,' I shout, without getting up, hoping maybe he's brought biscuits.

It's a good thing I'm lying down. If I'd been standing up, I might have keeled over when I saw it was Grace. Grace never comes into my room. She perches on the edge of my bed without being invited.

'Hi,' I say.

'So, Mum and Dad busted you about your gig last night then?'

'Yeah . . .'

'It's a shame,' she goes on. 'I was going to say I wouldn't grass on you if you wouldn't grass on me.'

'Yeah, I guessed as much. Don't worry – I didn't say anything. Who's the girl you were with?'

'Robyn.'

'Is she your girlfriend?'

She shrugs but looks me dead in the eyes. 'Yeah. It's not a big deal. I'll tell people at some point. So don't you go thinking this is some big emotional sisterly coming-out thing. I'm not hiding it; I just think that sort of thing is a bit old-fashioned, that's all.'

I burst out laughing; I can't help it. 'OK. Fine. It's up to you. At least you can stop calling me a lesbian now.'

'Nah, I might still do that. You look like way more of a lesbian than I do, so it's kind of ironic really. By the way, your band were no Dirty Harriet, but you weren't bad. I thought that girl Viv was a bit try-hard – but you can actually play. I was shocked.'

'Thanks. Are you just being nice to me so I don't tell Mum and Dad your big secret?'

'No, I don't really care if you do. It's not just a phase,

so they're going to have to know some time. I just can't face the idea of them being all *cool* about it. I think it will actually make their year. Having a gay daughter is so hip these days, didn't you know?'

'You're so right!' I actually guffaw. 'They're going to love being all *awesome* about it. Dad will probably make you a lesbian-themed playlist and Mum will want to invite your girlfriend round for, like, Vietnamese food or something.'

'Oh god,' Grace moans. 'They're going to love Robyn. Seriously, she's going to be their new favourite daughter. It's going to be so cringe. She's really into Riot grrrl music and, like, gender politics and stuff. She reads all those boring feminist books that Mum's into. I put up with it because she's hot, obviously. We only went to that gig you were in last night because Robyn is obsessed with that band Dirty Harriet. Give me some Beyoncé and a bit of good old-fashioned objectification any day.'

I'm surprised – Grace is saying this with something that sounds like fondness. She sounds almost soft when she's talking about Robyn. Like an actual, nice human being.

Without me realizing it, while we've been talking, Grace has shuffled up to my end of the bed.

'What are you watching?' she asks. 'Put something good on, will you? Have you got the new *MIC* on catch-up?'

Before I know what's happening, somehow Grace and I spend all of Sunday afternoon cuddled up on my bed watching crap on my iPad, chatting and actually having a pretty good time.

'Don't you dare tell Mum and Dad,' she says. 'Imagine – us two getting on for once *and* a gay daughter; they'll think Christmas has come early or something.'

Things I could do with my life

- Go back to school and finish sixth form. That shouldn't seem so bad – so why is it that I really, really don't want to?

- Go on Jeremy Kyle. 'I Kissed My Best Friend's Boyfriend and I Don't Know What to Do with My Sad Life!' Viviane *might* even be prepared to join in if I convince her it might be her 'big break' into a career of TV stardom.

- Um, join the circus? Not very bendy and scared of lions, so maybe Incredible Bearded Lady could be a possibility after a few days of no tweezers.

It's a Monday and I have nothing to do. I know it's half-term, but I'm still conscious of being in limbo and it feels weird.

Mum's going to West Grove today to speak to the head about whether they'll let me go back. I can't imagine it's going to be an easy sell – 'Yes, I know Elizabeth didn't do that well in her GCSEs and went mad in one of the exams, but now she's been kicked out of sixth-form college, so please can you let her come back? Of course she'll make up all the shit-tons of work she's missed.' Hmm. I know what I'd say.

I'm half hoping they won't let me back in, but I have literally no idea what else I could do, so I know I'm just being stupid. Besides, my mum is very persuasive, so I'd better get used to the idea.

It's ironic that I might be going back to West Grove now that I have no friends there any more. Then again, I have no friends anywhere.

In fact, the only person who seems to be talking to me these days is Grace. Which is mildly unsettling, but better than the alternative. Her usual insults have a new tone to them that makes them sound almost friendly. It's not like we're in 'my sister is my best friend' territory, but it's nice to have her as more of an ally. It's definitely better to be with Grace than against her.

I'm busy watching films where people die at the end, to lighten my mood, when she drifts into my room.

'You know you're on the Internet,' she says matter-of-factly.

'What?'

'That whole onstage thing with your band and that girl Viv. Of course people filmed it and put it on Facebook and stuff. I mean, don't flatter yourself – it hasn't gone viral or anything. It's only really people in Brighton who are talking about it, people who were there or friends of friends and stuff, but it's getting quite a lot of comments. You might want to have a look at it.'

She drifts out again like it's not a big deal. My hands have gone clammy and I can feel the rising tide of panic.

I haven't looked at my Facebook or any of that other stuff since my GCSE meltdown at school. I even changed my email address and only gave the new one to my close friends – OK, basically Daisy and Jake and my parents. I said it was because I was sick of the embarrassingly rubbish Hotmail address I got when I was thirteen – 'lethal_lizzle', what was I thinking? – but that was only half the story. I couldn't face seeing what everyone must be saying about me.

But things are different now. I'm stronger than I was then, so I shouldn't be such a coward. I can take it, right? Right?

I take a deep breath. I'm not sure where to start, and I don't dare go straight to YouTube, so I go to Facebook. It's weird – I haven't been on it for months, but it still feels like a natural reflex action to type in my password, mostly because I would have to sign in and out every time on the family computer to prevent any potential sabotage of my account by Grace. I used to check it so much, it's like muscle memory. Some people probably have that for useful stuff, like playing tennis or running the hundred metres, but for me it's pointlessly messing about on the Internet. Great. Worthy.

I'm a bit taken aback by the number of messages and friend requests. Half of them seem to be from people I don't know. There is loads of old stuff that I've never even seen, a barrage of it. Most of it comes from Viv.

I click on to her page, and scroll through reams of selfies. Here on Facebook though, the selfies are broken up with rants – either blowing her own trumpet or bitching about other people. Mostly, it seems, me.

'sum people r so fake – u know who u are! When I'm rich and famous, ur gonna B srry!'

'WHY R PEOPLE ALL SO CRAP???!'

'Why does this always happen 2 me in the end . . . Friends always let me down because they r so jealous of me.'

The thinly veiled insults are all directed at me – she's even tagged me, as she knew I wouldn't see. Pathetic losers, sad little girls, 'crazy bitches' and how nobody can keep up with Viv's great ambition and musical talent. I can't seem to look away. I keep scrolling and scrolling, taking in hundreds of posed selfies and barbed comments. But as they go on, I find I feel less and less, and then nothing – it's like I'm immune to it now.

As I scroll on and on, I see that this was happening way before Viv even met me. As I keep trawling, I see a pattern forming: Viv seems to get through a lot of friends.

Her timeline is littered with 'best' friendships that seem uncannily to mimic our own relationship – loads of joint photos and statuses, over the top references to being BFFs and future band-mates and taking on the world together. Then, invariably, it sours.

I start to see that the problem may not be me. Jess, the bass player I replaced, seems to have had a particularly bad time. Equally, before Rex, Viv's profile seems to have had a constant flurry of relationship status changes – and her style changes with every one. I am taken aback to see that just a few months ago, before she met Rex, she had brown hair and was wearing completely different clothes. I keep scrolling until my eyes go blurry and I realize this is a pointless exercise.

None of this is real, none of it actually matters – I wonder why I've been scared of something as stupid as Facebook for so long. It's ridiculous.

Then I click on my unread messages and a name catches my eye, the first thing I have seen that has genuinely sparked my interest, amid all the negative stuff that I no longer care about.

It's from Jessica Taylor, 'Jess' from Saturday night – whose profile picture shows her wearing pyjamas and making a comedy face, playing a toy guitar.

> Hi Lizzie, I know we don't really know each other but I wanted to talk to you about something – hope that doesn't sound too weird. Please could you message me? Jess x

I have no idea what she could possibly want. But what have I got to lose?

It's barely an hour since I got Jess's message. I'm now on my way to meet her at a random Turkish cafe on London Road that she suggested.

I haven't had time to obsess – I literally jumped in the shower, threw on some clothes without overthinking matters for once and ran out the door. I couldn't resist shouting over my shoulder to Grace on my way out that I was meeting Jess from Dirty Harriet for tea. I didn't hang around to hear her shocked response.

Now, as I walk into the small cafe, I can see that I should in fact have shouted: 'Bye, Grace, I'm off to meet *all of* Dirty Harriet for tea – see ya later'.

The three of them are huddled at a small round table, all of them sitting on floor cushions that render them almost horizontal. On the little table there is crammed an impressive variety of tea and snacks. All three of them are talking loudly, laughing their heads off. They all look effortless but cool. They look like a real band.

'Hey, there she is!' Harry shouts.

She grins and waves at me enthusiastically. She's wearing an old L7 T-shirt – my dad would approve.

'Over here, Lizzie!'

'Hi,' I say, trying and failing not to sound shy.

As if they can sense this, they all go out of their way to include me. They are like a gang of really cute, enthusiastic puppies. Their energy is contagious.

'Here, sit down here next to me . . . Budge up, Lola.'

'Have you tried baklava before, Lizzie? It will rot your teeth right out of your head, but it's totally worth it.'

'Tea or coffee? The mint tea is pretty nice. We try to limit Harry to only one cup of Turkish coffee per day or she gets too hyper to function like a normal human being, so she's only allowed water from now on.'

'Hey, I'm hardcore – I can take it, man!'

'Yeah, right – what about that time you ended up breathing into a paper bag, telling us your hands had gone see-through? That was all because you'd had two coffees, dude.'

'Right, everyone,' Jess says gently, and we all listen to her. 'Let's all stop yelling over each other for thirty seconds so that Lizzie can actually hear herself think.'

'So, we do call you Lizzie, right?' Harry asks me, with a sly sideways look. 'I thought your name was Betty, but after the other night, I thought I'd better start calling you Lizzie in case I get knocked out.'

'*Harry!*' Jess exclaims. 'Don't mind her,' she says to me.

'Yeah, it's Lizzie,' I explain. 'Short for Elizabeth. Betty was just a nickname when I was in the band.'

'Don't tell me,' Jess said. 'It was all Viv's idea and she insisted on calling you that at all times.'

'Er, yeah – how did you know?' I ask.

'Oh, I know all about that one. She tried to make me call myself Jessa for a while, said it sounded more exotic than plain old Jess.'

'It was part of her weird, controlling plan to make Jess into her clone.' Harry makes a face and mock-shudders.

'And I can't believe you fell for it, Jess.' Lola shakes her head. 'That girl is stone-cold evil.'

'Well, what are you supposed to do when the queen bee of the school suddenly wants to be best friends?' Jess asks. 'I was flattered for about five minutes. I didn't realize what she was really like.'

'This sounds familiar,' I say tentatively.

'Yeah, she does it all the time,' Jess says. 'I wasn't the first and you won't be the last. She's only out for herself; she just wants to control people as part of her grand master plan. She seems so nice when she wants something, but it never lasts long. None of her friendships do. She's a vampire.'

'Not just that,' Harry says with surprising venom. 'She's a bully. She was horrible to us all through school. Always calling us weirdos and freaks. Everyone sided with her, because they thought she was cool and they were scared of her. Thank god people saw through it in the end.'

'But . . . I don't think it's her fault,' I say, not wanting to get drawn into a bitch-fest. 'I feel kind of sorry for her. I think she's got problems. She's had a difficult life.'

'Oh, has she spun you some of her fake sob stories?' Harry says. 'Well, I wouldn't go worrying about Viv. She lies all the time, always trying to make herself sound more interesting. She's from the perfect family who spoil her rotten, but she's always bitching about everything. I just can't believe they got her her own flat.'

'It *is* annoying,' Lola agrees. 'She left St Cath's because she'd burned all her bridges there – people got sick of her bullying and she wasn't the coolest girl at school any more. Now she's trying to reinvent herself with her new boyfriend and her band and everything. But I believe in karma – people will see through her in the end.'

'Anyway,' Jess interrupts, 'enough of the negativity. We're not here just to bitch about Viv. Sorry, Lizzie. I just wanted you to know that you're not on your own; you mustn't blame yourself. It always goes wrong in the end with Viv. I found out the hard way too. You're lucky you got out when you did.'

'Well, I didn't feel that lucky when she laid into me and kicked me out of the band in front of a room full of people! But maybe it's one of those silver linings I've heard so much about.'

'That was pretty brutal, even for Viv,' Harry agrees. 'And that's kind of what we wanted to talk to you about. So, can we take it you're not playing bass in her band any more?'

'I think that's safe to say,' I agree.

'What did you think of our set the other night?' Lola asks.

'I loved it. It was amazing. Honestly. Amazing.'

'Well, that's good,' says Harry. 'Because if you're at a loose end now, we wondered if you might like to play with us instead.'

'But you already have a bass player,' I say, looking at Jess. 'You don't need me.'

'Well, the thing is,' Lola says, 'we thought you were

the best thing on that stage the other night.'

'Except for us of course,' chime in Harry and Jess, almost in unison.

'But you already have a bass player,' I repeat. 'I mean, it's amazing you think that . . . I can't believe it, but—'

'I'm really a guitarist,' Jess explains. 'I'm only playing bass in the band because we needed a bass player. If you were there, then it would free me up to play guitar – which is what I really want to do. Having two guitars would really beef up our sound.'

'We've got a slot booked at Electric Studios tomorrow afternoon,' says Harry. 'So we could have a jam and see how it goes – can you come?'

'What, like an audition?' I say.

'Well, don't worry. We won't be sitting in a line, pressing buzzers, shouting "next!" and "don't give up the day job" . . . But I suppose, yeah, kind of.'

'We always go to Woody's afterwards, for chips and milkshakes,' Lola adds. 'That's just as important as the rehearsal part. Maybe even more important.'

'Look, you guys . . . I'm so flattered and I'd really love to. Seriously, I can't tell you how much I would love to do this. But I can't.'

'Why not?'

'The thing is, I'm not good enough to jam. I can't even really play. I can't read music; I don't even know what the different notes are called – I figured it out with colour-coded stickers. And I might as well tell you – all that stuff Viv said about me being "mental", that's all true too. I'd love to do it, but this is all too much. Sorry. I just can't.'

I guess that's that then.

Then Harry bursts out laughing and the other two follow suit. Before I know it, I'm joining in.

'What, you think we want some annoying music-college nerd who can play the twelve-bar blues? No way!'

'We'll see you at Electric Studios tomorrow at two, Lizzie.'

Dirty Harriet: The (Wo)manifesto

1. We are not snobby about our taste in music and adopt a cheerfully no-brow policy to popular culture in general. Our influences include (but are not limited to): Haim, Robyn, Prince, Babes in Toyland, Neneh Cherry, Wolf Alice, Horse Party, Jack Lucan, Bat for Lashes, Patti Smith, cheesy chips, Madonna, John Waters films, Le Tigre, Bananarama, Courtney Barnett, Courtney Love, Kanye West, Kim Kardashian, Andy Warhol, Iggy and the Stooges, the Spice Girls, Yoko Ono, milkshakes, writing bad poetry, our nans.

2. While playing music we refuse to wear clothes that make us feel too cold, uncomfortable or vulnerable in any way. NB this includes shoes in which we cannot: a) dance like idiots; or b) run away if necessary.

3. If you come to a Dirty Harriet gig, please abide by the following guidelines: don't stand right in front of someone shorter than you; if you must take pictures, don't be a dick about it (better yet, just enjoy the moment); have fun; maybe make some new friends – people are nice!

4. Please don't turn up and expect a 'normal gig'. We are not professionals. We are mostly making it up as we go along. Please bear with us!

I've been up pretty much all day and night. I can't just turn up there with no clue what I'm doing, looking like a total idiot and embarrassing myself. So, I've been on the Dirty Harriet website, listening to their songs on a loop, attempting to play along and coming up with ideas.

I'm completely fried, and some of their songs have proved totally beyond my skills. The songs have a kind of spontaneous tribal element to them that is difficult to replicate. I'm going to have to wing it and hope for the best. Still, I'm actually hopeful that it won't be a complete disaster. The songs are amazing and I'm feeling inspired, even if I don't always have the technical skills to back it up.

'What the fug are you wearing?'

Grace is lounging in the doorway, obviously pleased with herself for having sneaked up and given me a fright. In a way, I'm quite relieved that our new friendliness hasn't actually changed much of anything. It's nice to know where you stand.

'What do you mean, what am I wearing? It's a dress.'

'Um, yeah. It's a bridesmaid's dress from Auntie Caroline's wedding three years ago, and you appear to be wearing it with a hoodie and trainers. And in case you hadn't noticed, that lipstick makes you look like you've recently drowned. The matted hair isn't exactly helping either.'

'It's a look I'm trying out,' I reply airily.

'For what? A shit school-play version of *The Little Mermaid*, with you as Ursula the Sea Witch crossed with Cinderella's ugly sisters?'

'Yeah, that's amazing – how did you guess?' I stick my tongue out at her. 'No, I'm just trying something out – this is my new look.'

And it kind of is. While looking up all the songs to learn for my not-an-audition for Dirty Harriet, I had time to flick through the whole of their website. Not a selfie in sight, there were instead pages of blog posts about the band's inspirations, musical favourites and general opinions on life. All of it is hilarious, inspiring and pretty wonderful.

So I have made an executive decision just to go for it. My bass playing, singing, dancing, my outfit – the whole shebang. I'm just going to go full-on, balls-out crazy. Let's face it, that's who I am – and it's better than some shy little wallflower stuck in denial and never doing anything. I've had enough of that to last me a lifetime.

'No, seriously,' Grace says, 'where are you going dressed like that? The Mad Hatter's tea party?'

'Is that some cool new Brighton cafe?' I shoot back. 'No, actually – I've got an audition-slash-jamming-session to join Dirty Harriet as their new bass player.'

I swear Grace's jaw actually clangs to the floor, cartoon style. I know I should really keep this quiet, to save myself from the humiliation when I don't get in and am left back at square one, but it's worth it to see the look on Grace's face. Just for a second.

'No, you're not. You're making it up. They already have a bass player.'

'That's exactly what I said. But they want me to join. I'm going to rehearse with them at Electric Studios this afternoon.'

'OK. The outfit kind of makes sense now. Kind of. Oh my god, wait till I tell Robyn. She *loves* Dirty Harriet so much it's actually creepy. She's going to crap herself with excitement.'

'Nice. Well, I've got to go – wish me luck.' I strap my bass on to my back and head out the door.

'Lizzie? Good luck. But, by the way – if Mum and Dad find out about this, they're going to kill you. After that whole "getting chucked out of college" thing. Don't worry – I'll cover for you! You are going to owe me so big.'

Thanks to Grace, I set off for Electric Studios with a smile on my face and almost a spring in my step. Or that might be thanks to being back in my trusty old Converse high tops rather than Viv's too-big heels. And this surprisingly comfortable old bridesmaid's dress I found at the back of my wardrobe – it's bright yellow and has a most pleasing sticky-out net tutu underneath. I truly love it. Which is ironic, since I hated being a bridesmaid when I was thirteen, so I spent most of Auntie Caroline's wedding hiding in a cupboard eating sugared almonds until I was sick. She's divorced now anyway – hopefully nothing to do with my terrible bridesmaiding skills.

For the whole walk to the studio, I keep my headphones plugged in, blasting out the Dirty Harriet tracks I've downloaded to my phone. I even find myself singing along as I bounce down the street.

When I arrive, nobody turns a hair at the sight of me – I just fit right in. It's really kind of miraculous.

'Are you with Harry and the gang?' asks an affable chap with a beard and a Mudhoney baseball cap, looking up from the Sherlock Holmes novel he is reading. 'They said you were coming. Go ahead into Room Three, on the left. Give us a shout if you need anything.'

'Thanks.'

'No worries. Don't be nervous – they're a cool bunch of girls. Bonkers, but sound. My money's on them to win that Battle of the Bands contest – they're going places.'

I can't believe I'm about to audition for a real band, one whose reputation seems to precede them. A couple of months ago I had never picked up a bass, and I'm still not completely sure what all the notes are. Still, everything I hear makes me a little bit more convinced that this is what I'm supposed to be doing; I want to be friends with these girls and make music with them. I'm prepared to work so hard to make it happen; maybe I'll really be able to do it.

As I open the door to Room Three, I am hit by a reggae beat layered under punk-guitar feedback and Harry trying to rap. I register that the guitar noise is coming from Jess, who has pre-emptively abandoned her bass – which is now all down to me. They grind to a ramshackle halt as I come in. Harry rushes up and hugs me.

'Glad you're here, Lizzie. We're trying out something new and it's total crap. I can barely stand to hear it myself, so we can't possibly inflict it upon a paying audience.

We're having fun, though. Just come and join in.'

'You can plug in here, and help yourself to Haribo *here*.' Lola gestures in turn with one drumstick. 'I can't get through a rehearsal without a sugar fix.'

While I faff about and get myself set up, the others start playing again. It's not regimented but it sort of works. Instead of overthinking it, I just take a deep breath and start playing along – anything that I feel might work. I look over at Lola and her drumsticks are flying, her hair in messy bunches keeping the same time. We get into a groove between us, my brain is entirely focused on rhythm, while the guitarists do their own thing and Harry sings made-up words over the top.

We keep going and going, eventually getting heavier and faster until Harry, whizzing around the room like a whirling dervish, literally keels over. She lies on the floor and groans into the microphone.

'Enough, enough,' she croaks. 'Must have . . . cheesy chips and strawberry milkshake.'

'Come on, Harry,' Jess says. 'We've still got time booked. We should run through a few of the songs for Saturday. We haven't got long, you know. We need to practise while we can.'

'I know, I know . . .'

Harry stands up and she's all action again, shoving a handful of Lola's Haribo into her mouth.

'OK, we'll do "Jellyfish" and "Diner Waitress", then after that maybe "Your Friends All Hate You . . ." Lizzie, just try and join in and see how you get on, yeah?'

Lola counts us in and we're off. Live, the songs sound at least as good as they did when I first heard them at the gig. Even just with four of us in a rehearsal room, the energy is huge. I have to admit, it does sound even better with two guitars. Jess is great – she's really going for it, even launching into a full-on guitar solo at one point. I just hope they think I'm good enough. I'm managing to keep up, playing it safe at first, then getting into it, and I think it's working.

I'm glad I spent so much time listening to the songs; I still have to work hard to keep my wits about me at all times. They don't seem to play a song the same way twice, so I have to think on my feet and have a go at improvising.

We're all having fun, but it's serious as well. They all really know their stuff though – in their own ramshackle way.

During the last song, Lola gets so carried away that one of her drumsticks flies out of her hand and sails halfway across the room, hitting Jess in the head.

'Keep going, keep going!' Harry shouts, still playing. 'Pretend it's a gig.'

Lola finishes the song with only one stick, and does a pretty good job of it.

'Note to self,' she says as we finish. 'Keep spare drumsticks in my pocket when we do the gig.'

'We've only got a few minutes left,' Harry informs us, glancing at her watch. 'Let's do our last number before we go and get chips.'

'It's become a little tradition,' Jess explains. 'At every rehearsal, we finish up with a cover of a pop song. Just for fun.'

'We do a good 1D,' Lola tells me. 'We actually played "You Don't Know You're Beautiful" at a gig once – it went down a storm. Seriously.'

'Can we do a Taylor Swift, please?' Harry asks, practically jumping up and down. 'I bloody love Taylor Swift.'

She starts singing the first line slowly and picking out the basic chords on her guitar. Lola puts a beat over the top and we all start to join in, working it out between us, getting it a bit wonky and wrong, but to my amazement it's actually recognizable. We pick up steam and Harry starts singing properly. It's definitely a weird version and the song has never sounded like this before, but somehow it works. More to the point, it's really fun.

'Ladies and gentlemen, goodnight!' Harry shouts, bowing to an imaginary crowd. 'Time for chips. Next stop Battle of the Bands – the final!'

We start packing up and getting our stuff together. The others are chatting as they faff about.

'I'm so sweaty,' Lola says, wiping her face with a towel out of her bag. 'I should have brought a spare top with me but I forgot.'

'You always say that,' Jess says. 'No spare top, no spare drumsticks . . . you're so disorganized.'

'Anyway, I bet I stink more than you,' Harry pipes up cheerfully, and sticks an armpit in Lola's face. 'See!'

'OK, you win!' Lola laughs. 'I surrender. Wow, you actually stink.'

'Yep. Pity those other poor souls in Woody's this afternoon.'

I can't bear it any longer. I feel like I'm going to explode.

'So, how did I do?' I practically shout.

They all look at me as if they're surprised. Then they look at each other and nod.

'You're in,' says Harry. 'Of course.'

'That was a great jam. You did brilliantly,' says Lola. 'Didn't you realize?'

'Well . . .' I don't know what to say. 'Yeah. I suppose so.'

'And I got to play guitar.' Jess grins. 'I've never had so much fun.'

'Come on,' Harry says. 'We'll buy you chips to celebrate.'

Woody's is a 1950s diner with booths and a jukebox but a very English seaside feeling to it. It's loud and bright and great. The waitresses wear pink uniforms and seem to know all of the band, saying hi and waving cheerfully when we troop in.

We pile into a booth and order loads of food and gigantic milkshakes. Harry proclaims that she is starving and orders extra onion rings for herself. Lola jumps up to put songs on the jukebox – lots of old girl bands, and classic pop like the Beatles, the Faces and the Kinks.

'Ah, I want to be Keith Moon when I grow up,' she sighs as 'Substitute' by the Who comes on.

'Hmm, I want to be Freddie Mercury crossed with Courtney Love,' Harry says. 'Imagine if they could have been my adoptive parents – that would be my dream come true.'

'My dream come true involves Jackson Griffith, a hotel room and the world's biggest box of Krispy Kremes.'

'That's not very feminist of you, Jess,' says Lola.

'No, it is,' Jess insists. 'I'm going to eat the doughnuts while he reads to me from *The Female Eunuch*. It's going to be seriously hot. What about you, Lizzie? Who are your favourites? What are your influences?'

'Well, loads of stuff . . .'

Instead of feeling embarrassed and put on the spot, we're soon discussing bands and other music. We're all enthused and sparking off each other. I don't care about sounding cool. I even admit my dad's weird love for Abba and it triggers a flurry of agreement ('They're amazing pop songs, and those girls were classically trained!' notes Harry). We love classic grunge bands, Japanese pop and we think Kim is as important as Kanye. Harry even gets a little notebook out of her rucksack, where she writes down some of my recommendations so that she can google them later.

'It's my favourite thing, discovering new music,' she says. 'I can spend literally days getting into a YouTube black hole. So how come you know so much about music?'

'My dad kind of got me into it. I've always loved music,

but I only started playing a couple of months ago with Viv and Rex. Well, unless you count some very unsuccessful violin lessons when I was ten – which I don't. How about you guys? You've all been playing for ages, haven't you?'

'I'm the same as you,' Lola says. 'My mum used to be a singer and my dad plays drums in a jazz band. I wanted to do something different so I played really bad acoustic guitar for a while and started a folk band at school. Then I realized I actually really loved drumming and that's when it all fell into place.'

'I don't have hipster parents like you two,' says Jess. 'I think the only records in the house when I was a kid were my mum's Take That albums. I had to make it up as I went along, playing guitar in my bedroom. Then I had my short spell playing in Viv's band – shudder – and now here I am. Oh, and we haven't told you – Harry's a child prodigy!'

'Shut up. I am not.'

'She is,' Lola says. 'Bona fide. Don't listen to her. She doesn't like us talking about it because it draws attention to the fact she's still only fifteen. She was this music genius and got a scholarship to a fancy music school when she was only eleven.'

'And then I discovered Nirvana and I dyed my hair green and pierced my own nose, and joined this band my brother was in. So I left the school and came back to normality.' Harry finishes the story with a roll of her eyes. 'I still love classical music and I play the piano just for fun, but I don't think I'm cut out to be a soloist. I'd rather be in a band and have a life.'

'You're only fifteen?' is all I can think of to say.

I can't believe that the self-possessed, confident and cool Harry is even younger than I am.

'Yeah.' She makes a face. 'Sixteen in December, but I got moved up a year in junior school so I've always been the youngest. It sucks.'

'Because she's a child prodigy!' the others chorus.

'Shut up!'

'But you've got a tattoo, and you're so . . .'

Harry laughs. 'The tattoo's drawn on. My brother's an artist and I got him to do it in permanent marker before the gig. I wish it was real. I've been trying not to shower too much ever since so I can keep it on as long as possible.'

'Stinker!' Lola chimes in for good measure.

'Did you all meet at school?' I ask.

'Well, Lola and I are cousins,' explains Harry. 'So we've basically been forced to be friends ever since we were born. Then we met Jess at St Catherine's. We saved her from the evil clutches of Viv.'

While we've been talking we've managed to demolish several plates of chips and other snacks, plus suck up milkshakes to their noisy dregs. The jukebox has been playing non-stop retro-cheese. The afternoon seems to have disappeared.

'I've got to go!' Harry suddenly exclaims. 'I'm supposed to be home for dinner by six. You coming, Lola?'

'Yeah, I'd better get back as well. We might as well walk that way together.'

'So, Busy Lizzie,' Harry goes on, shrugging into her

fake fur coat, 'are you definitely up for joining us? We might seem all silly and frivolous, but we actually take this really seriously. We all love music, and the band, and each other. Are you in?'

'I am so in.'

I have never wanted anything so badly in my life. I want to be in a band with these girls more than I wanted to be friends with Viv, even. More than I ever wanted Rex to kiss me.

'We practise at least three times a week and we split the cost of studio time equally. Every band decision is a democracy. Nobody is the star; we all have an equal say. We all help to update the website and all that stuff. Basically, we all have no life. But that's OK because we didn't exactly have glittering social lives to begin with. We're all music geeks.'

'But that's OK too,' adds Lola, 'because it's always the music geeks who win in the end. Every cool rock star in the canon was once a music geek. That's the law.'

'So,' Harry says to me, 'we'll see you at practice again on Thursday and then it's the gig on Saturday. Yeah?'

'Um . . .' I pause as I realize my enthusiasm has made me get totally carried away. 'Hang on a minute – did you say the gig on Saturday?'

'Of course,' says Harry. 'You knew that. It's the Battle of the Bands final. I know it's uncool of me, but I'd be so stoked if we won. Just think of that free studio time . . . None of us has bought any new clothes since we were about twelve, as all our money goes on records, instruments and studio rent. As you can probably tell just by looking at us. At least it's made sure we're in no danger of being objectified.'

'Hang on – can we go back to the whole Battle of the Bands thing, please?' I say, trying not to sound as panicky as I feel. 'I thought maybe I could join *after* that.'

'No time like the present,' Harry says. 'We need you for the gig, and it will be a cool way to introduce our newest member. If you're in, you're in. You've got to go for it.'

'But isn't it against the rules?' I say weakly.

'Ha! You don't actually think Mad Jack McKray cares about *rules*, do you?' Harry scoffs.

'Like we said, every band decision is democratic,' Lola says. 'We took a vote; you lost. You're playing with us on Saturday.'

'I'm not ready,' I protest. 'If you lose, it will be my fault. I don't even know all the songs yet.'

'If *we* lose, you mean. And I really don't think we will. You know some of those songs better than we do.'

'Well . . . OK.'

Harry whoops loudly, making everyone else in the place turn around and stare at us even more than they have been. Then she starts banging on the table with both hands until the others join in.

'One of us . . . One of us . . . One of us! One of us! One! Of! Us!'

They keep it up at the top of their voices until we all collapse laughing and they envelop me at the centre of a massive, sweaty group hug.

Dirty Harriet: The New Line-up!
By Tuesday Cooper.

Three have become four in Brighton's best new Riot grrrl disco punk outfit! Lizzie Brown, formerly of Viviane, is Dirty Harriet's new bass player. Jess Taylor will now play guitar, alongside singer–guitarist Harry Jackson, and Lola Cane on drums.

Harry said, 'We've been wanting to beef up our guitar sound for ages, but we were waiting for the right person to come along. Lizzie is definitely the right person. She's a unique bass player with her own style and she's a good egg. She's one of us!'

The full new line-up will be competing in the Battle of the Bands final on Saturday night. Dirty Harriet took the first round by storm and are favourites to win the whole competition. But, as we saw last time, anything could happen – watch this space!

I'm still feeling full of excitement at being officially in the band, not to mention full of chips and onion rings and all round good vibes. Life feels good. The sun is shining as I leave Jess on the corner, with hugs and promises to be in touch before the next band practice.

There's just one thing still bothering me. I know what I have to do, much as I do not relish the prospect, because I don't want to let it keep bothering me. I feel I owe it to her to tell her at least.

So instead of going home, I carry walking into the Lanes. Until I am outside Viv's flat. It's an idyllic day in Brighton – everyone but me seems to be on holiday, strolling at a leisurely pace, but I am on a mission.

I press the buzzer before I can change my mind. Then I have to wait on the doorstep for an age, wondering if she is actually home. I press the buzzer repeatedly, just in case. I hope I'm right that Viv should be in at this time but Rex should be out working at the cafe – it's her I want to speak to.

A blonde head appears at the window and I have to wait another agonizing few minutes while I guess she decides whether to speak to me. Eventually the door opens.

'Betty.'

Her arms are folded, her eyebrows arched. I try my best not to feel completely intimidated.

'Viv, I—' I begin.

'You'd better not come up,' she interrupts me. 'It's a tip. Rex is in the middle of moving out, not that it's any of your business.'

'Rex is moving out? Look, Viv, I . . . I have to tell you—'

She looks at me pityingly and laughs out loud. 'I already know, Betty. Grow up. Rex moving out is nothing to do with you. You only kissed; it's not like you had sex. In fact, you can't seem to *give* it away, can you? I tried to get Dave to go out with you, but he wasn't really interested. I really tried to help you, you know.'

I flinch, but I do my best to recover and say what I came here to say. Just get it done and get away.

'I came here to tell you that I'm joining Dirty Harriet as their new bass player.'

If I'm an open book, Viv is an impenetrable encyclopedia. The look of surprise that crosses her face only lasts literally a split second before she manages to hide it. I can see from her expression, once and for all, that we are not the same, not in any way. Rex was right about one thing – I am nothing like Viv.

'I expect you'll fit in well with those girls,' she says faux-sweetly. If I didn't know her so well, I might not even pick up on the malice. 'You go well together. You're so similar to them. I expect they've been telling you all sorts of things about me.'

What? I only say it in my head. *That you're a bully and you use people and I'm not the first person you've tried this with. You pick on people weaker than you and try to turn them into puppets, then drop them when it suits you. That you lie about everything.*

I didn't need them to tell me the things I worked out myself in the end, even though it took me a while. That you made me

275

feel bad about myself and like I was all wrong and I needed to be better, more like you. Like I couldn't even be myself. I was just someone you could control.

I think you must be really insecure to be like this. You seem so confident, but maybe you're not. Maybe I should feel sorry for you. Maybe.

'Yeah, they've told me a little bit,' is all I say out loud, matching her tone.

'Well, I'm pleased for you,' Viv goes on, sounding anything but. 'I've got loads of people interested in me after our gig. I'm speaking to a manager about putting me together with a new band.'

'That's great, Viv. I hope it works out for you,' I say.

From the way she's looking at me I suddenly can see what it is. My crime wasn't kissing Viv's boyfriend, even though I still feel terrible about that. It was learning to play bass and getting better than her. She wanted me to join her band, but I was supposed to know my place.

'I'm going to go now,' I say.

'Bye, Betty.'

'It's Lizzie actually.'

Despite everything that's happened today, it's still pretty early when I get home. My mum is never here at this time. I feel vaguely uneasy when I see her smartest high heels kicked off in the hallway, her best Vivienne Westwood jacket hanging on the end of the banisters ('Every woman needs a pair of high heels and a decent jacket') and hear Radio 1 coming from the kitchen. Neither my dad nor

Grace would ever listen to Radio 1 – my dad's not cool enough and Grace is too cool.

Worryingly, she appears to be chopping vegetables as she sings along with Little Mix. My mum never cooks. My dad does the cooking; my mum orders takeaway.

'Hi?' It comes out as a question.

'Hi, darling. Glad you're home. Good news.'

She wipes her hands on a tea towel and turns to me, looking ridiculously beautiful and put together. I have basically seen my mum every single day of my life, and somehow I still manage to feel a tiny bit intimidated by her and how inferior she can sometimes make me feel. I don't even know why – in my house there has always been a divide: my mum and Grace, my dad and me. It's like the Sorting Hat of genetics: we might all live under the same roof, but we're in different houses. Grace is definitely a Slytherin.

I feel like I know what the 'good news' might be and I suddenly and inexplicably want to cry.

'Good news?' I croak.

'I've been to the school this afternoon, to speak to Ms Wilding. That's why I'm dressed up like Margaret Thatcher.'

'What did she say?'

'Well, I'll admit I had to lay it on pretty thick, but she's agreed that you can go back to West Grove. It's still early enough that you won't have to wait for the new school year. You can go back next week, after half-term.'

I try so hard to raise some enthusiasm, but the threat

of tears in the back of my throat just won't go away. Mum has obviously gone to a lot of effort on my behalf.

'Didn't she want to talk to me?' I ask.

'I thought it would be for the best if I went in there and spoke to her first. So we could have a proper meeting. I explained the situation and she was quite understanding. She said that they could make an exception and find you a place. You can speak to her and to your teachers when you go back there on Monday.'

'What did you say about me? What did she say?'

'Well, obviously I just explained the situation. I said that you hadn't coped well at college, and we talked about everything that happened . . . before that. Obviously she knows some of your history with these sorts of, ah, stress issues. We agreed that being back in a more structured environment would be much better for you. They know you there; I'm sure they'll be very supportive. We all decided it's for the best.'

That 'we' seems to include everyone but me. I know I haven't exactly earned the right to have a say in this, but nobody has asked me how I feel about any of it. It's funny, at one point I wished I could go back to West Grove and at least be with Daisy and Jake, but after everything it now seems like it would be a backwards step. I feel like I'm ready to move on.

There is something profoundly depressing about my mum doing all this on my behalf. That she had to make people feel sorry for me in order to get me something I don't even want. The idea makes me feel beyond weird.

But there's nothing I can do. I had my opportunity and I royally messed it up.

'They've been very generous, considering,' my mum goes on. 'You could look a bit more pleased about it.'

'I am,' I say, trying to summon a smile to my face as there is literally nothing else I can do. 'Thanks, Mum.'

'Now, I'm making a stir-fry to celebrate. It's still your favourite, yes?'

Stir-fry has never been my favourite dinner in my life. I don't even like it that much. If I had to, I'd say it's only OK. My mum likes it because she is always on a diet. I have literally no idea where she got this ridiculous notion from.

'Thanks,' I repeat, with as much enthusiasm as I can muster.

Band Memo: 'The Hippie Ideal' (Don't laugh, OK?
Harry x)

Dear Members of Dirty Harriet,

On the eve of the Battle of the Bands final, we, the
undersigned band members, vow to our past and future
selves that we will not let the outcome of an arbitrary
contest affect us, our self-esteem, our friendships or our
music.

If we lose, we will not take it to heart. We will not
change what we do for anyone. We will continue to do
what we love and to have fun. We will not blame each
other, no matter what happens.

If we win, we will not let it go to our heads. We will
not become egotistical monsters. We will continue
to do what we love and to have fun, and we will not
change for anyone (see above).

We will do our best and support each other.

We will be awesome.

We are the mistresses of our own fate!

Peace & love,
Harry
Lola
Jess
Lizzie

Luckily I've hardly had time to think this week. It's been a blur, all leading up to the gig.

When I haven't been at band practice with the girls, I've been listening to the songs and playing along until deep into the night. We're all getting excited. The energy is making us all brim with new ideas – even me – that we can't wait to get on with once the gig is over. It's the first time I've ever been in an atmosphere where I have felt like I don't have to worry about looking stupid or getting it wrong, which have always been my biggest fears in life. It's fine just to have a go, nobody is judging. We're all having fun.

It's helped to block out everything else, which I'm trying not to think about. The week passing in a blur means that the gig is nearly upon us, but so is my return to West Grove. Not so much the return of the prodigal son, but the final humiliating surrender of the world's biggest loser.

Daisy and Jake aren't speaking to me, so it's not even as if I have any friends to go back to there. They're still ignoring all my messages. Thank goodness for the Dirty Harriet girls – if it wasn't for them I'd be feeling pretty lonely and friendless.

The gig is tonight and I am not thinking about anything else now. Harry might spontaneously combust, she's got so much nervous energy building up about the whole thing; she can't wait to get out there. The other two are more like me – a combination of excitement and pure terror.

We meet at Woody's beforehand. I've decided to wear my ridiculous yellow bridesmaid's dress again, my short haircut slicked back and spiked at the front rather than perfectly blow-dried into the styled little bob it was supposed to be. We're all piled into a booth, wearing our crazy gig outfits. I like the idea that we look like a band – our differentness marks us out as much as the instruments and equipment stacked up around our table.

'Urgh, I can't eat anything before a gig,' groans Jess. 'As soon as it's over, I'm going to stuff my face with every single noodle in this town.'

'It's her post-gig ritual,' Lola explains. 'Jess can never sleep after a gig so she stays up watching kids' cartoons in her pyjamas and eating her own body weight in noodles.'

'Sounds like a good one – I could do with some proper food after all this,' I agree.

All I have managed is a gigantic bowl of melting ice cream – good for soothing the nerves but not great for nutrition, I suppose. It's got maraschino cherries in it, but I'm not sure that counts towards my five-a-day.

'I don't know what the issue is personally.' Harry shrugs as she bites into a giant cheeseburger. 'Anyone want my gherkins?'

The rest of us literally give a collective shudder. The thing is, none of us, not even Harry with her massive burger and chips, is here for the food. It's something to do, somewhere to go – to be a team and get prepared for the evening together.

'Good luck!' the waitress shouts after us when it's eventually time to leave.

Harry is skipping down the street, being even louder than usual; so much so that it makes me wonder if it's secret nerves or genuine excitement. I decide it's the latter – she's not scared of anything, and she is bouncing off the walls.

At the venue, the atmosphere is much more serious than last time. Maybe because there are fewer bands playing tonight there aren't so many people hanging around the venue before it opens, so it's less of a party atmosphere. Or maybe it's because we're down to the final three that the stakes are raised and everyone has become more serious. Everyone but me has literally battled their way here – by rights I shouldn't even be here. Because there are fewer bands, each act has to play more songs this time – there's a lot of added pressure and a lot more to think about.

However, at the same time I'm much more relaxed and having a better time. Playing with Viv, Rex and Dave, I always felt like the inferior one; I was worried about doing things wrong and messing up, not for myself but because I was trying to please them. Now it's a different kind of pressure, but a much better one. I like being responsible for myself and being part of a band of equals. Even though I'm technically the new girl, I feel like I fit right in.

When Jack McKray walks into the venue – with an entourage and wearing a gigantic silver cowboy hat – the bands are all so on edge you can practically hear the collective intake of breath across the room.

'Gather round, gather round,' he says, perching on the side of the stage like a punk-rock pixie. 'You've done all right to get this far, but – let's face it – some of that last lot were pretty dire, so don't go congratulating yourselves too much just yet. I still want a bloody brilliant show tonight. No passengers allowed. Got it? Good.'

This is like the opposite of a pep talk. I can actually feel the people around me deflating. Luckily for all of us in Dirty Harriet, Jack's not telling us anything we don't know – and we've all agreed that winning should not be the aim. There are more important things to think about than obsessing over things we can't control – we just want to do ourselves proud.

'Let's get on with it,' Jack goes on. 'Based entirely on my own personal preference and bias – so don't even start trying to tell me *it's not fair*, because this is the music industry: of course it isn't bloody fair – the running order tonight will be Skyfall, Dirty Harriet, Dream Genies. I'd say "good luck" but if you're actually any good, you won't need it. Obviously we'll be announcing the winner at the end of the night and we'll want to talk to them. So I might see you later. Most of you – probably not.'

'Right bang in the middle . . .' Harry muses. 'Not bad.'

'Not great though.' Jess grimaces. 'Last would be better.'

'It is what it is.' Lola shrugs philosophically. 'There's nothing we can do, so we'd better make the best of it.'

'We might as well enjoy the musical stylings of the

very derivative and kind-of-sweet Skyfall then!' Harry declares. 'I quite like the one with the indie haircut and the Adidas trainers.'

'That could be any of them,' I point out.

'Exactly!'

After the soundchecks are all finished and the venue opens up properly for the night, it starts to fill up. I might be imagining it, but I am sure I see a few people looking over at me, as if they recognize me from the last gig and remember what happened. It makes me feel a bit uncomfortable and I try my best not to let it throw me. Inadvertently, my fingernails start digging into my palms, even with so much to distract me.

The venue is pretty full by the time Skyfall go on. I begin to see a few faces I know in the crowd.

I'm so stunned that for a second I think I might be hallucinating when I see Daisy and Jake walking towards me. Although it's no wonder I do a double take as they don't look like their normal selves at all – obviously styled by Jake, they are both wearing muscle vests and ripped jeans, with bandanas tied around their heads.

'Oh my god, what are you doing here?' I shriek.

'We're here to support you on your big night of course,' Jake says. 'And I hope you appreciate what we've done – I mean, *look* at us. I thought we ought to make the effort, since we're at a quote-unquote "rock club". I made a Pinterest board and everything.'

'Of course I appreciate it,' I say, hugging them both. 'I'm so sorry about everything. I've really missed you both. I'm a terrible friend.'

'I'm sorry too,' Daisy says. 'I was jealous. I overreacted. I suppose we'll have to get used to Betty.'

'Actually that's the thing,' I tell them. 'Betty's dead. I've killed her, like Ziggy Stardust. Lizzie's back.'

'I'm not sure about all this murder talk, or who Ziggy is,' Jake tells me, 'but it's nice to have Lizzie back. We heard about what happened with your friend Viv, so we thought you could do with the moral support.'

'And guess what?' I tell them. 'I'm coming back to West Grove after half-term. So everything's going back to normal.'

They don't look as enthusiastic about this as I'd hoped.

'You're kidding?' says Jake, making a face.

'Ugh, why would you want to do that?' Daisy asks. 'I'd stay away if I were you. It's still as dire there as ever.'

'Long story,' I tell her. 'It's all decided, thanks to my mum. End of.'

'Whatever,' Jake butts in, 'I like this whole Bridesmaid of Frankenstein look you've got going. Very post-apocalyptic chic. *Tank Girl* meets royal wedding.'

Daisy suddenly makes a strange squeaking noise and clutches at my arm.

'Oh my god, Lizzie,' she shrieks directly into my ear. 'Who is that *gorgeous* guy who's walking straight towards us? You have *got* to introduce me. I'm getting this very weird feeling that this is fate. I'm having an out-of-body experience.'

Jake rolls his eyes. 'Calm down, love,' he mutters.

Harry, standing next to him, overhears this and bursts out laughing.

'Don't tell me you're as cynical about romance as I am,' she says to him. 'Surely that's a scientific impossibility.'

'Try me,' he shoots back. 'I didn't even cry at *The Fault in Our Stars*. Serious. I have a heart of stone. By the way, I love your paisley-print dungaree shorts. They're a bold choice with the stripy tights. I admire that kind of risk-taking.'

'Actually they were pretty much the thing that smelled the least-worst off my bedroom floor earlier today. Sorry to burst your fashion bubble, but I actually couldn't give a crap.'

'Ooh, insouciant grunge chic. Love it. You're like a young Marc Jacobs, a true pioneer.'

'Well, if you think the same about my music, then I'll be your new best friend. Come on, I'll introduce you to the rest of the band.'

Meanwhile, Daisy's claw tightens around my left arm, nearly cutting off the circulation.

'Daisy! I've got to play bass with that arm tonight – go easy on me!'

She grabs me even harder. 'Seriously, I've got to know who that gorgeous boy is. Oh god, he's coming over, he's coming over . . .'

'Breathe, woman!' I instruct her before I look up to see who it is.

Honestly, he is the last person I expected to lay eyes on at this point.

'Hi, Dave.' With Daisy practically swooning next to me, I wave him over and grin at him in a slightly inane and very overenthusiastic way, to hide my awkwardness. 'How are you?'

'Decent. You?'

'Um, fine. Thank you. Look, I don't know if you've heard but I'm . . .' I gesture at the stage, vaguely.

'That you're Dirty Harriet's new bass player? Yeah, I know. Congratulations. I think it's awesome. They're really cool girls and I have a feeling you'll probably fit in better with them.'

'Yeah. Thanks. So, after last week . . . what about you?'

'Well, that's the end of Viviane The Band, I think. I'm going to concentrate on Breakfast of Champions. I heard that Viv's had some interest from a manager who's putting together a girl band. I think they're going to try to make her Sexy Spice or something.' He makes a face. 'Look, I feel like a dick. I had a thing for Viv, and that's why I joined the band. I was stupid.'

'Yeah, I think we both were actually. I totally understand how you feel.'

'Well, at least she didn't embarrass me by calling it out onstage. I mean, I knew it was pretty obvious you had a bit of a crush on Rex, but he definitely led you on. It wasn't fair of either of them. I'm totally over it now – it's a shame it happened the way it did, but I think we're both better off out of it to be honest.'

'I agree,' I say emphatically. 'And the thing with us, er . . . Viv trying to get us together . . .'

I make a face and am actually pleased to see he's doing the same.

'Let's forget it, yeah?'

'Great plan,' I agree.

Dave laughs. 'Anyway, I reckon your new crew are going to win tonight. Maybe you can give Breakfast of Champions a support slot when you go on a big headlining tour.'

'Deal. And I expect I'll see you in the guitar shop. You can help me when I need new strings because I'm still crap at restringing and I'd be too embarrassed to ask any of those other scary guys in there.' We shake on it. 'Hey, by the way – have you met my friend Daisy? I'm sure you two will really get on. I'd better go and get ready for our set.'

'Hi,' Dave says awkwardly. 'So, Daisy . . . That's a pretty name. Have you got any pets?'

'Actually, I have a rabbit and three guinea pigs. And a cockatiel. I love your T-shirt by the way. Who are the Sex Pistols exactly?'

I leave them to it and join my band. It's not long until we have to go on.

Rex:

Good luck tonight, Lizzie. R x

As we go out on to the stage I have only one thought in my head: it's OK. If I mess it up, it's OK, it doesn't matter. It becomes a mantra and it's strangely relaxing. It feels completely different to walking onstage last time.

Harry, Jess, Lola and I take our places and get our instruments set up. I sling my bass around my neck, my pick in my hand, looking out into the indistinct blur of the packed crowd.

'Hi. We're Dirty Harriet – make my day, punks!' Harry shouts out to a roar of excitement.

I look over at Lola and she gives me the nod.

'Five, six, seven, eight . . .'

And we're off. Harry's singing and screaming and strutting and even climbing up on top of the speakers at one point. Jess is shredding her guitar, making noises I've never heard before, stomping on her pedals and swinging her hair around wildly, a massive grin on her face the entire time. Lola is a tiny powerhouse, keeping solid time even as she flails madly, her drumsticks a blur.

As for me, I lose all sense of space and time, but somehow I'm totally focused. I'm in the zone. My hands are moving of their own accord, but that's only because they're being telepathically instructed by the feelings that are welling up in me through the music. I'm hearing it more clearly than I've ever heard anything before. I know I'm dancing along as I play, but I don't even care what I look like.

This is the same visceral, uncontrollable feeling as when I saw Dirty Harriet play here last time. When I was completely blown away by the music and thought I had never encountered anything like it before in my life. Only this time I am not just experiencing it, I am creating it. I am not just watching the storm outside, I am right there at the heart of it. Seriously, this must be what taking drugs is like, only better. And without the whole 'being illegal and potentially killing you' thing.

I don't ever want it to end, and I'm shocked when it does. It's like no time has passed at all, before I hear Harry shouting out to the audience again.

'We've been Dirty Harriet. I'm Harry, this is the awesome Lola on drums, Jess the amazing guitar virtuoso . . . and our newest member, the bass goddess Lizzie. We all love you, thanks for being so fantastic – enjoy Dream Genies and have a great night!'

I walk off the stage in a total daze. I feel buzzed that I've done it, like I've absorbed some of the energy and excitement of the audience – I can still hear them cheering and shouting, even as my ears ring with bass reverberations.

We troop offstage, dragging the most reluctant Harry behind us, still waving and blowing kisses at the audience. I can tell we all feel the same. We've all got the same bug.

We collapse into a mass, sweaty hug. In fact, I hadn't realized how sweaty I was until now – it's dripping off me, and we all look like we've just run a marathon. Without exception, we've all given it absolutely everything we've got.

Still in a daze, we head into the audience as the

Dream Genies go on and start setting up. It's weird – even though it was hideous, at least last time I was here in the competition I knew it had been an unmitigated disaster and that was it for Viviane. This time, the sense of excitement and apprehension is still hanging in the air as we have to wait to hear how we did. But that isn't the part that matters. I know we did brilliantly.

However, now I've left the stage, I am desperate to do it all again, to do whatever it takes. I wish I could do that every single day of my life. It dawns on me, properly, for the first time, that if we win, we'd be a step closer to doing that. I have never thought of myself as ambitious before – that's not what this is about – but it strikes me that this could actually change my life.

I *want* my life to be changed. I'm ready for it. Now that we've played so well and the crowd obviously loved it, I can't shake the sneaky feeling that we are actually in with a chance of winning. I can't quite leave the idea alone.

Still, there's nothing else I can do now. We've done our bit. I grin inanely at people as they congratulate us, sticking close to the other girls, feeling a bit overwhelmed. When Harry hands me a bottle of cold water I'm so grateful I almost weep. I gulp half of it down in one and pour the rest over my head, not caring about my make-up, slicking my spiky hair back.

Jake runs over, shouting his congratulations and dancing along with us, hugging Harry at the same time as he hugs me.

'You two are so sweaty,' he points out. 'You'd better

not drip on my new trainers.'

'Where's Daisy?' I ask him.

He bursts out laughing and gestures across the room. In a dark corner, Daisy appears to have her tongue halfway down Dave's throat and he is definitely not putting up any resistance. In fact, they might be asked to leave at this rate – they are looking way too into their snogging for it to be appropriate in a public place.

I'm inwardly congratulating myself for introducing them, when I see another familiar face. Everything is all happening a bit too quickly now – so many people and not enough head space to process it as my brain is still filled with music.

'You were pretty awesome,' Grace says, not deigning to hug me – probably because she is the only person in the room who isn't dripping with sweat – but she does nudge me with one bony elbow instead. Typical Grace – it actually hurts a bit, but it seems to be meant affectionately so I'll take it.

'You were good,' she says. 'I'm pretty impressed.'

'Thanks, Gracey.'

'Listen, I know I said I'd help you out with the parentals, but I just want you to know – I was most definitely *not* trying to organize some sort of cheesy teen-movie thing, but . . .'

'Oh god, what have you done?'

'You know, the cheesy teen-movie thing. The girl sneaks out to do, like, a dance show when her parents have forbidden her from going, or – I don't know – plays in a band when she's just been kicked out of college . . . and the parents come and watch, and they see how good she is, so instead of being disapproving, they're all like, "Wow, you were so great, we just didn't get it, of course you can go to the prom with the captain of the football team!"'

She at least has the good grace to look mildly guilty as she points to a table towards the back, where my parents are sitting. My mum looks a bit out of place and uncomfortable in her wrap dress and stilettos, but my dad looks like he's thoroughly enjoying himself. He's wearing his jazziest cardigan and doing some very enthusiastic seat dancing to Dream Genies.

'I suppose I'd better go over there . . .'

I have no idea what to expect. Just because my dad is excited to be out and listening to live bands doesn't mean I'm not in big trouble. In fact, I'm pretty sure I must be in big trouble. It's all right for Grace – she's taken my place and is chatting to Harry while I have to go and face the music. Literally.

'Hi,' I say awkwardly, standing over their table.

'Lizzie, is that your bridesmaid's dress from Auntie Caroline's wedding?' is my mum's first question.

'Um, yeah. It's kind of this new thing I'm trying out.'

'Well, that's pretty obvious . . .'

'Lizzles, Dirty Harriet are great. You girls remind me of the Slits or the Raincoats. Great stuff. Your singer is a bit like a young Kathleen Hanna, and your drummer is up there with John Bonham. And you! You've really learned to play – this hasn't turned out like the violin lessons at all!'

He and my mum exchange a look I can't read.

'Nick!' she says in a warning tone, and then turns to me. 'You've had a lot going on that we haven't known about, haven't you?' She sounds confused rather than angry. 'I understand that you're growing up, but I think we need to have a talk, don't you? I think we'd better all get home. Let's go.'

'Yeah, OK,' I agree automatically.

'Hang on a minute,' my dad cuts in. 'I'm quite enjoying these Dream Genies – they're like a young T. Rex. And most importantly – they haven't announced the winner yet. I think Dirty Harriet are really in with a chance.'

Harry comes running over, with Grace and Jake, plus the rest of the band in tow.

'Hi, you must be Lizzie's parents,' she yells. 'Sorry to interrupt – but Dream Genies are finishing up, and apparently they'll be announcing the results straight away.'

We all look towards the stage. The catsuited singer of the Dream Genies kicks one skinny flamingo leg out into the air and swings his feather boa as the last notes of their set ring out.

'We've been the outrageous, fabulous Dream Genies – goodnight and stay beautiful!'

They strut off the stage, leaving a trail of glitter behind them. Jack McKray bounds on.

'That was all right, wasn't it?' he cackles into the microphone. 'Thanks to all our bands tonight – some more than others, but you three were definitely the best of a bad bunch from round one! Now, I've got a few of my mates in the audience; you know, dodgy music-biz types. Believe it or not, we're in unanimous agreement, which hardly ever happens – I haven't had to bribe anyone *or* punch anyone. We're all agreed that tonight's winners should be . . .'

Everyone laughs as he does a long, torturous reality-TV-style pause. He plays up to it, putting it off and not uttering another word. It actually starts to get painful. Jess and Harry are both clutching at my hands, and all of us are in a little huddle. Forget what we said about winning. From the looks on their faces, I guess they actually care as much as I do. Even my mum looks like she's holding her breath and keeping her fingers crossed.

'All right, all right . . . As I was saying, tonight's official winners are . . . DIRTY HARRIET!'

My feet are actually pulled off the ground in a fierce group hug, and a huge cheer goes up in our corner and throughout the room. We actually did it.

'We actually did it!' we all scream, hugging and jumping up and down.

Propelled by Harry, we pile on to the stage and swarm around Jack.

'Calm down, guys.' He laughs and backs away as we threaten to engulf him. He hands us his card. 'My details are all on there. My office, nine o'clock Monday morning. Be there. Got it? Good.'

'Mad' Jack McKray – musician, producer, promoter, legend

Jack McKray was born and bred in Stoke Newington, London. He became well known as the keyboard player in the underground dance/punk band Slutz, which he formed with three school friends. Slutz became an unlikely success, crossing over from the underground to the mainstream with their surprise hit 'Dance Like a Crab', which reached number one in the UK chart in 1985. An eponymous album soon followed, which also reached number one and spawned two follow-up singles (neither of which was as successful as their predecessor).

The band decamped to the Sussex countryside to record their 'difficult' second album. The album did not materialize, and rumours of partying and spiralling costs abounded in the press. Slutz imploded soon afterwards, with reports of in-fighting. Fans would eagerly anticipate arguments and scuffles onstage between the band members, and Slutz were dropped by their management company midway through a European tour. Their second album, *Twisted Cucumber*, was eventually released after the band broke up and was widely considered a flop.

'Mad' Jack moved to Brighton, where he made a new name for himself as a gig promoter and manager. He has had several big successes as a manager, and he produced Lily Ella's smash-hit breakthrough album *20*. He is also a talent spotter for the record label Pop

Boutique, founded by his former band-mate Keith Harrington. Still regarded as something of a maverick within the music business, he has become known for finding new acts and propelling them to mainstream fame.

He lives on Brighton seafront, with his wife Saskia, editor of *Brain Candy* magazine, and their twin sons.

I wake up on Sunday morning with aching shoulders and my sweaty hair still plastered to my face, and it takes me a second to remember why. I drag myself out of bed and catch sight of myself in the hallway mirror on the way to the bathroom – in my Batman pyjama bottoms and an old stained T-shirt with a picture of a pug on it ('pugs not drugs'), my hair a legitimate mess rather than in any way a hot mess. I do not look like a cool, battle-winning musician in any possible universe. Maurice the evil cat follows me into the bathroom and watches me suspiciously as I pee, as if to confirm that I am definitely not a future music star.

'Maurice, you're freaking me out,' I say out loud.

I don't bother getting dressed or cleaning my teeth or anything before I head down to the kitchen. I have to admit, this is primarily due to the fact that I am absolutely, stomach-rumblingly starving and I am pretty sure that's the smell of my dad's corned beef hash wafting up the stairs.

'Morning . . .' I say, hoping to set a cheerful tone as I sit down at the kitchen table.

The radio is on as usual, but instead of her usual copy of the *Observer* – which has been my mum's breakfast reading material every single Sunday in living memory – she is poring over her iPad. I peer over and see that she has googled Mad Jack McKray and is reading the odd excerpt out to my dad, as he stirs a giant frying pan on the hob.

'That's Slutz with a z,' she calls out helpfully. 'And then apparently he moved to Brighton and set up the "legendary" club night Infrared Riding Hood . . . Oh, it does say here that he launched the career of that band who won the Mercury Prize last year. Hmm, and he has a guest show on BBC 6 Music. That's pretty impressive.'

'I'm not sure there's anyone still alive from a former punk band who *doesn't* have a show on 6 Music these days,' my dad grumbles. 'I'm surprised I haven't got one. I *should* have one really. Lizzles, can you stick some toast on while I do this? We'll be ready to eat in five.'

'Let's not wait for Grace,' my mum suggests. 'She'll probably be asleep for hours yet. I think the three of us really need to sit down and have a chat.'

'OK . . .'

I go about buttering toast and making myself a cup of tea, hoping that I am not letting on how uncomfortable this is all making me. By the time the three of us are sitting at the table with plates of my dad's – admittedly amazing – corned beef hash in front of us, even though I want to get this conversation underway, I am so hungry I immediately start shovelling food into my mouth.

'So, Lizzie,' my mum begins, 'obviously your dad and I have been discussing what happened last night and what happens next.'

'Ffnarr hrar,' I reply, through a mouthful of hot potato.

It's probably for the best anyway, even if I could speak in coherent words and sentences. We all know it's never a good sign when it's my mum who starts doing the talking.

'Clearly we've been very worried about you and how you're coping and taking responsibility for yourself, given the situation at college,' she goes on, and her serious tone makes my heart sink.

I know what is coming and I know I can't fight it. Given everything that has happened, I don't have a leg to stand on. I guess the band will have to go back to the line-up they had before I came along. Jess can play bass; they will be fine without me.

It's just that I wanted to do it so much. I don't know if *I* can go back to how I was before.

'I just think this is all too much for you, Lizzles,' my dad blurts out, sounding overemotional. 'Your band's great, but you're so fragile and the music industry is just brutal . . . It's not for you, Lizzie.'

I feel for my dad, as he sounds as if he might burst into tears at any moment. However, if even he is not on my side with this then I can seriously abandon all hope.

'But the thing is—' I begin, determined to at least try to argue my point.

My mum holds a hand up to stop me talking.

'The thing is, Lizzie,' she says, looking over at my dad, 'it's also a brilliant opportunity.'

'What?' my dad and I ask in stunned unison.

'It is,' she repeats, then looks at my dad. 'It *is*, Nick. Lizzie, I know your heart isn't into going back to school to do your A levels, is it?' she asks me.

'Well,' I squirm, 'not really.'

'Exactly. There's no point doing it if it's just going to be a waste of time. Qualifications are important, but not if it's nothing but a box-ticking exercise. You have no idea what you want to do after that, or whether you want to go to university. Now, I don't know the first thing about music – as you know, my favourite band is Coldplay. Nick, don't laugh. You said that Lizzie's band's good, yes?'

'Yeah, they're good. Different, energetic; I was genuinely impressed,' my dad says. 'But so are loads of bands. It's really tough out there.'

'True,' my mum agrees. 'But Lizzie is sixteen and she has her whole life ahead of her. My suggestion – if it's what you want, Lizzie – is that I come to the meeting with you on Monday and see what happens. I'll deal with the school and we can take it from there.'

'Mum, that's amazing.'

My mum knows me a lot better than I realized, but my dad still looks very worried.

'Can I come to the meeting too?' he asks. 'After all, I know a lot more about music . . . and I really fancy meeting Mad Jack McKray.'

'Only if you promise not to speak,' my mum replies. 'You're not to get all star-struck and carried away. If this Mad Jack character has any plans for the band, we need to make sure that Lizzie gets a good deal.'

Grace strolls into the kitchen and helps herself to coffee as she sits down, yawning extravagantly.

'You all look in a good mood,' she says. 'So I take it you're not going to kill Lizzie. Wow, I actually did a good deed – you're welcome, family. So, is now a good time to tell you that my girlfriend Robyn is coming round for dinner this evening . . . ?'

To Do Today

- Go to meeting with Mad Jack McKray.
- Impress him so much he wants to sign our band.
- Avoid having to go back to West Grove.
- Embark on my new life doing everything I have ever dreamed of?

Mad Jack McKray's office lives up to his name. It's in the basement of his house, which is one of the big fancy ones on the seafront, but the outside of the house is painted bright orange and has a giant disco ball and a mannequin with one leg missing in the front garden. We knock on the main front door, which is opened by a lady who seems to be juggling a mobile phone and two babies as she wrestles to invite us in. I guess this must be Jack's magazine-editor wife – I've been googling to find out all about them, and she sounds very high-powered. She obviously has tastes as eclectic as her husband's, as she is wearing a long gold dress and Crocs, but somehow she makes the combo look very chic. The hallway is painted a lurid fluorescent pink.

Even at this weird house, we must look like a very motley crew here on the doorstep. The girls in the band, including myself, are crazily excited and barely able to contain ourselves. Harry is wearing a top hat especially for the occasion. My dad, in his cardigan, has come round to the idea and is possibly more excited than we are – it turns out he was quite a fan of Slutz back in the day and even went to see them at the Shepherd's Bush Empire once, so he's totally overexcited to be coming round to Mad Jack McKray's house. My mum, wearing killer heels and her Vivienne Westwood jacket, is clutching a briefcase and looking fearsome. I'm trying to feel less embarrassed about her presence by imagining she's my lawyer or something, instead of my mother. The other girls in the band seem very impressed with her anyway.

'Hi, I'm Saskia,' the lady says with a harassed smile,

holding her iPhone away from her mouth for a second. 'Down in the basement, just follow the dreadful racket you can hear through the floorboards . . . Now, as I was saying, we need to get those samples from Japan in for the December issue, pronto . . .'

She disappears into the open-plan kitchen, where there seem to be a lot of other people milling about. This house is awesome. I listen for a second and realize that there is a distinct bass thump emanating from below us.

'He's got great taste,' my dad whispers to me. 'That's the Stone Roses. Listen to that bass line, Lizzie! Amazing stuff.'

We follow the bass line down a very rickety dark staircase to the basement. There are no windows and it is painted black and sprayed with graffiti – more toilet wall than Banksy artworks, it has to be said. The music becomes deafening, and as my eyes get used to the gloom I realize that the small space has quite a few people filling it up.

'Team Dirty Harriet, welcome to the madhouse!' Jack bellows, taking the needle off the record on his turntable with a screech that makes my dad wince. 'Come in, come in.'

We troop in. My mum and Harry grab the available chairs and the rest of us kind of perch on the floor, as that's what Jack is doing. Except for my dad, who happens to grab a nearby space hopper to sit on, then instantly looks as though he regrets it but can't quite work out how to get out of it.

'So, gang – let's do some introductions,' Jack says, indicating the two random strangers sitting on a tatty old sofa. 'I take it you met the missus and the sproglets upstairs. You all know me, unlucky for you. Obviously I'm the top dog around here, but I think you lot might turn out to be quite interesting, so I've invited a couple of mates along as well. You'll recognize this ugly mug over here – this is Keith, also known as head of Pop Boutique records.'

The head of a record company – I try my best not to squeal out loud and to keep my face in a vaguely neutral position on hearing this news. I don't even dare glance at Harry.

'Pleasure to meet you,' says Keith with a nod.

Although he and Jack are allegedly childhood friends and were in their old band together, on first impression I can't imagine two people more different. Jack, with his crazy outfits and bouncing off the walls, is the opposite of Keith, who is wearing an expensive-looking black polo neck and has an air of Zen about him. I bet he does yoga.

Jack goes on. 'And this lovely lady is Sadie Steinbeck, a tour manager.'

Sadie Steinbeck doesn't say a word and barely raises an eyebrow. In fact, she looks like Botox might have rendered her eyebrows incapable of movement. With her over-the-knee pantomime boots and her raccoon eyeliner, she has a mildly terrifying air about her. I wonder, not for the first time today, whether this is all a really weird dream.

Jack carries on talking. 'Now, I know you're all Dirty

Harriet but I haven't the faintest idea who's who, so you'll have to jog my memory. I'm crap with names, so I won't remember them anyway – I did a lot of acid in the late 80s and I've had trouble with my memory ever since. Don't do drugs, kids – that's my first bit of advice for you.'

'And don't eat the yellow snow,' Harry says. 'That's mine. I'm Harry, by the way. This is Lizzie, Lola and Jess, and—'

My mum promptly interrupts. 'And we're the band's current management team, so we're here to look after their interests. I'm Annabel and this is Nick.'

'We're Lizzie's parents,' my dad blurts out, unable to help himself and earning himself a death stare from my mum.

'That's cute,' Sadie Steinbeck says in a clipped New York accent, sounding as though she actually thinks it's anything but. I try my best not to visibly cringe, as the others don't seem to care.

She goes on. 'So, Jack got me looking at your website and I really like your sound. It's raw, it's fresh – it needs some work, but it's totally different to anything else out there. I like that.'

'You've got a lot of potential, but you need work,' Keith agrees, nodding seriously. 'If we go for it, it's going to take a lot of hard graft. This is a tough business. Are you prepared to put in the effort?'

'Yes!' we all chorus with maximum enthusiasm, like a whole bunch of school swots.

'Hang on – hard work is fine with us,' Harry cuts in.

'But when you say we need "work", what does that mean, exactly? I'm fine with the hard labour bit, but this sounds suspiciously like you want to change things. That bit I'm not so sure about.'

I'm glad Harry's here to say this sort of thing so that I don't have to. Even my mum looks impressed.

'I'm with you,' says Sadie. 'You're going to need that kind of determination and self-worth in this industry, believe me.'

'We are not going to be talked into dumbing down or sexing up,' Lola says. 'You should seriously know that about us.'

'The music is the most important thing,' I contribute.

'And our friendship,' says Jess. 'This band is a democracy. Nobody is the star of the show; we're all equal.'

'We don't want to change any of that,' says Keith. 'We're talking about evolution here, not revolution. We want to keep you as you are, but to refine your sound so it's the best it can be.'

'Look,' says Sadie, 'not to blow smoke up your ass here, but we think you're pretty great. This isn't about changing you.'

I can't help it. I can't try and be cool; it's impossible. I can't believe that proper, professional people are saying this about us. I break out into a big cheesy grin and can't resist looking at the others to see that they are doing the same.

'So your prize from the other night is a studio session,'

Jack explains. 'But what we want to do is go into the studio and record an EP, first off. I'll produce you and we'll release it on Pop Boutique.'

'What's an EP?' asks Lola.

'It stands for extended play,' I explain automatically, without thinking. 'It's usually four or five songs – more than a single but less than a whole album.'

I realize that everyone is looking at me and I can feel myself blushing. My dad and Jack both nod at me with approval.

'Exactly that,' says Jack.

'There's a studio down in Dorset we'd like to use – it's in the middle of nowhere and it's residential, so we'd go there for a week or two and put the tracks down,' says Keith. 'We'll promote it through Pop Boutique and you can do a session on Jack's 6 Music show. All that jazz.'

'We'll organize a tour to coincide with the release,' says Sadie. 'Small to medium-sized venues to start with – clubs and universities, that kind of scene. Then we'll look into getting you a support slot with a major act, and expanding into other countries, a European tour and then maybe the US.'

My brain is literally going to explode. I can't believe these words are being thrown around all of a sudden. These things are being said about a band that involves *me*.

'What do you think?' asks Jack. 'For a start, what's your set-up? Are you able to do all of this?'

'How *old* are you guys anyway?' Sadie chips in.

At this, for the first time, all of us look at each other sheepishly. When something seems too good to be true, it's usually because it is. Are we going to ruin this by admitting that we are a bunch of clueless schoolgirls and Harry is actually a fifteen-year-old 'child prodigy' with a drawn-on tattoo?

'This is all perfectly possible,' my mum replies smoothly on all of our behalfs, and this time I'm definitely grateful she's handling it. 'We'll need to have some internal meetings and work out the details. Here's my card – if you can draw me up a proper proposal and email it over, I'll organize everything at our end.'

'Great,' Sadie says, smiling at my mum. 'I think we can all do business together. This is very exciting.'

Amid all this excitement, I just feel really lucky to have my mum on my team. She looks over at me and gives me a barely perceptible wink, over my dad's head.

'Have you got any questions for us at this stage, girls?' asks Keith.

This is where I should probably come out with some insightful and well-informed question but my mind has gone blank. We all look at each other and make faces, trying to think of anything. Given the circumstances, it's impossible – I have no idea. We shrug and burst out laughing.

'Yes, I have a question,' pipes up Harry. 'Can we have milkshakes and cheesy chips on our rider, please? And loads of mayo. And salad cream.'

'Ew, not mayo!' I reply, forgetting where I am and that

there is a roomful of important people present. 'Ketchup, and ketchup only, on chips – we're not savages!'

'What about the salad cream?'

'Heathen!' Jess and Lola join in.

'But we are going to get a rider, right?'

'Well, here's to Dirty Harriet and their many future condiments,' Jack cackles. 'I've got a feeling we've all got a bit of an adventure on our hands.'

'Come on, punk – make my day!'

The future is dazzling for new Brighton band Dirty Harriet. Good thing they're wearing ironic vintage Ray-Bans. Tuesday Cooper reports from the frontlines of the new Riot grrrl revolution.

'We don't want to be like anyone else, sound like anyone else, look like anyone else,' states Harry Jackson, lead singer of Dirty Harriet.

That could be the band's manifesto – it informs everything they do, and it's true that they are truly unique on today's music scene. Although they already have an *actual* manifesto. You can read it on their website. It states to the world that they embrace all musical genres (even the uncool and the cheesy), their music is what matters (*not* their looks or fashion sense) and includes instructions to (in short) 'have fun, be nice' at their live gigs. This might sound like basic common sense, but it's also depressing how rare this kind of thinking is in this newfangled world of multimedia entertainment.

Dirty Harriet's sound is totally modern and new, but the band members themselves hark back to a time when the music world was a happier place (i.e. my beloved rose-tinted decade of choice, the 90s). Their image and ethos is as tough as the original Riot grrrls, and their ambitions are just as huge.

'It's all part of the whole thing,' explains

drummer Lola Cane. 'The music, the messages on our website, the fact that we try not to buy into the whole boring "sexy/fashion" trap. The band is a democracy and our politics include our audience.'

'The music is the most important part,' says bass player Lizzie Brown, 'but that ties into the fact that we just want to be ourselves and do our own thing. I have never felt as much myself and as empowered as with these girls.'

Guitarist Jessica Taylor agrees that the F-word – feminism – is key to the band's dynamic. 'We've all been around our fair share of girls who just want to be the star and tear each other down. That's not what we're about. If we can set a good example by playing music and respecting each other, then we're happy.'

They point out that their name is a part of the manifesto – a female version of the old-school cinema badass Dirty Harry, played by Clint Eastwood.

It's an attitude that's paying off. All of the members have played in other bands before, but they have only recently come together as a foursome. They have already won Brighton's Battle of the Bands contest, as a result of which they will be recording an EP next month under the Pop Boutique label, produced by the legendary 'Mad' Jack McKray, who is responsible for launching so many young hipster careers that surely stardom must beckon for Dirty Harriet.

Although they are all still sixth-form students who require parental permission to sign their record contracts, their heads are firmly screwed on. It looks like they may have to study on the road, as they show no signs of slowing down any time soon.

The EP will be followed by a tour that includes dates in London, Manchester and Brighton. Their live shows are an uninhibited, fun-filled spectacle not to be missed, so I'd recommend catching them in a small venue while you still can.

Even though the news has started to sink in – *this is really happening* – my head is still spinning. After we left Jack's house, we all went for celebratory noodles. Even now I'm back home, in my bedroom and wearing my pyjamas, I'm still trying to get my head around it all.

'Lizzie!'

My dad's voice drifts up the stairs just as I've got into bed and prepared to watch Netflix until I fall asleep. I can't begrudge him anything today, but I really wish I didn't have to move. My bones are tired.

'Coming!' I shout back, peeling myself out from underneath my nice warm duvet.

It's no great hardship – hopefully he just wants to share some more of his many thoughts and feelings about the band, or maybe he's even made me a delicious late-night snack. My dad has been known to get a very sweet tooth at this time of night.

The first instinct I have that something is amiss is when I come down the stairs and see my dad's quizzical face staring right at me. He's just standing there in the middle of the hall, all twitchy and eyebrows.

'Lizzles, you seem to have a – er – visitor?'

It's a split second before I even see Rex. The sight of his face – here, in my house – automatically makes my chest well up with hopeful joy. Until I tell it not to, and it only half listens. Then I register the shock of seeing him here – *here*, in my *house*, with my *dad* – and it makes my brain shut down instantaneously.

I can't seem to raise my eyes up off the floor, where

even the sight of Rex's black Converse next to my dad's slippers is too weird to comprehend. Then I see my own manky bare feet and remember that I am wearing my pyjamas, with my face scrubbed shiny and my hair scraped back most unflatteringly.

'Um, hi, Rex,' I say, looking apologetically at my dad.

Rex looks uncomfortable and shifts from foot to foot. 'Yeah. Sorry, to, um . . .'

The atmosphere couldn't be any more awkward if we tried.

'I was hoping,' Rex goes on, and my heart disobeys me yet again, 'that we might be able to talk. Maybe.'

My dad clears his throat. 'I'll leave you two alone,' he says finally. 'Not in your bedroom though, Lizzie. Stay downstairs, OK?'

I nod and try my best not to die of embarrassment right there on the spot, but shoot my dad what I hope is a reassuring little smile as he slopes off. After he has exited the hallway, Rex and I just stand there and stare at each other.

'Would you like a cup of tea?' I ask him.

'Yeah. Thanks. That'd be good.'

The cosy, slightly messy kitchen and the whirring of the dishwasher is quite comforting. Better than standing there like a couple of sad orphans in the draughty hallway. As I bustle about, filling up the kettle and getting mugs out of the cupboard, I start to feel at less of a disadvantage. I am surprised to realize that, after all those bass lessons, being in close physical proximity to Rex isn't actually that weird. Even when he is leaning against the kitchen counter and looking at me and generally being the most gorgeous thing ever to have been in my kitchen, including Grace.

'Rex, what are you doing here?' I even build up the courage to ask out loud, as I hand him a cup of tea.

From all those bass lessons, I also know that he takes his tea very strong, with half a sugar and only the slightest splash of milk. In fact, he told me it's Pantone 470C. The perfect cup of tea is very important to Rex.

'Well remembered,' he notes, brushing my hand and looking into our cups like he's reading our fortune. My breath catches in my throat, in spite of myself, but I soon recover, by throwing open a cupboard and basically shoving my face into it.

'Ooh, we've got some of those dark-chocolate ginger biscuits.' I shove the whole packet at him. 'They're not up to your home-made standard, but they're insanely delicious!'

'Lizzie . . .' He grabs my hand and pulls me next to him, forcing me to stand still. 'You asked me what I'm doing here. I needed to talk to you.'

'Why?'

'Because I'm sorry. Because I'm stupid. Because I messed everything up.'

'Are you saying this because Viv broke up with you?'

'No!' he practically shouts. 'I mean, it was mutual. I messed things up all round, but mostly I messed things up with you. I mean, I wanted to say this at the gig –

I started to, but you rushed off.'

I look at him from behind my teacup, no idea what to say.

'I really like you, Lizzie,' he goes on. 'I didn't realize how much. I'm an idiot. I mean, we have so much in common and I love hanging out with you. You're so cool.'

'I'm really not,' I argue automatically.

'You sneaked up on me,' he says with a shrug. 'I only didn't notice because you're always *saying* you're not pretty, you're not cool enough, whatever. Then I realized I was looking forward to seeing you every day. And now . . . I've missed you.'

He looks at me until I have to look away and stare into my cup of tea.

'You do know this isn't going to make me swoon straight into your arms like we're in a Brontë novel or something, right?' I tell him, making a face. 'I'm not the type.'

'I like you, deal with it. Anyway, I already know you're cooler than that. No swooning expected, honest.'

'OK . . . But you came to my house uninvited in the middle of the night. You've got to admit, that's a pretty grand gesture. You could have just, you know, *texted* or something. Don't go thinking that you've earned a big dramatic reaction, OK?'

Even though I'm in my pyjamas in my parents' kitchen, I feel weirdly comfortable. Comfortable enough to make jokes and not feel pressured to kiss him, and it's nice. He thinks I'm cool. Maybe that's enough for now.

'So I thought maybe we could go out some time,' he says.

'What, like on a date?'

'Yeah. On a date. Why not? Dinner and a film. I'll even buy you popcorn if you like.'

'Actually I don't like popcorn,' I tell him. 'It's just like crunchy air. I much prefer those really gross nachos with the plastic cheese and the –'

I'm trying to prove a point – that he can't win me over that easily – but he bursts out laughing and I relent and join in.

'Lizzie, I'll even buy you a hot dog if you really want. And I object to them on principle.'

'Seriously though . . .' I'm reluctant even to say it, and to risk putting a stop to him grinning at me like that, 'I just don't know about this. After everything . . . I'm not sure.'

His face falls on cue. 'Yeah. I had a funny feeling you might say that.'

'I mean, maybe we could just hang out, as friends, and see how we get on . . . ?'

'Do you know what?' he says. 'I'll admit I'm not used to being turned down when I ask girls out – but that actually sounds really good.'

'Cool. So . . . friends?'

'Friends.'

We shake on it.

'Now, as you can tell from my glamorous outfit,' I say, 'I'd better get to bed.'

'I'll text you tomorrow, see what you're up to. You know, just as friends.'

'Goodnight,' I insist with a laugh.

As I wave him off and close the front door behind him, I turn around to go up to bed and see my mum at the top of the stairs.

'Mum! Were you *spying* on me?'

'Well, I wanted to get a look at this mysterious boy courting you in the kitchen. Your father's useless; he couldn't even tell me what he looked like. I approve, by the way – Rex is very cute.'

'Mum, please stop talking!'

'Plus, obviously I was keeping an eye on you and poised to intervene if things started getting out of hand. I was expecting a bit more than a *handshake* to be going on down here, but it turned out I didn't have to worry. I don't think I'd have been able to resist a boy like that at your age. Honestly, your generation are very odd. But well done, Lizzie.'

Lizzie:

You're both still coming to the party tonight, right? Come over early so I don't look like a loser!

Daisy:

Defo. I'm wearing my new Sex Pistols T-shirt. I got it on the Internet. I'm really excited!

Jake:

Snap. Well, I mean I'm also excited. I will not be wearing a Sex Pistols T-shirt.

'Seriously, we were *so* right about Mum and Dad,' Grace groans, hogging my bedroom mirror and putting on another layer of lipgloss. 'So right that I'm actually embarrassed for them. They're so tediously predictable.'

I can tell she's more pleased than she's letting on, but she's definitely right. We're convinced the party they are throwing tonight is as much in aid of Grace's coming out as it is to celebrate Dirty Harriet being signed. My parents love any excuse for a party – my mum so that she can buy an expensive new dress and devise cocktail recipes, my dad so that he can craft a much-pondered playlist and bake cheese straws. This is a double excuse for a party.

We all went to Jack's office and signed the contracts this afternoon. It was really cool – we were all there, all four of us with our parents this time, and my dad took photos of us signing on the dotted line. Jack and Saskia even had us a cake made with 'Dirty Harriet FTW' iced on it in loopy rainbow letters. It was from some weird healthy cake company, so it was made with fruit sugar and wholemeal spelt flour, and it tasted vile, but it was lovely of them. We all ate it anyway, obviously.

They've all been invited to my parents' party tonight. My dad has gone totally overboard as usual, and the guest list has spiralled out of control, while my mum panics about how so many people are going to fit in our small sitting room and whether we should make them all take their shoes off. (No, is my dad's firm answer on that front.)

At least my dad's 'the more the merrier' attitude means I've had free rein with my own invites. Not that

I've exactly become Ms Popularity or anything, but it's nice to be able to have the rest of the band there, and Rex, plus obviously Daisy and Jake. This entailed one more guest, as predicted by Jake. Ever since the Battle of the Bands final, Daisy and Dave (or the Double-Ds, as Jake has christened them) have been utterly inseparable. I am finding it hard to imagine what they can find to talk about – surely Chester the Labrador has been exhausted as a topic of conversation by now. Maybe he nods and listens to his headphones while she talks about reality TV, or maybe they are happy just snogging each other's faces off in silence – but somehow I'm not surprised that it works. They obviously really like each other.

'Is the guest of honour excited?' I ask Grace.

She rolls her eyes at me in the mirror. 'Like you would not believe. Robyn and Mum have seriously become BFFs. They're even following each other on Instagram. It's so messed up. If Mum and Dad approve of her too much, I might be forced to break up with her.'

'Very funny – of course you won't. You *love* her.' I make an exaggerated kissy face in the mirror.

'Shut up. Anyway, we'd better get downstairs – she'll be here any minute and I can't leave her to fend for herself.'

'Yeah, plus we can get a head start on the party snacks. Good plan. Let's go.'

My parents are still getting used to this sort-of truce between Grace and me. My dad in particular seems to think it's some kind of cruel trick; he looks up in slightly suspicious surprise when we walk into the room together and both converge on a vast bowl of our favourite wasabi peas as if it's the cornucopia from *The Hunger Games*.

'If you can eat twenty of these in a row, I'll give you a fiver,' Grace suggests.

Just as I'm debating whether I can do it without my nasal passages actually catching fire, my dad starts to shuffle out of the room.

'I'm going to go and put on my party cardigan,' he tells us. 'Shout upstairs if the doorbell rings and I miss it – I've got "Get Lucky" cued up for when the first guests arrive. It's a classic, always sets the perfect tone.'

Sadly for him, he doesn't even have time to put his jazzy party knitwear on as the doorbell rings immediately and 'Get Lucky' has to go straight on. As Grace predicted, Robyn is in the first wave of guests and my dad is delighted to see her.

Rex is close behind her, bearing a box of home-made brownies and wearing an MC5 T-shirt that has my dad in raptures. I wave at him from across the room and leave them to it.

'Is the future pop star in the house?' Jake shouts as he comes into the room and wraps me in a hug. 'I expect I'll need to be on a guest list next time I see you. And you'd better put me on it, if you value your life. I'm hoping some of your new-found fame might rub off on me.'

'Actually I think it's my eyeliner that has rubbed off on you,' I say, wiping his black-smeared cheek. 'Sorry.'

'Hey, I've got an idea – how about you give me a job

as your on-tour stylist? No offence, but I think you could do with my help.'

I laugh in his face. 'No deal – sorry. I'm *expressing myself*, OK? This is part of my art now. And this from a man who's wearing culottes. Don't give up the day job, dude.'

'Hey, back off, Beetlejuice.'

In fact I'm wearing the Beyond Retro dress that I bought especially for my first day at college. It's been relegated from pole position as my favourite dress by now, but I still like it. Jake and I are both still laughing when Daisy finally appears, with Dave at her heels. She has a faint smear of lipstick that goes all the way up to her left eyebrow, with none left on her lips; Dave has a matching fuchsia-pink smear halfway across his face. As she hugs me with one arm, and Dave mumbles a friendly hello, I notice that they don't let go of each other's hands for a second.

The girls from the band have arrived en masse along with them.

'We found these two snogging out in the street like the world was ending,' Jess explains. 'So we dragged them indoors.'

'Oh god, is this what I'm going to be stuck with when you run off to the studio and away on tour?' Jake wonders. 'I'm going to be starved of any sensible conversation – Daisy barely comes up for air these days. Suddenly I wish you were coming back to West Grove after all, Lizzie.'

'Oh, come on,' Daisy protests. 'You're always too

engrossed in your phone and taking selfies to hold a sensible conversation at the best of times.'

'You'll all have to come to lots of our gigs then, so you don't go out of your minds with boredom,' says Harry.

I'm enjoying my dad's party playlist and concentrating on the snacks while they all chat around me. I've just chucked a mini hot dog into my mouth whole, when someone thumps me on the back and makes me choke.

'Watch it – can't have the bass player choking on a hot dog before we've even recorded the EP,' Mad Jack cackles, appearing out of nowhere in a camouflage jumpsuit and gold high-tops. 'It's hardly a rock 'n' roll way to go, is it, Mama Cass?'

'Good luck going on tour with this lot,' Jake says to Mad Jack. 'Are you sure you're ready for this?'

'I've worked with Pete Doherty and partied with Courtney Love,' Jack chuckles. 'I think I can handle a bunch of schoolgirls.'

'You reckon?' Harry asks, feigning outrage.

'With you lot, it's going to be like going on tour with St Trinians,' Jack says.

'Well, you know what they say –' Harry shrugs – '"What goes on tour stays on tour." I'm not even sure what that means, but I just like saying it because *we are going on tour*!'

'That sounds so rock 'n' roll,' Lola agrees.

'Yep,' I chip in. 'We're going on tour – with our crazy new manager and my parents. *So* rock 'n' roll!'

'That's rock 'n' roll Dirty Harriet style, Lizzie! We're

mavericks, we're breaking the rules!'

The four of us look at each other and laugh, but it's true. We're doing things our way, being ourselves. I'm not too nervous about it, or even embarrassed that my parents are coming on tour with us now (well, not much). I get to play bass, hang out with my friends and be the person I'm supposed to be. I can't wait.

Acknowledgements

Hugest gratitude in the world to my awesome editor Rachel and my amazing agent Caroline. SUCH MASSIVE THANKS.

Thank you to all the lovely humans at Macmillan – especially Bea, Kat, Jess and George – and to wonderful Jo at Hardman & Swainson.

Thank you to my genuinely extraordinary family, who have helped and supported and been fabulous, always: all of you, but especially Mum, Dad, Katy, Nan, Fiona, Peter, Nick, Ian, Jocelyn, Niki, Chris, Karen, Carrie, Leslie and Lillian.

Staunchest love to my awesome soul gang: Ruth, Annabel, Ali, Lou and Neil. Not to sound melodramatic, but I actually couldn't have got through this without you.

About the Author

Eleanor Wood lives in Brighton, where she can mostly be found hanging around in cafes and record shops, running on the beach, pretending to be French and/or that it's the 1960s, and writing deep into the night. She used to make a photocopied fanzine, moved on to embarrassingly personal blogging and has written for magazines like *Elle*, *Time Out* and *The Face*. She has a fringe, is fond of eyeliner and wishes she had a dog.

You can read her blog at
http://eleanor-wood.blogspot.co.uk
or chat to her on Twitter at @eleanor_wood